T
PERFECT
HOUSE
FOR MURDER

A gripping murder mystery full of twists

LINDA MATHER

Jo and Macy Mysteries Book 6

JOFFE
BOOKS

Joffe Books, London
www.joffebooks.com

First published in Great Britain in 2023

Cover art by Nick Castle

ISBN: 978-1-83526-082-1

CHAPTER ONE

The minister blessed the baby and she wriggled and whimpered. An audible sigh resounded around the country church, and the phone in Jo's pocket vibrated urgently. Not just one call, but two, in quick succession. Unfortunately, it was in the pocket that rested close to Teddy's hip, so she knew he'd felt it too. He didn't react, and she resisted looking at it. The minister beckoned the parents and godparents towards the font. Teddy, as one of the godparents, got to his feet to follow his brother and his wife and their tiny daughter, Lela-May Scarborough, who remained fractious in her mother's arms. Jo, knowing he was nervous, gave his hand an encouraging squeeze as he left the pew.

It wasn't until they were released into the fresh sunshine that Jo was able to view her missed calls. She sheltered inside the old stone porch while Teddy posed for photographs with the other godparents. Both Hanni and Macy had called: her oldest friends, the two people who understood her best in the world and who rarely phoned her.

In Hanni's case, this was because they saw each other most days. Jo often helped her friend out at the Rivermill Bookshop, which Hanni ran. It was largely due to Hanni's support, together with her local Mind, Body and Spirit

1

network, that Jo had become established as a professional astrologer, and she never forgot her friend's help. David Macy, her ex-boss, was simply elusive; she hadn't heard from him in months. While she was staring at the phone, Hanni called again. Jo answered quickly, keeping her voice low.

'What is it, Han? I'm at the christening.'

'Oh. Oh, of course you are.' Hanni hesitated, but only briefly. 'I'm sorry, I had to call. I need your help, Josephine.'

'What is it? What's wrong?'

'I've stumbled across something, which was meant to stay hidden. Something terrible. It's — it's a person and they are dead, Josephine, and I think they might have been dead a while.' Hanni's voice faded and then returned, breathless and fast. 'I'm meant to be cleansing the whole space, so I couldn't leave out the cellar — even though they said it's not in use because it's been flooded. As soon as I started down the steps, I sensed it was something far worse. Then I saw a plastic bundle on the floor under a shelf and—' She stopped, then started again. 'As soon as I realized what it was, I — well, I'm sorry, but I ran out of there.'

'Are you sure you've found a body? I mean, what did you actually see?'

Her friend's voice came back at her, still soft but filled with dread. 'I know what it is. It's a human body. I just don't know what to do.'

'Where are you?' Jo could hear birds chirping in the gaps between Hanni's words, so she knew her friend was outdoors. She remembered Hanni had said something about a 'spiritual cleansing' but, as Jo had no idea what this meant, she hadn't asked for details. Hanni was a crystal healer in addition to running the bookshop and, although they were close friends, Jo didn't pretend to understand much about her friend's speciality.

'I'm at the New Navigation pub at Stokesly,' Hanni was saying. 'Sarah, she's the landlady, asked me to do some cleansing work because they have been experiencing . . . well, I don't know what it is, but she's worried that it's poltergeist activity. I've been here all morning and have smudged every corner of every room with white sage. I couldn't miss out the cellar—'

'But, Hanni, what did you actually see? It was probably dark in there. You could be—'

'It was a human form, wrapped up.' Hanni's shudder was audible. 'And I can't go back in there. I've told Sarah and her husband, Gary, but he doesn't want to tell the police. They're both terrified of any publicity. I left them arguing about it, which is why I came outside. But if they don't call the police, I'm going to have to, aren't I?'

'Yes. Obviously, they've got to tell the police,' Jo hissed impatiently. 'They really don't have any choice.'

'Yes, I know. I just needed to hear someone say that.' Hanni's voice gathered strength. 'Sarah and Gary are going to need some help with this. Josephine, do you think you could come and talk to them? I'm sure you can convince Gary it's the right thing to do.'

'Not now, no. Just tell them they have to phone 999,' Jo said firmly. Then, when her friend fell silent, she added, 'Look, if you message me the location, I will try to get there and help out if I can. You'll be OK, Hanni.'

'I know I will. I'm just a bit shaken, that's all.'

Teddy was looking around for her when she stepped out of the dark porch, blinking. 'They want some family pictures,' he said, tugging her hand towards the beaming, well-dressed group around the baby.

'I'm not family,' Jo protested, her phone safely stowed in her pocket.

'Don't be silly,' Teddy smiled, adding with a sharp look, 'Who was that on the phone?'

'It was my sister, Marie,' Jo said quickly, wide-eyed. 'She sounds upset about something. I'm sorry, but I'm going to have to go and see her.'

'To Coventry? Now?' Teddy's open face registered astonishment. 'What can she be so upset about? Is it your parents? Are they OK?'

Jo's parents were both elderly but in good health, and Jo couldn't bring herself to say otherwise, so she muttered, 'I don't know, but I'll be back as soon as I can.'

'But you'll miss the lunch.'

'I've seen the important thing. You know, the actual christening.'

'At least stay for the photos,' he insisted. Behind him, Teddy's elder brother was waving as frantically as he could while holding a small baby.

She gave Teddy a gentle shove — 'Look, you're needed' — and stepped backwards into the little crowd of family and friends. She could feel a guilty heat rising to her face. She hardly ever blushed. But then she didn't often hang around in a churchyard in a print dress and heels admiring a baby either, she reminded herself. She snapped a few pictures as Teddy posed with his equally handsome elder brother and Lela-May. Both men had a golfer's tan and a sportsman's build, but Teddy was the one who made his living at the game. Andy was an accountant. Both were blond with clear blue eyes, which smiled easily. Jo and Teddy had been together for over two years, and Jo never got tired of looking at him.

As she watched Teddy's family form around the baby for a series of official photographs, she realized, a little guiltily, that she didn't actually know any of them very well, and this was entirely her own doing. Teddy often tried to involve her in family get-togethers — especially lately — but, fond though she was of him, she often wished that he did not belong to one of the locally renowned Cotswold families, and managed to avoid them when she could.

However, today he was determined to include her in the family photographs. Despite her mild protests, he drew her alongside him, with the result that in the photos she looked reserved and uneasy. Her curly dark mane had been tamed for the occasion, and the warm red of the summer dress had been well chosen by her sister, Marie. But Jo's expression did not match the Scarborough smiles.

Given the honour clearly bestowed upon her by being invited to the family lunch, Jo should probably have felt worse about never actually reaching the hotel. But oddly, as she drove down the lush valley lanes under glorious blue skies, all she felt was a sense of escape. The New Navigation, where Hanni had been carrying out the spiritual cleansing, was only fifteen minutes away from the country church where the Scarborough family were gathered, but it gave her enough time to listen to her other message. This was from David Macy. His voice through the car speakers was lethargic and uninflected as ever, and yet gave her a sudden sense of his presence.

'A bolt from the blue, I know,' came his familiar dry tones. 'But I'm on your patch and I wondered if you fancied meeting up for a drink or a coffee? I'm seeing a guy in Cheltenham this afternoon, so if you're around later, say, after three, let me know. I'm at the Hotel du Vin.'

She hadn't liked lying to Teddy, but if she'd said she was responding to a plea from Hanni, he wouldn't have understood why she had to go. And she would certainly not reveal the invitation from Macy. Teddy had wisely never asked too many questions, but he knew that she and Macy had been lovers. What he couldn't comprehend was that both Hanni and Macy were old friends, who hardly ever asked anything of her, so when they did, it was as important as family. If not more so. *Therefore it wasn't really a lie*, she told herself, as she drove towards the address Hanni had sent, which appeared to be alongside a canal near the little cluster of houses which made up the hamlet of Stokesly.

The pub squatted behind a tight bend in the lane just over a hump-backed bridge. As she slowed, she saw a slight figure leaning over the brick parapet, peering down to the canal below. They turned swiftly as she passed and stared blatantly into her car. Jo was aware of a young, pale face peering out of an over-sized black hoody. Jo stared briefly back into the judging gaze of a teenage girl. But then the treacherous bend needed her attention and the moment went out of her mind.

5

The old inn lay directly below on the canal bank. Its white-painted brick and square green umbrellas in the large beer garden at the back were a landmark for passing barges or walkers on the towpath, but it had been taking drivers by surprise for over 150 years, and she had to make a quick swerve into the car park. It seemed deserted, with only one other car parked. A blackboard beside the gate explained that the pub was closed for *Temporary Renovations*. As she slid out of the seat, she noticed first Hanni's bike, leaning against the fence, and then Hanni herself on the path which ran down the side of the pub towards the beer garden. Her friend's elfin face was translucent with shock and her dungarees were stuffed into mud-spattered wellies, which looked too large for her.

'The police are on their way. Gary finally called them,' Hanni said as she walked, stiff with anxiety, to meet her. 'And they wanted to send an ambulance. But it's far too late for that.' She pushed her short fringe off her forehead and breathed out. 'Believe me, I'm so thankful to see you.'

'I'm not sure what I can do.' Jo looked around her, tilting her head to look up at the bridge. The young figure in the black hoody was no longer in sight. Behind the white walls of the pub, the canal could be seen, still and glinting in the sun, and, on the opposite bank, a row of quaint cottages with flowers tumbling out of their garden walls and the tops of trees behind them. Jo brought her eyes back from the idyllic summer scene to Hanni's ashen face. 'How do you know this body has been there a while? I mean, are we talking years?'

'Not judging by the newness of the plastic tied around it but I can definitely say that all life and energy has long gone. And there's the smell.' She brought a delicate hand to her mouth, almost gagging at the memory. 'But I'm worried for Sarah and Gary. Will you come and talk to them about what happens next? They run the place, and are desperate to keep it all as quiet as possible. I said I had a friend who is a private investigator who might be able to help them.'

'Well, I've only just finished training, don't forget. I'm still an astrologer first and foremost. If you want an actual, experienced PI, we'll have to call on Macy.'

'At least you've come across this sort of thing before. The police told them not to go anywhere near the body, so they're waiting in the lounge.' Hanni took a step towards the gate which led to the pub entrance, but Jo hesitated. She didn't spend too long wondering what made Hanni think she had previously found dead bodies in cellars. Instead she put a hand on her friend's arm. 'Hold on. They've waited a while, a few more minutes isn't going to matter. Show me where you found it.'

'Why? You can't — The police will be here soon.' Hanni glanced quickly behind her down the path. At the side of the pub, a door stood ajar. Jo saw it shift slightly in the light breeze as she began to walk towards it. With the white une-ven wall of the pub on her right, she passed a small lean-to shed where logs were stacked, and came to the door, with Hanni following slowly.

'That's the back room of the pub.' Hanni spoke in a lowered voice. 'They don't use it every day, only when they're very busy. The door to the cellar is in that room. Gary said I didn't need to go down there because it's been flooded with all the rain we had a couple of weeks ago. But obviously, I had to clear that space too, or the negative energy will just gather there, so he lent me these boots . . .' Her voice faded as Jo reached the shabby door.

Jo noticed a keypad lock on the door frame, but it gave easily under her hand. The wood grated slightly on the stone-flagged floor. 'Come on, we've only got a few minutes,' she said.

Hanni held back. 'I really can't.'

Jo looked over her shoulder. 'This is the only chance I'm going to get to know what we're dealing with, which is important if I'm going to help Sarah and Gary. You don't have to come with me, just keep an eye out for the police. And give me the wellies.' Jo leaned against the wall and discarded her high-heeled sandals, then grabbed at the boots and pulled them on.

'I want to make as few new traces as possible,' Jo was saying, while Hanni stood over her, shaking her head.

'Gary went in after me, and he saw it too,' Hanni said. 'He confirmed it's a human body, and Sarah finally talked him into phoning the police. They'll be here any minute.'

'Just tell me where to look,' Jo said, 'and shout if the police come.'

She slowed her breathing before stepping over the threshold. With her intake of breath came a meaty, sweetish smell that made her falter for a second. Blinds at the high windows shaded the room and, after the bright sunlight, at first she only saw blocky shapes, including a large round table in the centre and a clutter of furniture around the walls. As she entered, the shapes solidified into battered brown tables and chairs against the walls. Dimly, to her left, she made out a huge set of wooden wings hanging from the wall above an old sideboard, cluttered with fat church candles and bowls.

'There's a door on the back wall,' Hanni's voice reached her from outside. 'That's the door to the cellar. Down there, you can see shelves on the wall to the left, behind the other steps. It's under the bottom shelf.'

The door was ajar and a gassy, rotting smell crept up the cellar steps. A bare bulb lit the staircase, and at its base she could make out, straight ahead, low tables with metal kegs stacked below them and plastic crates on top. As she descended, she noted that along the left wall, another steeper set of stairs with metal runners led down from a trapdoor. Behind them, she could make out the lines of shelves, fixed to the brick walls. The mouldering stench deepened and hit her throat. She had to stop for a second to cough and swallow hard. After that, she tried to hold her breath.

The dim bulb reflected in ripples and puddles on the cellar floor and she fumbled with the torch on her phone. It painted a shaky cone of white light across the floor, leading towards a long, lumpy plastic shape under the bottom shelf.

She could see the plastic was thick and transparent and tied tight, but there were gaps along the side and she could make out the fabric of a coat, and a matted piece of hair. As she stepped onto the damp, uneven flags of the cellar floor, she realized the puddles were not just water, as the torch beam threw back the oily sheen of a thick viscous substance leaking from the body.

CHAPTER TWO

As Jo swept the torch beam over the plastic, the contours revealed the shape was human. The crease at the elbow, the hump of the shoulder. The head was hardly visible at all, covered by the hood of a heavy, waxy coat. As she moved her torch, she realized that the shadows on the hood of the coat were, in fact, stains: a dried, dark, bloody patch.

She advanced carefully, not touching anything except her phone, which she held out in front like a wavering shield. The bright light picked out new details. Folded off-white sheets or tablecloths were stacked on the shelf directly above the body in zipped plastic packets. She realized that the corpse was actually wearing the coat with the hood pulled up: she could see the seam at the base of the hood, just visible through the plastic. And then something white on the floor: the fingers of a hand sticking out through a gap in the nylon rope used to tie the bundle. It was a feminine hand with clean, neat, unvarnished fingernails, Jo noted, trying to concentrate on the practical details to suppress a wave of near panic.

'Jo! They're here,' Hanni's high-pitched cry pierced the dark room behind her, and Jo nearly dropped her phone. She turned sharply and stumbled up the steps, clumsy in the large boots. The square room above now seemed light compared to the claustrophobic dimness of the cellar. She stomped across the wooden floor, crashing her hip into the corner of the sideboard, suddenly grateful for the rush of warm air outside.

'The police car has parked at the front, so they can't see us. Are you all right?' Hanni snatched back the boots as soon as Jo sat down. 'I will say I saw your car and went to meet you. You've only just got here, OK?'

'All right.' Jo was coughing and trying to breathe deeply, and felt relieved at her friend's unexpected presence of mind, as she was still reeling from what she'd seen. She shoved her feet into her sandals and raced up the path behind her.

As they turned towards the pub entrance, Hanni virtually collided with a stocky man, who was heading in their direction. 'I was wondering where you were. The police are here and they'll want to see you.'

Hanni caught her breath and launched into her explanation. 'Gary, this is my friend Jo Hughes. She just got here. I told you, she is setting up as a private investigator and may be able to help.'

The publican turned to look at her. He was middle-aged with a face made more inscrutable by narrow eyes and skin that looked like it was used to the sun. 'Any help is welcome,' he said briefly. 'The brewery are going to crucify us for this, so we need to avoid all publicity, if we can.'

'Well, my best advice right now is that you tell the police everything you know,' Jo said, taking a leaf out of Macy's playbook. 'Don't be tempted to hold anything back. Be completely open with them.' She was very aware that Macy didn't always stick to his own rules, but it was sound advice and had generally served them well over the years.

Gary Robart pushed open the front door, 'We'd better go on in. Sarah won't like dealing with the police on her own.'

A nostalgic smell greeted Jo as she stepped through the porch into the pub. It took a minute or two for her to pin down the memory. The lounge bar was fitted with an old-fashioned, high-coloured carpet. There was a fireplace against the outside wall, chintzy seats and plenty of polished wood. The air smelled faintly of beer, woodsmoke and polish. It wasn't until she saw the horse brasses laid out ready for cleaning that she identified the sharp scent of brass polish, which recalled Sundays as a child in Wales, helping her grandmother clean the ornaments while hearing all the family gossip. It was a comforting memory, but here, in contrast, she was confronted by the slightly ominous sight of two police detectives standing beside a corner table, where Sarah Robart was sitting with her cigarette poised over a glass ashtray, elbow resting at her side and her features hazy behind the smoke. The woman had a striking face: expressive green eyes accentuated by short, spiky black hair. Contrary to what her husband had said, she looked at ease. 'Do come in, one and all,' she said drily as they entered. 'Gary, you'd better make some tea.'

'Not just yet, thanks all the same.' The male DC's eyes roved across all of them and came to rest on the landlord. 'A few questions first. Gary, you made a call about a discovery in the cellar. Would you like to fill us in?'

Jo, purposely bringing up the rear, took a discreet moment to brush some mud from the path off her dress. She recognized the female plain clothes officer as DS Diane Watts from previous dealings with the Stroud police. DS Watts was in her thirties, like Jo, and they shared other similarities, Jo recalled, being equally strong-minded and persistent. She supposed that, as a local PI, she was going to have to get to know the Stroud police. She knew Macy always maintained good contacts in the Birmingham and Coventry forces. Given the hard stare she was receiving from DS Watts, Jo doubted that this was a good moment to start.

'Yes, that was me,' Gary Robart was saying. 'Detective Constable Williams, I'm sorry to bring you round here again. I know we've had to report some strange activity in the past, which we think might be poltergeists. We're still suffering from the unexplained noises at night, banging and mirrors that fall off the wall and smash. That's the reason we've asked Hanni here, in fact.'

Sarah interrupted him, briskly. 'Get to the point, Gary.' She met the jaded gaze of DC Williams. 'Believe me, we'd rather just be getting on with business quietly,' she said. 'My husband called you when Hanni came to tell us she believed she'd found human remains in our cellar.'

'The cellar's been out of action since the floods last month. I've had to store stock in the back room,' Gary explained. He paused and swallowed. 'Anyway, obviously, after we'd spoken to Hanni, I went down to investigate—' His stiff delivery came to an abrupt halt as the door at the back of the bar opened.

They all turned as a stocky woman strode towards them, clasping a wooden tray stacked with tea mugs. 'Thought you might need sustenance,' she announced. 'Tea with sugar is good for shock.' The woman's doughy face registered the disapproval that seemed to be a permanent fixture of DC Williams' expression, but ploughed on. 'Oh. Sorry if I got it wrong but, well, I don't mind admitting I'm shocked, even if no one else is.'

'Don't worry about it, Maureen,' Sarah spoke up. 'The officers don't want a brew, but I'm sure the rest of us appreciate it.' To the two police officers, she added, 'This is Maureen Toomey, who cleans here for us.'

'I can see your efforts, Maureen,' DS Watts smiled, pointing to the brasses laid out on a table by the fireplace. 'And thank you for the tea. I will have some, thank you.'

'Can't take the credit for them, I'm afraid.' Maureen placed the heavy tray on the table in front of Sarah. 'Nora does the brasses.' She began to hand out generous mugs of tea. No one declined, and DC Williams helped himself to sugar.

'Can I ask you to remain with us, please?' He pulled up a seat for Maureen, who sat down and looked at her watch ostentatiously. 'I do have another job to get to. I'm a carer at Stokes Avon residential home,' she added, straightening her shoulders under DC Williams' gaze. 'My shift starts at two thirty, so if I can't be there on time, I need to let them know.'

'Noted.' The officer turned back to Sarah and Gary. 'Now, can you confirm if there is anyone else in the building? Any other staff? Or anyone else we need to know about?' When they assured him there was no one, DS Watts asked, 'So who is Nora?'

'Nora Hutchinson.' Again, it was Sarah who responded. 'She's just a nice kid who likes to help out. She gets bored at weekends, so I give her some little jobs to do. She lives in the cottages on the other side of the canal with her father and her little brother. Number three.'

While DC Williams scribbled this down, Diane Watts took charge of the questioning. 'We'll need to talk to her,' she said, with a brief instructive nod to her colleague. She looked at the small group seated in front of her. 'But first of all, which of you is Hanni Light? Will you explain what happened, please? And start by telling us, what is your role here?'

A visible shift of discomfort passed between Sarah and Hanni, although they were careful not to look at each other. Once again, Sarah Robart spoke first. 'We asked Hanni in to cleanse the pub — it's not a physical clean, you understand. Maureen does that daily, of course. It's more of a spiritual cleansing, which you perform with white sage smoke, to clear the place of any negativity.'

The police officers received this information stony-faced. Jo could sense waves of disapproval emanating from Maureen, who folded her arms and sat back in her chair, but Hanni lifted her chin, her voice soft but clear. 'My name is Hanni Light, and I work with crystals and healing energies. Space cleansing is a service I offer.'

'You know we sometimes hold paranormal events and invite ghost hunters and the like,' Gary Robart appealed to DC Williams, whose expression radiated scepticism. Jo felt her own eyebrows rise and she looked across at Hanni. Why had her friend not mentioned this? But Hanni's attention was fixed on Sarah. 'The place is haunted. I mean, we are used to living with that. There is the ghost of an engineer, who drowned by falling off the bridge. It's well documented,' he added, defensively. 'Anyway, if you do have spirits around, it's a good idea to have the space sort of cleaned up regularly. Well, Hanni has a technique to do this, so we are giving it a try. It's like a sort of exorcism.'

'It's not.' Hanni and Sarah spoke in one voice.

'I've heard of it,' DS Watts said, surprising all of them, including her colleague. 'But go on, Miss Light. Please, can you just tell us what you found? Starting with when you arrived here today, and including timings if you can.'

Hanni sat upright at the end of the bench seat beside Gary and Sarah and recounted her day. 'I got here before nine o'clock and started the cleansing straight away. I live over at Slad and cycled here. I can easily carry all I need on the bike, and I wanted to start early because the process takes time. It's called smudging, and I use the embers of white sage, assisted by feathers and mantras. I began upstairs in Sarah and Gary's flat, and worked downwards through the building.'

There was a little pause, and Jo, sensing there was something left unsaid, determined to get the full story from her friend later. Hanni explained how she had cleansed the front rooms of the pub and the living quarters upstairs by lunch time. 'That just left the back room and the cellar which leads off it. Gary told me it's been flooded, but I had to cover the whole space, otherwise—' she looked at their faces and sighed — 'otherwise the negative energies will simply gather there. So I borrowed Gary's wellies and went down the cellar steps.' She paused momentarily. 'I left the side door to the pub open, as you have to provide an exit for those energies that are not beneficial.'

'Go on.' DC Williams kept his voice neutral, although his expression remained cynical. 'What did you find?'

'In the cellar, there are some old shelves attached to the wall, and under the bottom one . . .' She took an uneven breath. 'It was on the cellar floor under the bottom shelf,' she went on. 'The person is wrapped up in plastic, but I could tell from the . . . the shape.' Her eyes, large and shadowed, flicked across to Jo for a second. 'Then I came up here and told Gary, and I also called my friend Jo because . . . I-I was in shock and I knew she'd know what to do.'

'And did you call the police immediately?' DS Watts broke in.

'Of course,' Gary said quickly. 'Well, after I'd had a look for myself. Just to check, you know. It's definitely a body, I'm afraid, but God only knows how it got there. Then I called you.'

'I don't know how we're going to come back from this,' Sarah said, taking out another cigarette and holding it, unlit. 'We've had some lean months, and now we have this to deal with.'

'I'm sure you appreciate we have more questions,' DS Watts said abruptly. 'But first, we'd better take a look. Miss Light, would you like to show Detective Williams—'

'I can't,' Hanni shook her head so violently that her short, fine hair flew around her ears. 'I showed Gary. He knows where it is.'

'All right.' DS Watts nodded at her colleague, which surprised Jo, who was watching closely. 'You go with Mr Robart, and I'll stay here and get down a few more details.' She drew out a chair but didn't sit. Instead, her eyes settled on Jo. 'So as I understand it, you arrived after the discovery of the body, if that's what it proves to be. It's Jo Hughes, isn't it?' DS Watts sounded pleased with herself. 'Astrologer/detective, if I am not mistaken? So, how come you are here?'

'I'll settle for astrologer,' Jo said, deciding now would not be the time to promote her putative new career as a PI. 'It's as Hanni said. She called me shortly after she found . . . it. She was obviously upset, so I came over as soon as I could.'

'I really don't think there is anything you can add to the inquiry at this stage,' Diane Watts said, 'and, to be frank, the fewer people here the better. So you are free to go, although we will need a statement from you in due course. I would simply ask you not to discuss anything you've heard today, as it is part of an active police inquiry.'

Hanni looked wide-eyed across the table at her friend while DS Watts turned towards Maureen. 'Given you have another job to get to, er . . . is it Miss or Mrs Toomey?'

'It's Mrs Toomey,' Maureen answered, her tone polite but resigned.

'We can see you at the station tomorrow, too,' the detective went on. She gave both Jo and Maureen a dismissive nod and turned to Sarah Robart.

'I need you to fill in a few gaps for me,' Diane Watts was saying as Jo left the group, taking her time. Neither Gary nor DC Williams seemed in any hurry to leave, she noticed, as she waited by the door while Maureen went to retrieve her coat and bag from the kitchen. Although, who could blame them?

Suddenly, a shadowy figure rushed across the other side of the stained-glass panels. As Jo hesitated, a workman charged past her, shoving the door inwards, his bare muscly arm catching her shoulder.

'What's going on? I saw the police car and, I'm sorry, but I had to know—' He pulled up short as the circle of faces around the corner table turned to him. He put a hand to the tousled hair on top of his head. The gesture made him seem young and gauche. Actually, he was a little older than herself, Jo guessed, so a bit too old for the 'lost boy' look, but he was attractive and probably used to getting away with it. From behind the newcomer's wiry form, she noted his heavy-duty work shorts and reinforced boots, and recalled seeing a glimpse of scaffolding on the end cottage across the canal.

'Matty, what are you doing here, mate?' Gary broke in, agitated. 'We don't know ourselves what we've found—'

'And you are?' DS Watts asked. At her hip, her radio crackled and she silenced it.

'Matty Sullivan. I'm working for Leah Ellerman on the renovation of her cottages over the canal.' He lowered his hands to his sides and levelled his shoulders, but his heightened anxiety was palpable. 'Look, this is out of order, I know, crashing in here like this, but can you please just tell me what it is you've found?'

'I found it,' Hanni spoke up unexpectedly. 'All we know is that it's a human body, and I found it in the cellar.'

'Is it a woman?' Matty Sullivan demanded.

DC Williams responded just as quickly. 'We don't know, but it's obvious you have some suspicions of your own. You'd better tell us what they are,' he said. Although DS Watts said nothing, Jo had the distinct impression that she would have handled the interruption differently.

Matty Sullivan drew himself onto the balls of his feet as if ready to fight. Jo, shifting position slightly, saw that the ridges of his strong cheekbones were flushed. 'I believe it is Leah Ellerman.'

Jo watched the colour drain from Sarah Robart's face, while her husband shook his head as if unaware of what he was doing. Maureen's square jaw visibly dropped. No one spoke, though, and Matty Sullivan went on, keeping his voice calm. 'I've been worried about Leah for days. I've messaged her and called her I don't know how many times, but I've had absolutely nothing back. I need to talk to her about the building work and — well, it's unusual.' He came to an abrupt halt. 'I knew I should have told someone,' he added.

'Matty, stay calm. It can't be Leah — she's in London.' It was Maureen who spoke first, her voice aiming to reassure, but Jo heard a shudder of dread.

'No, it isn't Leah Ellerman. Apparently, it's been there some time.' Gary spoke with conviction.

DS Watts held up her hands in a 'stop' gesture, her irritation now obvious to all. 'Let's not speculate any further, please. Mr Sullivan, we will need you to give a statement. Now we need to investigate the scene, please, DC Williams?' Her colleague had the grace to look abashed. She went on, 'I will continue to get details from Mr and Mrs Robart. Mrs Toomey, Miss Hughes, I think you were on the point of leaving. Please don't forget my request not to disclose any details of what you've heard.'

DS Diane Watts couldn't have made it any clearer that Jo's presence wasn't welcome, and even she couldn't find an excuse to linger. She slipped out of the pub and into the garden with the sun warm on her face and legs, while inwardly, she felt chilled and slightly queasy.

'Are you all right?' She had been aware of Maureen following, heavy-footed, and now turned to find her at her elbow. 'It might be best to sit for a minute before driving anywhere,' the woman said. She was about forty-ish with a stoic, earnest face and flecked brown eyes behind metal-framed spectacles.

'No, I'm fine,' Jo assured her. 'Especially now I'm out in the fresh air. It's just that I can't seem to get rid of the smell.' She quickly realized her mistake and hurried on. 'How about you? You seemed to know the woman they're talking about. Has she been missing a while?'

Maureen nodded slowly. 'Yes, I know Leah. I work for her. If it *is* her. Personally, I wouldn't set any store by what Matty Sullivan says. And, if he's as worried as he makes out, why didn't he tell someone? We'd be better off waiting for the official police report.' She looked again at Jo. 'You're sure you're OK? Because I really do have to go. I have to be over in Stokes Avon by two thirty.' She hunted for her car keys in a capacious bag. 'I know it's not far, but the boss is unforgiving.' She shot Jo a wry grin.

'I've worked for bosses like that.' Jo smiled back reassuringly. 'Though you've got a pretty good excuse today.' As they left the pub by the old-fashioned wooden gate, Jo glanced back along the canal. The pub's square white-brick shape sat beside a lock, on the other side of which the canal's water level plunged, leaving a steep drop from the hump-backed bridge. Now, sitting on the black-and-white lock gate, staring into the glassy water, was the young, dark-clad figure she had passed on the bridge earlier.

'That's Nora Hutchinson.' Maureen followed Jo's gaze. 'Lord knows what she finds so interesting about the place, but she's always hanging around the pub.'

'She's the one who's helping out with the brasses,' Jo said.

'Yes. Sarah sent her home as soon as your friend told her what she'd found.'

'Well, she hasn't gone home,' Jo remarked, as they walked towards their cars.

'Oh, she's never there if she can help it,' Maureen said. She offered a hurried goodbye and made a beeline for the small blue car on the far side of the pub car park. Jo noticed that there was another car park beyond it, clearly fenced off. Gary Robart was now leading DC Williams along the pub side of this fence, towards the gently swinging door, which Jo had left open.

Jo shuddered to herself and looked at her phone. It was 2.15 p.m. She could re-join Teddy at the hotel, or wherever he was. On the other hand, it would take her about half an hour to drive to Cheltenham and stroll into the Hotel du Vin, which would be perfect timing for the end of Macy's meeting.

CHAPTER THREE

In fact, she arrived early, and David Macy was still very much occupied. She saw him immediately, dark and still, his long legs crossed and his sparse shape framed by one of the eau-de-nil velvet wing chairs in the hotel lounge. His expression was so intent that she knew he hadn't noticed her, so she selected an armchair of her own, from which she could observe both Macy and his client. When a waiter arrived, she ordered herself a strong coffee with hot milk and sat back to reflect on her unusual day so far.

She was almost immediately distracted by Macy's client: an athletic-looking man, maybe in his early fifties, which would make him about twelve years older than Macy. He was blond and still handsome, wearing a smart business suit, but she noticed that his corporate blue shirt eased out over his trousers, and his cheeks were an unhealthy cherry colour, which clashed with his blond hair. Paradoxically, there was an energy about the man, which suggested he'd rather be out on the sports field than sitting in front of china teacups. His broad back filled the chair, and he shifted in his seat as he talked. Macy, she noticed, hardly spoke, but this was nothing out of the ordinary.

There was no doubt that the uneasy stranger had an undeniable presence. And, taking all these details in, meant that she avoided answering the question: what on earth was she doing here? She knew she should be with Teddy, taking her turn at admiring the new baby. Andy's wife, Nikki, had placed Lela-May briefly in Jo's arms while they waited to go into church, but Jo had looked so alarmed that Nikki had quickly retrieved the squirming bundle. Jo had felt relieved. She'd never had any idea what to do with babies. Now that her nephews were teenagers, she sometimes felt she understood them better than their mother, Marie, but when they'd been babies, she had been clueless.

Thinking of her sister gave her a pang of guilt. Marie would be furious if she knew she'd been used as an excuse to escape the Scarborough family lunch. Of course, all of Jo's family had loved Teddy since Jo had first introduced them two years ago, but when she watched Teddy and Marie chatting quietly together, she couldn't avoid the feeling that they were planning her future. All the same, she chided herself, she should not have lied to Teddy. And she should certainly not have driven to Cheltenham on a whim. *I should just go home*, she decided, as she sipped her coffee in its delicate cup. *This was a bad idea*. After all, she was sure Macy hadn't seen her.

As she made this decision, the dynamic between the two seated men suddenly shifted. The blond stranger was leaning forward, his large hands splayed open, making emphatic gestures. Macy's expression was closed, apparently unmoved, but Jo felt sure his client was not used to being refused. With his blond hair and round face, he resembled a petulant, ageing cherub. She couldn't help but invent a scenario. Maybe the cherub suspected his wife of cheating and wanted some evidence? But she knew Macy didn't like such cases and, even if his agency took them on, he wouldn't deal with them himself. No, for Macy to come out to Cheltenham for a face-to-face meeting meant this was either an important client or complex new work. Jo favoured the former. A significant business client, she decided, judging from the expensive suit and charismatic air, who had come to Macy with personal problems, therefore crossing a boundary. This would explain the fleeting look of distaste she had seen cross Macy's face.

The two men were suddenly on their feet, facing each other frankly and shaking hands. Against Jo's expectations, it seemed like a deal had been done. The client did not hang around, however. After a brief nod, he was on the move, striding past her. *Wanting to shake the dust from his heels*, Jo thought, and wondered why that phrase had occurred to her.

'Hello, you,' came the familiar voice at her side. 'Practising being a proper PI, are you?'

She turned to Macy, hoping not to show how pleased she was to see him again. 'It's been a while.'

'There's been a pandemic,' he said. 'No one has seen anyone.' He looked around him at the couples and family groups enjoying their afternoon teas. 'Fancy a walk?'

She fell into step with him as they strolled through the lobby and out onto the pavement, shaded by horse chestnut trees. She knew he was still thinking about his meeting and the distracting, uneasy man who had just rushed past her.

'What was all that about?' she asked eventually. 'And who was the sulky cherub?'

He frowned at her, taking a turn into a garden square ahead of them. 'What do you mean? What cherub?'

Jo sent him a look. 'Your new client. You told me you were meeting him.'

'Did I?'

'Don't be annoying,' she said. 'I haven't seen you in months. Don't let's fall out in the first few minutes.'

'OK, we'll save it till later,' he said, adopting a nasty tone. 'How are your plans to set up a rival business going?'

Jo exerted all her patience. It was a warm, sunny day, and the roses were out in the square as they entered through a little gate. She had lied to her boyfriend and driven out of her way to meet Macy. She really didn't want to fall out with him. 'No need to worry on that score,' she said. 'I was never going to rival Macy and Wilson. I am just me, working in the sleepy Cotswolds, whereas you run a well-established private investigation agency in the Midlands. Plus, it's not a great time to start a new enterprise. The astrology business is doing better than ever, though, thanks for asking.'

'Good, I'm glad to hear it.' He found an empty wrought-iron bench and dropped onto it, still pensive.

'So, tell me about your meeting,' she said, sitting beside him, and, when he didn't answer, she just waited.

'I mean it, Jo,' he said eventually. 'Drop it, OK? You didn't see anyone today.'

'Then why invite me? You told me you were meeting a new client.' She paused as her mind presented options. 'Is he famous? Is that it? Are you afraid I'll recognize him? Or is he a spy?' she added. 'We are in Cheltenham after all. Is he a James Bond-type from GCHQ?'

'Now *you're* being annoying.'

'Only because you suddenly don't trust me.'

They lapsed into silence, both staring at the peach-coloured roses in the round bed in front of them. Jo decided to give it one more try. 'I thought he looked ill at ease, your client,' she observed. 'And he was very quick to leave once you'd shaken hands on the deal. Maybe he was worried you would change your mind.' This last was a moment of inspiration and she knew she'd struck a chord when Macy's dark eyes came up to meet hers.

'I won't change my mind,' he said. 'Look, it's not that I don't trust you, Jo, but you've just got to forget about that meeting. Let's just say it's an unusual case. Can we leave it there?'

'I've already deleted it,' she said. Although they both knew this wasn't true.

'Tell me what you've been up to instead.' His sudden, positive tone sounded a little fake, and she responded with an eyeroll but all the same addressed his question.

'I've witnessed both ends of the life cycle today,' she said. This had sounded quite clever when she'd thought of it in the car driving over, but out loud it just seemed strange and drew a frown from Macy.

'Birth and death? How so?'

'Well, I was at a christening this morning. Hence the outfit.' She waved a hand at her dress.

'I had noticed.'

'Teddy's brother and his wife have had a baby girl.'

'Teddy is still on the scene, then?'

'Yes, he is. And Rowanna?' Jo shot the question back at him. Rowanna worked at Macy and Wilson as a sort of office manager, and Jo had established that Rowanna and Macy had been an item for a while.

He nodded soberly and she went on. 'Anyway, I was coming out of church when Hanni rang me to say she'd found a body. Actual human remains. It was in a cellar in a pub where she was working.'

'I remember Hanni,' Macy put in. 'She runs the Rivermill Bookshop and does crystal healing and that sort of thing. It's not the sort of work where you encounter death.'

Jo granted him a look of moderate approval. 'That's right, and she was quite shaken up. Today she was meant to be "spiritually cleansing" the pub because they've had some ghost-hunting events there and some other weird stuff happening, which they are calling "poltergeist activity".' She emphasized the verbal quote marks to indicate her low opinion of such an analysis. 'The landlady, Sarah Robart, contacted Hanni — I think her husband Gary just goes along with anything his wife says. Anyway, they called in Hanni to help with, I don't know, getting rid of any unexplained nastiness, I suppose.' She waited for the raised eyebrows, but he just nodded.

'Go on.'

'Well, if you ask Hanni to do something, she will be thorough about it,' Jo said. 'She insisted on visiting every corner of the building, and even though Gary told her the cellar was flooded, she went down there and found this human body — female, I think — under a shelf.' Jo was unable to resist a small shiver and hoped he hadn't noticed. She had no intention of revealing to anyone that she had sneaked down to have a look at the body. It now seemed a weird thing to have done, even to her.

'Well, that justifies her fee. A corpse must produce a lot of negative energy,' Macy said, and, for the first time, she saw a hint of light in his eyes.

'So, of course, she called me.'

'Of course.' He began to smile back at her. 'And what did Jo Hughes, astrologer and PI-in-training, recommend?' This time his teasing was gentler.

'I told her to inform the police and let them get on with it. And that's what's happening now. In fact, they sort of chucked me out,' she laughed. 'I hope you approve?'

'I do approve. Never get mixed up in anything if you can leave it to the police.'

'But Hanni is mixed up in it,' Jo said more seriously. 'She's going to be a key witness. And so are these friends of hers, the Robarts, who run the pub. Hanni thinks they may want some help with dealing with it all.'

'If there is anything Hanni needs, just let me know. I can recommend a good solicitor, and I know a bit about what's involved in a coroner's inquiry.'

'Thanks,' she said. 'I might take you up on that.' She thought for a second and then added, decisively, 'If the Robarts ask me to act for them, I'll accept. After all, it would be my first solo case and I need the practical experience. Even if they can't pay me, it would be worth it to get established. I expect you had to work for nothing when you were setting up in business.'

He regarded her quizzically. 'You think?'

She laughed. 'OK, maybe not. But I have to start some-where, and it will help to build a reputation.'

'You've certainly been reading the textbooks,' Macy said. A frown crossed his face. 'I don't really understand why you want to get into this work as a career, to be honest. I'd get out of it, if I could.' He dipped his head in his hands for a moment or two, then looked up suddenly with a brighter expression. 'Come on, how about that drink now? Maybe not that stuffy hotel, but you must know a little cocktail bar?'

Somewhere to the west, a thin chime tolled the quarter hour and Jo looked at her watch unnecessarily. 'Oh, I don't think I can,' she said, continuing to avoid his eyes. 'I've really got to get back. In fact, I should go and talk to my new clients, and I really must get some time with Hanni to ask her about finding the body. I'm nowhere near getting the full story yet.'

'You must?' Macy said, regarding her with his opaque eyes. A minute passed, and then he said, 'Well, if business demands it, then you must. But if you need help with any of it, just give me a call.'

He walked back to her car and they parted with a hug and a chaste kiss. Even while she savoured the sensation, eyes closed, feeling his warm skin under the cotton shirt, a contrary part of her was also eager to get away. It was as if guilt had caught up with her on the bench in the rose garden, flung a net over her and dragged her homewards.

She drove home to Stroud, parked as near to her flat as she could, and called Teddy. She found herself making up a story about Marie being worried about her son, who was refusing to stay on at school to do his A Levels. This part was true, but Jo knew her competent and self-sufficient elder sister would never have bothered to call her about it. That unwelcome, flustered feeling returned and she halted in the middle of a rambling explanation, asking brightly instead, 'How is the lunch going? Is everyone having a good time?'

'Jo, it's four o'clock. Lunch was over hours ago. I went back to Andy's for a coffee and we played with the baby. It's hard to believe, but Lela-May wasn't a bit tired. While I was there, she learned to roll.'

'To what?' Jo was wondering if she should have just driven over to Teddy's, as he was at home. They had got used to spending an equal amount of time in each other's places.

'To roll over. Babies have to learn to do that, you know. It's an important stage in their development.'

'Oh, that's a good thing then. Shall I come over?'

She noticed an uncharacteristic hesitation from Teddy. He said he'd only just got home and suggested a pizza tomorrow night instead. Jo agreed, but felt unreasonably put out. They chatted idly while she walked towards her flat on the corner of Fleece Alley and King Street. She punched in the keycode for the outer gate, climbed the outdoor steps, past the bank's backyard door and in through her own front door, while still listening to Teddy enthuse about his little niece and how well she'd behaved at the hotel. She found her thoughts turning to her potential new 'case'. Having declared to Macy that she was going to accept it, she was now even more determined to do so.

'We missed you at the lunch though,' Teddy was saying. 'I explained it was about your family so it was understood.' A pang of guilt made Jo hasten to end the call and she wound up staring at a distorted image of herself in the chrome of the kettle. Her own treacherous dark eyes stared back, as she clutched her phone and frowned. If she was going to take on this local case, Teddy would have to know about it sooner or later, and she was fairly sure he was not going to like the idea. Being a PI was not a Scarborough sort of job, she thought, and decided to tell him over their pizza tomorrow.

'I'm in the police car,' Hanni said, when Jo called, her voice low and constrained. 'The officer is very kindly giving me a lift back to the New Navigation so I can collect my bike.'

'Oh, OK. They took you to the police station, did they? You had to sign a witness statement? I realize you can't say much,' Jo added quickly, 'but are you all right?'

Hanni assured her that she was, but Jo knew now was not the time to pursue it. Instead, she asked about Sarah and Gary Robart.

'They've gone ahead in another car,' Hanni went on. 'They will have to close the pub for a while. This is like an explosion in their lives and their business, and they don't know what to do for the best.'

'I will help if I can. Look, I can drive over there now to see them,' Jo offered. 'In fact, I'll meet you there.'

'That would be really good.' Although Hanni was still guarded, there was no mistaking her friend's relief, and Jo felt even more certain there was something her friend was keeping from her.

CHAPTER FOUR

Hanni was waiting for her outside the pub, hands in the pockets of her patchwork jacket. Gary's wellies had been exchanged for her own rope sandals, but her face remained wan and troubled. 'I wanted to ask you something,' she looked at her watch distractedly, 'but I've got to get home soon. I tried to explain on the phone, and I think I just worried them.' Hanni lived with her mother and sister, both of whom had been ill and, as far as Jo could work out, now seemed completely reliant on Hanni.

'Don't worry, I'll drive you. We'll get the bike in the car somehow. How did it go at the police station?'

'They took a statement and fingerprints and DNA samples.' Hanni bit her lip. 'Do you think I need to be concerned? Do I need a solicitor? Because I don't know any.'

'They haven't talked about charging you, have they?'

'No, of course not.' Hanni's voice rose in alarm. 'What could they charge me with? I wasn't trespassing. I had the publicans' permission—'

'You shouldn't need a solicitor if they've just taken a witness statement,' Jo reassured her. 'But if it comes to that, Macy has offered some help.'

'You've been in touch with David?' Hanni persisted in using Macy's first name, although Jo never did. 'That was very good of him.'

'What else were the police asking? Do they think it is Leah Ellerman, like the builder guy said?'

'No, they didn't say a word about that. We went through in detail about exactly what I'd found and the timings, which I was a bit vague about. Of course, I didn't say that you'd seen it too.' She paused and looked earnestly at her friend. 'You did see it, didn't you?' When Jo nodded, Hanni asked, 'What did you see?'

'I saw the body wrapped in clear plastic under the shelf. I saw her hand half-sticking out—' Jo shivered, although the evening air was balmy. 'It seemed quite slight. That's why I was pretty sure it was a woman. And she was wearing a hooded coat, like a parka.'

They both fell silent for a moment before Jo pursued her questions about the police interview.

'They asked lots of questions about Sarah's so-called paranormal evenings and whether I was involved,' Hanni said.

'Are you? And have they really got a resident ghost and poltergeist?'

'I don't have anything to do with any of that, but I'll get Sarah to explain.' Hanni sighed. 'Come on, we'd best go in.'

The blackboard outside the New Navigation now read 'Closed Until Further Notice'. Jo edged past it and Hanni tapped lightly on the front door. As she did, the sound of raised voices reached them: Sarah's voice shouting harshly was followed by the rumble of Gary's answering bass, both brought up sharp by their knocking. Hanni chewed her lip as Sarah called out, 'Come in, it's open.' In any other circumstances Jo might have been tempted to make an excuse and go home. But these were her clients and this was her case.

Sarah was in the same corner seat as when Jo had last seen her, holding another cigarette in her fingers and wearing an irritable expression which she didn't try to disguise. Gary paced around the bar. 'Don't just let people in — especially now,' he snapped at his wife. 'It could be the press — or anybody.'

'I knew who it was,' Sarah said.

Gary turned to Jo, his narrow eyes sharp with anxiety. 'I should explain that we can't afford to pay you anything. What we really need is someone to help us manage the publicity. We've already had the local press here in numbers this afternoon, and no doubt they'll be back tomorrow. The brewery are sending someone but they will likely do more harm than good.'

'You need to understand, it's my first case,' Jo said. 'And I'm not sure what help I'll be.'

'You need to work on your marketing,' Sarah said drily. She pushed back her chair and came to stand in front of Jo, resting her hands lightly on her shoulders. They were more or less the same height, and her greenish eyes looked directly into Jo's steady brown gaze. Eventually her face seemed to relax a notch. She turned to her husband. 'Gary, how about a brandy for our visitors? And for me, come to that. Jo, we may not pay in money but we are grateful, as Gary says. We always remember our friends.'

'Jo needs you to be completely honest with her,' Hanni said, accepting a shot of brandy. 'And she needs to know what happens in your paranormal evenings.'

'Our monthly spiritual sessions,' Sarah corrected, downing her drink in one. 'But not now, we're all too knackered. Maybe tomorrow?'

Jo took her brandy from the metal tray. 'And anything you know about how that body came to be in your cellar, of course.'

'On that, I don't have a clue,' Sarah said emphatically, 'but I am pretty sure Matty is right about who it is.'

Even her husband took a breath at this announcement, and Hanni sat down suddenly. Jo paused with her brandy to her lips. 'Go on.'

Sarah took a drag on her cigarette, lifting her round face away from the smoke. Jo noticed she had unusually lucid eyes, which shifted in colour, now seeming more hazel than green. Jo felt the other woman was enjoying the dramatic moment. 'I feel sure it is Leah Ellerman,' she said. 'She owns the end cottage. In fact, she owns all of them, but she lives in number five, at the end of the terrace. She's renovating each of them to let as holiday cottages.'

'Matty Sullivan has been working on them for about six months,' Gary supplied. 'He's building her an extension too. Her own personal gym, I believe.'

'What makes you say it's her?' Jo asked.

'I just know,' Sarah shrugged. 'It felt right when Matty said it, and I haven't seen Leah for a week or so either. Not that we care too much. I'm not going to pretend I like the woman.' She looked at them both defiantly and went on. 'I know she works in London and sometimes she stays over, but she's not normally away this long. Her car's gone too,' she added, eyeing their rapt faces with a certain satisfaction.

'And when did you notice her car was gone?' Jo asked, recovering first.

Gary gave a wheezy laugh. 'Sarah, you do realize you could just be making all this up to fit a story in your head, don't you?'

'I noticed about two days ago,' Sarah responded to Jo. 'But of course, I didn't think much of it then. Listening to the police and Matty, plus my own instincts, I just feel it's her—'

'You have absolutely no evidence!' Gary broke in, staring at his wife in exasperation.

Sarah shrugged. 'I don't need evidence. I'm not the fucking police, am I? Excuse my French,' she added with a nod to Jo and Hanni. 'But you have offered to help us, so I thought it best to tell you what I know. And I think you will find I'm not wrong.'

'Did you tell the police your theory?' Jo asked.

'No, I'm not inclined to make their job any easier. They didn't ask, and they had Matty bending their ear about it. I told them Leah's car was missing because they asked if I'd noticed anything unusual. No doubt they will know soon enough anyway. They've taken the body away to carry out their forensic checks — DNA and all that.'

Gary heaved an audible sigh and glanced nervously at Jo. 'I wouldn't be surprised if you changed your mind about helping us now.'

Jo got to her feet. 'No, I'm still up for it. I'll advise you as best I can, and if you cover my expenses, that's all I ask at the moment.' She held out her hand and Sarah shook it without hesitation. 'You probably need to warn any visitors not to talk to the press too,' she added. 'Are you expecting anyone tomorrow?'

'Only Maureen, the cleaner. She's due at seven o'clock but I'll call and tell her not to come,' Sarah said. 'The back room and cellar are still out of bounds anyway — even for us. The brewery said they were sending someone, but they didn't say when. I can't really put them off. Unfortunately.'

'What about your security arrangements?' Jo asked. 'I noticed there's another entrance to the cellar through a sort of trapdoor opening. The body was quite close to those steps.'

'That's the keg run,' Gary said. 'Those cellar doors open onto the path by the side here.' He pointed towards the back room of the pub, which lay behind the bar. 'Back in the day, they used to roll the kegs down the runners, but I am not keeping the same amount of stock these days and, since the cellar's been flooded, I've been easily storing it out the back of the kitchen.'

Sarah groaned. 'The police asked us endless questions about our security arrangements, as will the brewery chap, no doubt. Yes, we only have limited CCTV, and yes, the back door is often left on the latch, and no, we don't keep a list of who has the key code.' She sighed heavily. 'Suffice to say: could do better.'

Jo could see that Hanni was eager to get home, so she promised to call the Robarts in the morning and she and her friend walked back to the car and stowed her bike in the boot in silence. They were both so preoccupied with their own thoughts that they barely spoke during the drive, and the overcrowded hedgerows created their own darkness in the lanes. It was deep twilight by the time Jo reached Slad, where Hanni lived with her mother and sister in the family's farmhouse. Turning into the farm track, Jo couldn't resist asking, 'How well do you know Sarah?'

Hanni took her time answering as the lane twisted upwards into open land and a lighter dusk. 'Oh, I've known her for years. She was a member of the Mind, Body and Spirit network before me. In fact, she used to virtually run it, but then she fell out with one of the other women, who wanted to take over, and she left.'

'What did they fall out about?'

Hanni looked across at her. 'That's a strange question. This was years ago, Josephine. Long before you moved to Stroud. Sarah was more part of the town then. She had a stall in the indoor market and used to offer tarot readings. She might even have had a shop for a while. There was a woman who had more commercial ideas and they just fell out, you know, like committees always do. Sarah's not active in the network anymore.'

Jo drew up on the flattened grass in front of the low farm-house. Hanni's family had sold most of the land and had long since ceased to work the farm themselves. There was a single, low-voltage light in the porch and Jo thought she saw a curtain move in one of the windows. Hanni unbuckled her seatbelt and opened the car door. 'This is all so good of you, and thank you for the lift. Do you want to come in? Mum and April are always asking about you and would love to see you.'

'No, you've had a horrible day. Go and let them know you're OK and get some sleep.'

Hanni reached over and hugged her, but Jo thought she caught the sound of a small sob as her friend clambered out of the car. She still felt sure that Hanni was withholding something, which she had never suspected in all the years they'd been friends. The thought deepened her unease as she watched Hanni slip in through the front door of the farm-house. Then she reversed out of the drive and headed home.

CHAPTER FIVE

The next morning found Jo in her workroom at her flat, responding to emails about her astrology business. Paid work had to come first, and she had a few commissions outstanding and her monthly newsletter to write, which she wanted to publish before the summer solstice. She had also promised to draw up a natal chart for Lela-May. Birth charts for newborn babies always had to be handled sensitively, and this one bore the added complication of her being a Scarborough baby. She'd not heard from Teddy since the arrangement to meet for pizza and she decided to message him to agree when to meet. Remembering her brief rendezvous with Macy left her with a residual guilty feeling and she found herself taking longer than the text really deserved.

She started her newsletter, brought her social media up to date and had completed the calculations for the baby's chart when the doorbell rang. She left the printer churning out the diagram and went downstairs. DS Diane Watts was standing on her doorstep holding up her warrant card, which Jo thought was rather unnecessary.

'I have a few questions about the discovery at the New Navigation yesterday. Do you mind if I come in?'

Jo had been anticipating the police interview and hoped it might provide an opportunity to find out more information. However, she felt slightly wrong-footed by the call at her flat. There was something about Diane Watts that always put her on the defensive, and the woman's appraising glances as Jo led her to the sitting room did nothing to alleviate this feeling. DS Watts took the proffered seat on the sofa and brought her flat brown gaze back to Jo. 'This needn't take long. I just need to clarify your timings and actions at the scene.'

Jo consulted her phone for the exact time of Hanni's call and calculated that her journey from the church to the pub had taken about twenty minutes. She decided to say nothing about Gary's initial reluctance to call the police, not least because he was now a client.

'Why you? I mean, I don't mean to be rude, but you're an astrologer, aren't you? What did Hanni Light think you were going to be able to do? Why didn't she just call us, or at least tell the landlord, Mr Robart?'

'She called me after she'd told Gary. I think she just needed a friend.'

'I understand you were at a christening at the time?' DS Watts ostentatiously placed her notebook open on the coffee table. 'And Hanni Light was aware of this. So it wasn't exactly a convenient time for you, was it? In fact, I believe Miss Light called you twice, because you didn't pick up first time?'

'I was in church.' Jo tried to keep her tone level.

'Exactly. The Scarboroughs' new baby, I believe. Over at Winson? Beautiful old church, isn't it? And they went on to the Winson Manor House Hotel afterwards for lunch?'

That was the trouble with the Scarboroughs, Jo thought. *Everyone in this small town knew them.*

'So you must have had to leave early?' DS Watts persisted. 'Why did you do that? Why not just give her advice on the phone?'

Jo wrestled with this for a second. The honest answer was that she had been glad of a reason to escape, but she could barely admit this to herself, so she certainly wasn't going to say as much to Diane Watts. 'I knew Hanni was badly shaken and she'd asked for my help.' She settled on this as a good enough answer, adding, 'It was a horrible thing to discover, after all.'

'Do you believe in all that tosh about spiritual cleansing?' The detective changed tack, and Jo waited to see where she was going with it before responding. 'That sane business people like Mr and Mrs Robart would pay for such services is almost beyond belief, isn't it?'

'I don't know much about it,' Jo said, honestly. 'Anyway, I thought you said you understood it?'

DS Watts wrinkled her nose. 'I didn't say I believed in it. And let's face it, Jo, with possibly the best intentions, your friend has placed herself in a difficult position, wouldn't you say? She conned them into believing that a bit of smoke could get rid of so-called negative energy, which then gave her the right to snoop around the place all day. Every nook and cranny, that's what she said to us.'

'Hanni didn't offer. They asked her to do the cleansing. It's on her website as a service she provides.'

'I have to pose the difficult questions, Jo. I'm sure you understand,' DS Watts said. Jo found her superior tone even more irritating, but said nothing and her silence was rewarded when the detective's phone rang. Avidly listening in, Jo deduced that the station was calling to say some results were back. Possibly forensics, she guessed.

'Have you confirmed the identity of the body yet?' she asked as soon as the other woman had finished her call.

'I can't discuss that.' DS Watts packed up her notebook and prepared to leave. 'We'll have to continue this at the station. Can you come in and sign a statement this afternoon?'

'Is it Leah Ellerman?' Jo asked, and DS Watts' needled expression told her that both the builder and Sarah's instincts had been right.

'I'm not able to confirm or deny that,' the detective said quickly, the official mask back in place. 'But, can I ask, what makes you suggest that name?'

Jo led her back down the hall. 'I was there when Matty Sullivan, the builder, burst into the pub and announced it, remember?'

'That's little more than gossip.' DS Watts sighed. 'This afternoon at the police station, can we just stick to facts, please? See you at two thirty p.m.'

Jo watched as the detective crossed the short concrete bridge which led to the outside steps down to Fleece Alley, and wondered how she always managed to get on the wrong side of Diane Watts. If she was going to make a success of her first solo case, she would need the support of the police, she reminded herself, as she returned indoors.

A ginger cat took advantage of her distraction to stroll in behind her. Jo lived above a bank in a two-storey flat, which had once been their offices. She had inherited the cat from the bank too. The loose arrangement was that Halifax was fed by the bank staff during office hours and looked after himself at night. In fact, however, he visited Jo's flat any time of the day or night he could gain access. Although her flat was 'only rented', as Teddy liked to point out, she loved it and had so far resisted his suggestions to buy a place together. Macy had never made such offers, and nor was he likely to, she reflected, as she made herself another coffee. But if he had, her answer would have been the same.

She took the coffee upstairs to her workroom to see what an online search could produce on Leah Ellerman. There was some discrepancy about her age — either forty-one or for-ty-two — but the date of birth was 19 October, which made her a Libran. She had been born in Stokesly, Gloucestershire, and, as a schoolgirl, had some success as a junior showjumper. There were pictures of her with rosettes and trophies, proudly holding the bridles of glossy ponies. The only recent photo-graph of Leah was a corporate headshot with her straight fair hair in a smart bob, perfectly cut to accentuate an angular face. She was described as a VP at StadtBank, a German bank based in London. Judging by their organization chart, this was a senior position just below board level. Jo was trying to establish exactly what this involved by weaving her way through their complex website when Gary Robart rang.

He got straight to the point. 'We've got the media outside the pub again. Mainly local papers but some TV too. They are shouting questions at us every time we go out. It's doing my head in, Jo.'

'Don't go out,' Jo said. 'Don't engage with them at all. Anything you say will only add fuel to the flames. Are the SOCO people still there?'

'They say they are just finishing, but when they take the police cordon down, it's only going to get worse.'

Jo explained about her interview with DS Watts and promised she would go over to the pub afterwards. Gary seemed satisfied with this and assured her that he and Sarah would stay indoors for the rest of the day. The pub was, of course, still closed. Despite Jo's best efforts, however, it wasn't a short call and it meant she was almost late for her appointment.

She was shown to a waiting area and passed the time by reviewing her sketchy notes on Leah Ellerman. She recognized DC Williams as he bustled past, escorting a middle-aged man in a checked shirt into the office behind her. The man scanned the waiting room through heavy, square spectacles with an almost desperate look, as if he half-hoped someone would come and rescue him. Jo heard him tell the policeman that he had to be back home in half an hour, as his kids were due home from school, and she wondered if this was Nora Hutchinson's dad. She was leaving another message for Teddy, who had not yet replied to her earlier one, when she overheard a woman at the counter making a complaint.

'I shouldn't need to come and see you. I have things to organize: the registrar, the funeral, the wake. It will all fall to me, and I'm afraid this is just wasting my time.' The woman had a harsh, hectoring tone, which Jo tried to blot out. 'I need to speak to the officer in charge of the investigation. Someone who can make decisions, please. Quite honestly, you have been less use than a chatbot.'

At this rudeness, Jo couldn't help but glance up. The woman was large as well as loud, with a mackintosh draped around her shoulders. She wore wide trousers and flat shoes. The raincoat was a Burberry, Jo noted, and she had a cut-glass county accent, which marked her out as a certain, landed Cotswold type.

'Please can you just go and fetch the person investigating my sister's death,' the woman continued. This caught Jo's attention and, although a screen blocked her view of the officer replying, it became apparent that the loud woman had been asked to wait. She turned towards the plastic chairs where Jo was sitting and, looking through her rather than at her, heaved an impatient sigh.

'It's a pain, isn't it?' Jo said, looking at her watch for emphasis. 'I had an appointment here for half past two, but . . .' She lifted her hands to indicate that she was still waiting.

The other woman frowned as if mildly irritated to be drawn into conversation. 'I just don't have the time to spare. That's the issue.'

'I'm in the same boat,' Jo said with feeling, conscious that she hadn't even started the interpretation of Lela-May's chart. 'Are you waiting to see DS Watts too?'

'No, DCI Rose is the man in charge of my case. I've asked to speak to the organ grinder because I'm fed up with being fobbed off by monkeys. The police haven't answered any of my questions. They are fine if you want to splurge your feelings and cry all over them, but not if you ask them hard questions, I find. They tried to foist a Family Liaison Officer on me. What even is that? Some kind of social worker?' The woman rounded her eyes in horror. 'I gave a flat no to that notion.'

'I suppose that DCI Rose is a senior officer,' Jo said, keen to keep the conversation going. 'So, once you get hold of him you should be all right.'

'I doubt that very much—' The woman halted suddenly and tipped her head to one side. 'I say, you're not the young woman who found my sister, are you?' she asked abruptly.

'Because DS Watts is on the same inquiry. I'm sorry to ask, but if you were, it would save me an awful lot of time and trouble.'

'What do you mean, found your sister?'

The woman took a few steps in Jo's direction. 'I'm Irene Ellerman-James,' she said, as if that should explain everything. When it clearly didn't, she sat down a couple of seats away and met Jo's eyes soberly. 'I learned of the death of my sister yesterday. Her body was found in the cellar of a pub only a few miles from my house.' She came to a halt and her plain, wide face looked older and wearier.

Jo judged that the woman was at least fifty, which made her about ten years older than her sister. Her clothes and her manner were somehow middle-aged, and it seemed she was used to having things her own way.

'That is about all they will tell me so far. I don't know how she died or where exactly she was found, or by whom. I'm literally starved of information,' Irene went on, her voice and colour rising again. 'All I know is that a young woman found her. This will be all over the local press tomorrow and there are undoubtedly journalists out there who know more than I do.'

Jo had a brief flashback to the wrapped, oozing body on the brick, cellar floor and felt momentarily stunned as she grappled with the fact that she'd been staring at this woman's sister. She could understand her driving need for information. 'I am sorry,' she said.

The other woman blinked and nodded, pressing her eyelids briefly. 'Yes, well, you've just got to get on with whatever life throws at you, haven't you?'

'I am here to give a statement about . . . about the discovery, but I'm not going to be able to tell them, or you, very much,' Jo said. 'It was my friend who found your sister. She called me because she was very shaken up by it.'

'I understand she was a cleaner at the pub? The woman who found her?' Irene Ellerman-James was watching her closely.

'No, not really, not the actual cleaner, that's someone else. Hanni, that's my friend, carries out spiritual cleansing, and the landlady had asked her to perform this service on the pub. Hanni is a crystal healer and it's something she does.'

'Oh, I see.' Irene's expression did not match her words, but she rushed on to her next question. 'And do you know where Leah was? And how she was?'

Jo hesitated before answering, reluctant to share graphic details. 'Well, a little, but I would have thought the police should tell you.'

'It's like getting blood out of a stone, believe me.' It was clear that Irene would have asked more questions, but she was interrupted by the desk officer, who appeared in the doorway behind them, regarding them both with suspicion. 'If you'd come with me, please, Mrs Ellerman-James. Miss Hughes, DS Watts will be with you in a moment.'

'I'll be in touch,' Irene muttered, before getting to her feet. Jo slipped her business card into the woman's large, soft hand. Admittedly, the card related to her astrology business, but it contained the necessary details. She wasn't sure whether to believe Irene Ellerman-James. Surely a close relative couldn't know less than the local press? Later, when she had finished her statement, she asked DS Watts what information they were releasing to relatives and the media.

'We have spoken at length with her sister and there's a notice already out to the media with a press conference planned for tomorrow afternoon at two p.m.,' the detective told her briskly. 'Journalists may ask you for views, but we strongly advise you not to comment as it may hinder the inquiry. After all, we all want a swift conclusion.'

It was clear that DS Watts was going to stick to the official line and Jo left the station feeling as bereft of information as Irene Ellerman-James had claimed to be. She had promised to meet her new clients, but had little idea how she was going to be of any use to them. So, on her way, she called Macy.

'I could do with some advice.' She didn't like admitting it, but he had offered to help, so she ploughed on. 'It's about this case that Hanni has got me involved in. A woman's body has been found in a pub cellar and the police have completely clammed up about it. I am pretty sure it is Leah Ellerman, a woman in her early forties who lives close by and owns properties near the pub. But they haven't confirmed that officially. And they're not telling the relatives much either. What can I do to find out what's going on? I don't even know how she died, or how long she'd been there.'

'Do you *want* to know?' Macy asked. Judging from the sounds in the background, he was in the office. 'It's down to the police how much they share.'

'I feel like I'm at the back of the queue,' Jo complained. 'And I've got to tell Gary and Sarah something.'

'Maybe it's not information that your clients are after. But there is one thing you could try. Have you thought about going to the mortuary? If you can find out where your body is being held, I have a few contacts in that line of work, and they can be surprisingly well-informed.'

'OK, thanks. I'll try it. Anyway, are you OK? How is the Angry Cherub? You know, the mystery man you met in Cheltenham.'

There was a pause in which Jo very distinctly heard Macy close his office door. 'I told you there was no meeting and there is no mystery client.'

'You see, that's another example,' Jo sighed, staring out at the police cars and official-looking white vans surrounding the pub. 'No one is telling me anything.'

'Believe me, sometimes a little knowledge is actually a safer thing,' Macy said before he rang off. Despite how annoying he could be, Jo had to admit, she would never have thought of the mortuary as a source of information. Sitting outside the pub, she performed a few quick searches on her phone to discover where the body was likely to be held. Once she'd texted Macy with the name of the Gloucestershire mortuary, she braced herself to face questions from her clients. She had to weave her way through a little crowd of uniformed police and journalists who mingled amiably either side of the police cordon, but once Jo said she was expected by Sarah and Gary Robart, a PC let her through.

Although she would never admit it to him, it turned out that Macy was right. The publicans didn't particularly seem to want more information. They were sitting despondently at a picnic bench on a private patio at the back of the pub, out of sight of any journalists, or indeed police officers, as it was tucked behind the kitchen. 'It's like a goldfish bowl,' Sarah sighed. 'And I'm dreading the press conference. The brewery have said we shouldn't attend, but it might make us look guilty if we don't.'

'Guilty of what?' Gary demanded. 'Don't be ridiculous. No one can really think that we—' He broke off, shaking his head at the deserted tables in the beer garden in front of him. 'No, it would be mad to go.'

'I can go for you and report back,' Jo offered, and they seemed to accept this plan. 'I do have a few questions for you first, though.'

'Ask away.' Gary gave a resigned sigh. 'I swear to God, there is no question we haven't already answered a thousand times.'

Consulting her notes, Jo asked them about Leah's car, which Sarah said was a grey Hyundai Tucson. 'I just noticed about the middle of last week that I hadn't seen it for a while,' she said, off-handedly. 'She did go away now and again, so I didn't think much of it.'

'Where Leah parks is not on our land,' Gary explained. 'That actually belongs to the canal cottages, so she owns it and her tenants also use it for parking. There are no CCTV cameras there and ours only cover the pub car park and the garden.' He pointed ahead to the empty tables.

But Jo was staring across the canal to the little terrace. There were five houses in all. From this angle, she could see the scaffolding around the side of a new extension to the first house in the terrace more clearly. It was the cottage closest to the narrow lane, which ran along the back of the pub, over another bridge. Leah's car park must open onto this lane, Jo assumed, and decided she needed a thorough tour of both lanes, bridges and the canal cottages as soon as the police work was finished.

'That's Leah's house, isn't it?' Jo said, pointing to the scaffolding. 'I need to know about all her tenants in the other cottages.'

Sarah obligingly pulled a notepad towards her and began to scribble a list. At the top, she wrote: *Leah Ellerman, no. 5.*

'She lived on her own?' Jo asked, looking over Sarah's shoulder.

'Yes, she worked for a London firm. Sometimes she seemed to be working from home and sometimes commuting or staying over. She was a single woman, not accountable to anyone.' Sarah nodded, head down over the list, adding more dreamily, 'She was a lonely spirit.'

She handed over the list and Jo ran her eye down it. Number one, at the opposite end of the terrace, was noted as a holiday let and she asked who was renting it.

'We don't know her name but it's a woman on her own, and she's been here a fortnight or so,' Gary said, reading over Jo's shoulder. 'She's not been into the pub.'

'It's not what you expect from a holiday, is it? To have a murder inquiry outside your window. I need to go and see her before she decides to go back home,' Jo said. Next door to the holiday let, number two was noted as 'being renovated' by Sarah and, glancing up, Jo saw that a mound of topsoil was just visible in its tiny front garden.

'It's nearly finished apparently,' Sarah said. 'Maureen told me it should be ready in September.'

Gary poked a calloused finger at the note against *no. 3: the Hutchinson family.* 'Gil Hutchinson is a lovely guy. Single dad with two teenagers: a girl and a boy. Don't know how the hell he does it, but he copes brilliantly.'

'Just as single mums do, I expect,' Sarah commented drily. 'Mr and Mrs Lilley — George and Valerie — live at number four, next to Leah. They are more reserved and elderly. I see more of her than him. She often comes to my paranormal evenings.' She turned to Jo suddenly. 'I haven't forgotten that you want to know what they involve, so I wondered if you wanted to take part? We are due to have a session on Thursday night — why not come along? Hanni is welcome too, if she wants.'

Gary gave his wife a sharp look. 'Surely you can't be intending to hold Thursday's session? Not with the press all over us like a rash?'

'Of course.' Sarah lifted her shoulders. 'They will have got fed up by then, and they're not here at night anyway. People need the sessions, Gary. They rely on our evenings to give them sustenance for their loss and . . .' She paused. 'For all sorts of reasons, we must go on with them. I won't be beaten by this latest disaster.'

Jo accepted Sarah's invitation for the Thursday evening, although not without some inner qualms, and promised to be back in touch after the press conference. Exiting through the police cordon was almost as difficult as getting in. A few of the journalists asked her name and a local TV camera crew appeared to be filming, but one of the PCs told her not to be alarmed. 'There's nothing for them to report, so don't worry, you won't be on the telly tonight,' he grinned as he lifted the tape.

'How are Sarah and Gary?' a woman's voice called after her. Jo saw a tall woman break free of the little crowd and stride towards her. 'You must be a friend of theirs, or they wouldn't let you through. I know them both, you see, especially Sarah.' The woman kept pace with her on the way to her car. She was half a head taller than Jo, about the same age, with an English rose complexion and a Welsh accent. 'How are they doing?'

'Sounds like you know them better than me.' Jo felt the need to be cagey, as the woman was clearly a journalist.

'So, if you're not a close friend, why go and see them?' she persisted, jogging to catch up, a laptop bag bumping at her side. She watched as Jo unlocked her car. 'Look, I'm Alys Parry, and I've been covering this story over the last twelve months. You've probably seen it in the *Standard*. About the engineer ghost at the pub? More recently, I did a feature on the poltergeist activity. I'm in negotiation with a podcast team on that, and it was on local telly news.'

Jo hesitated. She remembered seeing something about a TV ghost hunt at a local pub, but it was months ago, and she hadn't connected it with the New Navigation. The journalist went on, 'Recently, they've been holding regular so-called paranormal evenings. And now a dead body. I like the couple — genuinely — and this could be either really bad or really good for them, publicity-wise. I can help them find a way through it.' Alys Parry paused. 'And you? What's your interest?'

'Jo Hughes. I really don't know Sarah and Gary very well — only through a friend. So I can't give you anything for your paper. It's not because I want to be difficult but because I really don't know anything.' Jo picked her way warily through truths and omissions, and still felt she'd said too much. She opened her car door.

'All right.' Alys nodded briskly, her long, bright hair flying out from her face. 'But this story has got a run in it yet, so maybe we can help each other out at some stage. There's a press conference tomorrow afternoon at St Luke's parish hall. Hope to see you there.' She stood back with a wave and Jo drove off, still wary but more positive. Maybe she wasn't as excluded from information as she'd thought. Alys Parry could turn out to be a good contact, although she would need to be managed, and Jo now had the list of Leah Ellerman's tenants and Macy's tip about the mortuary. There was also one person very close to home who was bound to know more about the Ellerman family.

* * *

That evening, when they were established at a corner table at his favourite bistro, Jo tackled Teddy about the Ellermans. 'You know all the local families, don't you?'

Teddy looked surprised. 'The golfers, you mean? I know all those. That's part of my job.' He glanced around the dimly lit restaurant, which was quiet on a Monday night. She noticed he seemed unusually on edge and felt a tingle of apprehension, which she tried to ignore.

'Not golfers, no. I mean the county types.' She pressed on with her questions. 'Those families who own show-jumping ponies and send their kids to boarding school.' Jo glanced at the menu. She had been surprised at his choice of the bistro, as she had expected their usual pizza place on a midweek night. 'In particular,' she went on, 'the Ellermans. Have you heard of them?'

Teddy frowned. 'Yes, I suppose so. Harold Ellerman ran a furniture business, and made his own artisan stuff locally, which sold all over the world, as I recall. But Mum knows them better than me. You know she was disappointed you didn't come to the lunch yesterday,' he added. 'She wants to get to know you better.'

Jo flushed. *Again.* It was her guilty conscience, she knew. But she was right to feel guilty about meeting Macy in secret, she reminded herself. Teddy deserved better. 'I know. I'm really sorry,' she said, beginning a stumbling apology, and was rescued by the waiter, arriving to take their order.

'Honestly, don't worry, I know it was important,' Teddy said when they were alone again. 'Family always has to take priority.'

As the olives, crusty bread, oil and vinegar were delivered, Jo tucked in, partly to cover her embarrassment. 'Going back to the Ellermans,' she said, tearing off some bread for dipping, 'what can you remember about them? Is their furniture business still going? Are they minted?'

'Yes, I'd say they are pretty comfortable. I went to a garden party once at their house in Stokesly. It's a typical Cotswold-stone manor house. A nice old pile, if I remember correctly. I played tennis there, and I remember they looked after their grass courts well.' He chose an olive thoughtfully and announced, 'Duncan Ellerman, that was the guy. He took over the business when Harold died. Affable chap. He was my tennis partner. Quite a bit older than me, but could still play. I think we might have won.' He grinned at her briefly and his handsome eyes crinkled. 'Don't ask me who we were playing against, because I have no clue. Anyway, why the interest in the Ellermans?'

'Oh, one of my clients mentioned them,' Jo said. She guessed that the news of Leah Ellerman's death would be out tomorrow, but it didn't seem the right moment for explaining, so she changed the subject. 'I started Lela-May's natal chart today.'

'That's going to be interesting.' A broad smile lit up Teddy's face and Jo couldn't help smiling back. 'She is going to be smart. We don't need the stars to tell us that. She can already tell who is speaking. You can see it by the way she looks at you. She has a different expression for every member of the family.'

'It was grizzly when she looked at me.' Jo laughed, but Teddy seemed in the mood to take everything seriously, and he reached over and took her hand.

'That's only because she doesn't know you yet.'

With a sharper stab of apprehension, Jo reached for her glass of wine and took a fortifying gulp while Teddy went on, 'In fact, she's such a delight, that having her around has made me think about what it would be like to start a family.'

'Oh.' Jo couldn't find anything else to say. It was not that the idea had never occurred to her. Of course she had envisaged a future for her and Teddy, even if the picture was rather blurry. She knew her mother and Marie could easily fill in the details for her, if asked, as they undoubtedly had a more defined plan for them both. As for motherhood, it had always seemed a possibility way off in the future, although she was aware that she was dodging the biological facts.

'I know that we'd have to do some conventional things first,' he said. 'Such as get married and buy a house together, but, before I got too carried away,' he paused and fidgeted with his wine glass, 'I thought I'd ask how you felt about it?'

'I don't really know.' Jo found herself floundering, and could feel her heart pounding as if she was in the midst of a sweaty workout. 'You and me? Married with a mortgage?'

He laughed. 'Well, of course, I've already got one of those, and you can't live like an eternal student forever, you know.'

'I don't—' Jo began, halted, and began again. 'I've got a business to run — two, in fact — and I've only just qualified as a PI. I want to get established in both . . .' She sighed. It sounded inadequate even to her own ears. 'Anyway, eternal is forever, so you don't need to say both.'

Teddy looked confused and she felt instantly guilty again.

'I'm sorry, it's a bit of a surprise,' she mumbled.

Teddy said, of course, he understood, and moved smoothly onto other subjects.

Lying beside him in her bed later that night, Jo found herself doubting whether he did understand. How could he? She didn't really get it herself. And, while she was being honest with herself, she had to admit it wasn't really the surprise she had claimed. Teddy had started a few conversations lately about their future, which had made her feel almost panicky. Until now, she'd managed to divert him onto other subjects, but that was a shabby way to behave, she told herself.

She pushed away the covers, went downstairs and made herself a peppermint tea while Teddy slept soundly. Halifax cadged some extra food while her tea was infusing and then sat with her on the sofa as she sipped it. At a loss about what to do or feel, she dug her phone out of her handbag and checked her messages. There was only one, which was from Macy: *The mortuary guy you need to see is Len Martell, so make sure he is on duty and mention my name. He is good on cause of death and amenable to chocolate biscuits.*

She laughed aloud and the cat turned his head to stare at her.

CHAPTER SIX

On her way to the mortuary in rural Gloucestershire the next morning, Jo knew she was taking a chance of Macy's contact being on duty — but then there seemed to be very little she *was* certain about. Since the conversation with Teddy last night, this included her own feelings and her own future. Teddy, finding her asleep on the sofa with the cat, had brought her coffee and toast before going to work, and she was grateful that he hadn't asked any questions. Thinking about her dilemma didn't seem to help, so, as usual, she applied herself to work and followed up Macy's message.

The mortuary was set a long way back from the hospital — for understandable reasons, Jo acknowledged, as her approach took her down a winding, single-track lane through dramatic Scots pines. She couldn't suppress a shiver as she locked her car and walked across to the discreet door in the low-rise building. She thought of Macy's question — 'Do you *want* to know?' — and she hesitated for a moment with her hand on the frosted-glass door. But she did want to know. She liked to think it was the same as the instinct which led her to follow a thread in a person's astrological data, looking for patterns and exploring gaps. Perhaps it was due to her own innate Virgo need for order. Whatever the reason, if there were unanswered questions, she was driven to resolve them. She turned the metal door handle and stepped inside.

A plumpish man in a white hospital uniform came slowly to the desk. When Jo saw that the name on his lanyard was Len Martell, she inwardly punched the air — Macy's contact was on duty. And even better, there was no one else around. As suggested, she told Martell that she was a PI working for Macy and Wilson and was trying to find information about a body brought in by the police two days ago. 'David Macy said you might be able to . . . to help . . .' She faltered a little towards the end, as she noticed a wicked glint in Martell's watery blue eyes. He had an egg-shaped head and very little hair, which made his eyes more prominent.

'Oh, so Macy has "people" these days, does he?' Martell crowed. 'He's too elevated to grace us with his presence, I suppose. You'll have to tell him to get over himself and get down here in person.'

'I'll enjoy that,' she said.

Martell deliberately looked her up and down. 'I believe you will.' He looked at her without blinking, which she found slightly disconcerting. 'I hear Macy doesn't work out of his little box of an office in Coventry anymore? I don't suppose he has to sleep over the shop these days either. He's got a swish place with teams of people doing the grunt work, I understand.'

Jo wondered how he'd come by this background on Macy, but said nothing. She was aware that her smile was becoming fixed, especially when Martell went on, 'Well, you can tell him that the only way he's going to get anything confidential from me is if he asks me himself. It's all covered by data protection now, you know. It's not like back in the day, and I don't have time to stand and chat either. All my time has to be logged on a spreadsheet nowadays. Even when I go for a pee.'

Jo was beginning to feel that chocolate biscuits were not going to cut it and tried to remember how much cash she had in her purse. She'd never bribed anyone in her life. *How much hard-earned cash was this information worth?* She had no clue, so gave Macy's approach another try. 'That's a shame, because I was looking forward to a good chat. Macy's told me a lot about how you've helped him in the past. He even told me your favourite biscuits.' She produced the packet from her bag, adding lamely, 'They're Marks & Spencer's.'

Len Martell continued to look unimpressed. 'What kind of a fool's errand has he sent you on anyway?'

'Well, actually, he hasn't really sent me.' Jo decided that a crash course in honesty wouldn't do any harm. 'I just asked him if he knew anyone who would help because—' She broke off and took another breath. 'My friend discovered a dead body on Sunday, and now she's a key witness. Because I've trained as a PI, I should be able to advise her, but it's hard to know what's going on.'

Martell nodded shrewdly. 'That's more like it. In this job you develop a nose for all sorts of smells, and I've got a sixth sense for bullshit.' He consulted the clock on the wall. 'I suppose I could make a brew. Everyone needs a tea break, after all.' He disappeared for a moment to unlock the door into the office space. 'You'd better come through,' he said.

Jo entered with some trepidation. While five minutes ago she had been delighted to find the place deserted, she now found herself looking around and listening out for any signs that someone else was nearby. There were none. As she followed Martell's stocky, white-robed form into his office, she realized that, not for the first time in her life, she was putting a lot of faith in Macy.

He bustled on into a tiny kitchen. Jo stayed by the door. 'I won't be able to show you the deceased, of course,' Martell called from the kitchen, where he was boiling a kettle.

'No, that's OK,' Jo said hurriedly. She couldn't resist a glance towards the double doors, behind which she assumed the bodies were stored. 'I've just got some questions.'

'So, what do you really do? Because you're not going to tell me you make a living out of Macy's line of work.'

'People do,' Jo said. 'As you say, he has quite a team these days. But no, not me. I'm actually an astrologer, working in

Stroud, where I have a little studio for consultations. People like to consult the planets about a whole range of things: the start of projects, compatibility, personality. All the big questions in life.'

Martell leaned against the door jamb, hairy arms folded across his uniform. 'Pisces sun, Capricorn rising, moon in Aquarius. That's my big three.'

'Intriguing.' Jo tried to hide her surprise. It wasn't often that she met someone so knowledgeable about their birth chart. 'That's a complex mix of signs: water, earth and air energies.'

'It explains the job.' He gave her a droll look and went to pour the tea. 'Aquarius is the mad scientist, and Pisces, the sign closest to death. Lots of my planets are in the twelfth house, too.'

'Pisces and the twelfth house are associated with the unconscious, not death,' Jo corrected him mildly.

He brought the tea mugs to one of the desks and Jo was forced to find herself a seat. He rolled an office chair over so he could sit beside her. 'Actually, I know that it's the eighth house which is associated with death,' he went on. 'Death and sex as a matter of fact.' Martell bestowed on her his watery, unblinking gaze. He nibbled some chocolate off his biscuit and then dunked it in his tea. 'But there isn't a house for murder, is there?'

'No,' Jo said, after the briefest of pauses. She was becoming very aware of how remote the mortuary was from any other buildings, and pictured her lone car in the car park. 'What makes you ask?'

'Because I've only got two suspicious deaths in at the moment,' Martell said. 'One is a straightforward stabbing on the Charwell Estate on Saturday night, and the other is — well, shall we say, more interesting.'

'Is it Leah Ellerman? Do you know what happened to her?'

'That's the one.' Martell nodded, clearly enjoying himself. 'Post-mortem hasn't been undertaken yet and, obviously,

I'm not a pathologist, so my information is limited to eyes and ears. Or all five senses, you could say.'

'What can you tell me about her?' Jo made herself drink her tea slowly, as her instinct was to gulp it down and get out of there.

'Her sister, Irene, identified her yesterday. Of course, you've probably heard of the Ellermans. They're local big wheels, but, despite the money, the elder sister hasn't aged well.' He dunked his biscuit again, shaking his head sadly. 'Now, Leah was a much more attractive woman. Fit-looking — you can see she worked out — but slight, about five foot three. Probably in her forties,' Martell went on. 'I can tell you that she was hit on the back of her head — probably more than once — with a degree of force. Something blunt like a baseball bat, I'd say. The most interesting features are the time of death and how she was wrapped. Heavy-duty plastic and nylon rope ties. It was a business-like job, and carried out straight after the act, I'd say.'

Jo tried to hide a shudder. 'Why the cellar?' she murmured. 'She was under a set of shelves, which were stacked with things like tablecloths, napkins, cutlery.' She halted, realizing she was revealing too much detail, but Martell didn't seem to have noticed.

'Maybe the body was in transit,' he shrugged. 'Maybe her murderer planned to move her elsewhere — to a prepared grave, say — but, for whatever reason, it didn't happen.'

'What do you mean about the time of death being interesting?' she asked.

'Well, it's at least a week, which is quite a while for someone who has, shall we say, a normal life. I mean, an old person living alone, or the homeless, that's more the type who get left lying undiscovered for a long time. These days, it's hard for someone with a life to stay off the radar. Or who had a life, I should say.' He chuckled at his own choice of words. 'Obviously, the police will get their official report, but I'm a pretty good judge. Certainly good enough for Macy. I hope you tell him so.'

'I will,' Jo assured him. She was torn between wanting to know more and a more basic desire to get away from him and the place. Trying to call to mind the shadowy cellar and the body, wrapped in the heavy plastic, she decided on one more question. 'I suppose there must have been a lot of blood?'

'Always is with a head wound. But this one was relatively clean. Of course, we don't get to keep the personal effects, nor the plastic wrapping and the rope. Personal effects go to the police forensic lab.' He turned to the computer on the desk in front of them. 'We send them photos of what we've handed over though, if you'd like to have a look? Hang on a minute.' He moved the screen and his seat towards her and Jo inched away.

After he'd searched through several emails, he brought a series of pictures onto the screen: a woman's jacket and shirt, both blood-stained, a smart midi-length skirt, which looked undamaged, high heels, underwear. Jo began to feel a little queasy. Martell's stubby body seemed to radiate heat and she edged even further away. He enlarged the photograph of the parka, which Jo remembered grimly. Now, seeing it in better detail, she realized it was a large and battered coat, out of keeping with Leah's business clothes.

'This caught most of the blood,' Martell said with satisfaction. He moved the cursor to the collar and hood of the parka to show the staining.

'Can we see what was in her bag?' Jo had glimpsed a photograph of a leather satchel big enough to hold a laptop. She made herself sit still while he searched for it.

'Was she robbed, do you mean?' Martell obligingly clicked back through the pictures. All the contents and the bag itself were numbered, and it was clear that a laptop, a purse and a phone were all present.

'The phone will be very useful,' he remarked. 'So, you've got your answer. Look at the amount of cash she was carrying.' He pointed to a wad of £50 notes. 'That figures. The Ellermans are not short of a bob or two, as I told you.'

'I wonder why the perpetrator hid the body, and what stopped them moving it,' she said, as much to herself as Martell. 'If that was their intention.'

'Ours is not to reason why; ours is just to do and die,' he announced, turning his egg-shaped face in her direction. Jo judged this a good moment to leave. He got to his feet when she did and she thanked him for his help. He held out a flabby white hand and she shook it reluctantly.

'Give my regards to Macy, won't you? What is he doing with himself these days, anyway? I mean, apart from work. He used to tell me all his woman troubles over a beer. I assume he has sorted those out now and found a replacement for the wife?'

'I've no idea,' Jo said, keeping on track towards the office door. She had known Macy had been married, although she couldn't remember who had told her and was certainly not going to discuss it now. She turned the handle, but the rein-forced glass door didn't shift.

'I need to unlock it first,' Martell grinned, holding up his pass.

'Well, go on then,' Jo said with asperity.

'As long as *you're* not the replacement,' he said, taking his time to scan the passkey. 'You're far too classy for him, and you can tell him I said so.'

The door gave suddenly beneath Jo's forceful hand. 'I will,' she said blithely, once she was the other side of the desk. *And that's not all I will be telling Macy*, she thought, as she stormed to her car. She was back on the motorway before she stopped fuming at her old boss for not telling her Martell was a creep.

* * *

'Yes, OK, I suppose he is a creep,' Macy acknowledged, his voice irritatingly calm through her car speakers. 'But was it useful?'

'Yes, but I'm not sure it was worth it. And you do realize he is obsessed with you, don't you?' she added, feeling that she had not yet done justice to Martell's unpleasantness. 'Knows all about your new office and your divorce.'

'He does? Well, I can't help the impact I have on people.'

Jo decided they both deserved a break from Martell. Instead, she asked Macy if he had any update on his new case involving the businessman she'd seen at the Hotel du Vin, who she still thought of as 'the Angry Cherub'.

'I don't know what you mean,' he said. 'I've got a ton of new cases, thank you very much. Do you want me to put you through to the team working on them?'

'My guess is you are looking after this one yourself,' she said shrewdly. 'I know you're not going to tell me anything, but I'll just keep asking occasionally. In case you need the independent help of a fellow PI, who also happens to be an astrologer. I hope you got his birth details, by the way.'

'There is no case, no mystery man, so no date of birth. Now, I have to see a lawyer about a court case.'

'That's OK, I need to go too. The police press conference is at two, and I've got to find the place yet.'

* * *

The Stroud police had selected a church hall only a little further up the hill from the station, so it was easy enough to locate, but Jo was surprised to be allowed in without question. Looking around the dusty room set out with wooden chairs, she saw that the front rows were already taken up by photographers, including a couple of local TV camera crews with a noisy crowd of journalists buzzing around them. There were ordinary members of the public too: a gaggle of young people with phones and tablets at the ready, who Jo took to be students, and some less easily identifiable people sitting alone or in pairs. She chose a seat next to an elderly couple, who exchanged polite smiles with her as they stood up to let her through.

There was no one yet seated in front of the blue constabulary screens, where a couple of techies were checking microphones and cabling. Jo was content to sit and wait, sipping her coffee from her favourite deli. She craned her neck as the room started to fill up and counted around fifty people. As Stroud was now her adopted town, she felt she should know some of them, but the only person she recognized was Alys Parry, who was hard to miss, being the tallest woman in the room, and having a loud laugh. Chatting to another journalist while checking her phone, Alys noticed Jo and waved her water bottle at her.

When the police cortege eventually filed in, Irene Ellerman-James brought up the rear of the procession and, as they took their places behind the microphones, she was steered to the end of the conference table. She sat heavily, pushing her microphone away and staring around the room as if she would relish a confrontation with her sister's killer. Apart from more make-up, she looked pretty much the same as when Jo had seen her at the police station — the same slouching posture and air of impatience. Of all the police officers beside her, Jo recognized DS Diane Watts and DC Williams.

A mild-mannered, middle-aged officer in a short-sleeved shirt and an ancient tie introduced himself as DCI Brian Rose, the SIO, and read from a press release, which confirmed Leah Ellerman's identity, describing her as an esteemed and respected landowner in the local community.

'Many of you may know the family,' he added, as Irene glared at the fidgety audience. DCI Rose asked people to come forward if they had seen Leah or had any dealings with her in the last two weeks.

'Does that mean you've placed the time of death within two weeks?' one of the journalists called out.

'We will open for questions in a moment,' DCI Rose chided in his soft Birmingham accent. 'Obviously, we don't have the exact time of death, but the last sighting of Miss Leah Ellerman was by one of her tenants two weeks ago, so we are most interested in her movements during this period.'

The questions, when permitted, seemed to Jo to be a bit bizarre. People asked about likely links to terrorism or serial killers. One journalist wanted to know if there was a connection to her job in London. 'I understand she works for a business consultancy. Do we know if she was involved in politics or organized crime?'

The most sensible question came from Alys Parry, who asked what lines of inquiry the police were pursuing. DCI Rose handed this over to his sergeant.

'We have started house-to-house enquiries and have taken statements from witnesses,' Diane Watts said, her expression even more ferocious than usual. 'When we have the full forensic reports, which we expect imminently, they will no doubt open up subsequent lines of inquiry.'

'What about the connection to the supposed haunt-ings at the New Navigation?' Alys Parry continued. 'Or their ghost-hunting events, which have been well publicized locally? As the body was found there, are you seeking expert advice on the paranormal?'

A ripple of interest hummed around the room. DCI Rose was quick to quell it. 'No such advice is required.'

'Is it true then that there was a crystal healer present when the body was found?' Alys persisted, and Jo held her breath. Undaunted when the police refused to confirm this, the journalist carried straight on to her next question. 'And did you know that the landlord and landlady of the pub, Mr and Mrs Robart, are consulting an astrologer?'

Jo tensed again, awaiting the response. Of course, she had told Alys Parry her name, so it would have taken only minimal research to find out about her business. Fortunately, there was nothing online about her new PI career yet.

'Mr and Mrs Robart are at liberty to talk to whoever they wish.' DCI Rose made the response, but his sergeant's eyes sought out Jo's in the audience and shot her a fierce look.

The elderly woman beside Jo had been sitting with her arm poker straight in the air for a few minutes and finally managed to catch the police officer's attention. 'Will you be investigating the tenants of the holiday lets that Leah Ellerman owns?' she demanded. 'We've got new people coming in nearly every week who could be any Tom, Dick or Harry.' The woman's voice rose as she got into her stride. 'To say nothing of the builders and various contractors, who are a different lot every other day. Are you looking into them too?'

From the defiant way she folded her arms, the woman sitting beside Jo didn't appear to be mollified by DCI Rose's assurances. The man on her other side, presumably her husband, leaned forward. 'This is no use at all, Val,' he muttered. 'We may as well go home.'

'No, no, we'll sit it out. There may be more to come yet,' his wife said.

He looked doubtful, and Jo, catching his eye, gave him a conspiratorial grin, as she couldn't help agreeing with him. In fact, she concluded that the whole press conference was a masterclass at not giving much away while at the same time seeking public help. If it wasn't for the warning note about how Hanni's and her own involvement in the case might be used by the media, it would have been a waste of time. She was pretty sure, however, as she covertly checked Sarah's list, that she was sitting next to the Lilleys from number four Canalside Cottages.

'That was a good question about the holiday tenants,' she murmured to the woman next to her as they stood up to leave.

She frowned at Jo suspiciously. 'If you say so. And you are?'

'Jo Hughes, I'm here on behalf of Gary and Sarah Robart from the pub.'

'Oh, you're a friend of Sarah's.' Her lined face immediately softened into a smile. 'I can see perfectly why she didn't want to come herself. I'm Valerie Lilley, and this is my husband, George. We live at number four. The last ones standing,' she added with a pugilistic air. 'Leah's renovations are working along the row towards us. Like the creeping death.'

'Val, it might be better to drop that line now,' her husband muttered. 'Given the circumstances.'

'So, you're her neighbours? And you haven't seen her at all in two weeks? Isn't that a bit odd?' Jo stayed alongside them as they patiently queued for the single exit.

'It was nothing unusual.' Valerie Lilley was clearly not short of an opinion. 'You never knew where Leah was from one week to the next. She seemed to be able to pick and choose her hours. It certainly wasn't Monday to Friday, nine to five anyway. Sometimes she was away a few nights at a time, sometimes she was "working from home". Although that can cover a multitude of sins, from what I gather.'

'You don't seem to like her very much,' Jo said. Out of the corner of her eye, she saw Alys Parry approaching, all smiles.

'We didn't have a problem with her. She always spoke very polite and considerate, and we exchanged cards and a glass of sherry at Christmas. In many ways, Leah was a very good neighbour and landlady.' George Lilley stepped in with this answer, taking his wife's arm. 'Now, we're on a meter, so we will have to shoot off. Excuse us.'

Jo watched them file out of the hall while mentally ticking them off her list of canal-side residents she needed to speak to. The Lilleys might have more to tell, but at least she'd made initial contact.

'I've got a minute now, if you're free?' Alys Parry arrived at her elbow. 'It really is only a minute as I have a phone call to make, but I know you wanted a quick word.' Somehow, the journalist made it sound like she was doing Jo a favour.

'Yes, thanks for dropping my astrology business onto the police radar,' Jo began. Turning to face the journalist, she noticed that the other woman was pregnant. Instantly, her conversation with Teddy came back into Jo's mind. She and Alys were of an age. If anything, the journalist was a little younger, and on her left hand Jo saw the flash of a diamond and a gold wedding band. *Was this what she wanted?* This question suddenly seemed all-consuming, and she lost the thread of what she'd been intending to say.

'I'm sure you're already on their radar. You've made a statement,' Alys said cheerfully. 'But, listen, you heard them.

DI Watts said it's the neighbours they're interested in. Though, personally, I wouldn't rule out the family. Meanwhile, I've got something that will pique my readers' curiosity: a crystal healer and an astrologer involved in the haunted pub. Sarah Robart is the gift who keeps on giving. I do need to ask, though, are you giving the Robarts astrological advice?'

'No. I told you, I met them through a friend.' The hall was gradually emptying around the two women and the techies were back on the podium, removing equipment.

'That would be Hanni Light, who found the body,' Alys supplied. 'You're both members of the Mind, Body and Spirit network, based in Stroud. I've looked you both up, as you'd expect. Sarah was also a member, once upon a time.'

'I can see you've got a story in mind, but I thought you said you were a friend of the Robarts. That kind of publicity is not going to help the pub.'

Alys gave her a sideways look. 'Think again,' she said. 'They've always lapped it up before. Ask them about their ghost-hunting nights. And when people lost interest in that, they suddenly had poltergeist activity. And it was through me that they got the local TV there, which was very good for their business, I can tell you. Look,' she paused, 'I really do have to go and make a call, but I've got a suggestion. I will let you see an advance copy of the story if you will get Sarah and Gary to talk to me. The Ellermans have brought down the portcullis on me. That's to be expected. Irene has retreated behind her Cotswold-stone walls, but the Robarts are just ordinary people, and they are usually more than happy to chat.'

Jo agreed that she would ask them. Alys seemed content with that and promised to email her the article in an hour or so. 'It'll be in tomorrow's *Standard*. Just a supporting couple of paragraphs, that's all. Honestly, it's nothing to worry about.' Alys beamed at her and Jo watched her stroll out, already consulting her phone.

She followed more slowly, aware of a troubling, unfamiliar feeling. Was she envious of Alys? Or was it fear? Either way, it made her uneasy, so she redirected her thoughts to the Ellerman case. Alys could be a good contact, she reminded herself, and worth staying the right side of. Meanwhile, she needed to warn Hanni that they were both going to feature in a story in tomorrow's paper. She guessed her friend would be closing up at the Rivermill and she hurried through the town, taking all the shortcuts she knew, to catch Hanni before she left the shop. When she reached the little café and bookshop at the corner of the old woollen mill, she saw her friend inside cashing up the day's takings. She still looked pale and worried, but when she unlocked the door, her first question took Jo aback.

'What's wrong, Josephine? You look like you've had a harder day than me.'

'Not really,' Jo said, and then found she was wiping tears from her eyes. Hanni drew her into the shop and Jo dropped onto one of the café chairs. 'There's really nothing wrong,' she insisted. 'Not compared to what you've been through.'

'It's your heart chakra which is out of balance,' Hanni said, eyeing her friend and placing a hand on her back below her shoulders. 'Just sit there and I'll make you some green tea, which is perfect for restoring emotional energy.'

'Teddy sprung something on me last night,' Jo said slowly, while her friend busied herself behind the counter. 'He wants us to settle down and have babies. I know that doesn't sound so terrible,' she sighed, 'but he asked me a really difficult question.'

'Teddy proposed?'

'No, worse than that.' Jo found a tissue in her handbag and blotted a stray tear. 'He asked me how I felt about it. And the thing is, I really don't know.'

'And if he had proposed?' Hanni asked. The grassy fragrance of the tea scented the air as she brought the mugs over and sat opposite Jo.

'Oh, that would have been easy. I'd have said no. It's not the right time for weddings and mortgages and all that malarkey. I'm still building my businesses and . . .' Jo faltered and came to a halt. She sighed shakily. 'But today I met a journalist who is pregnant and successful, and she looks really happy and sorted and . . . Well, how can you argue with that? I mean, that's what I want, isn't it? One day, anyway.' Jo groaned. 'Oh, and that's really why I came to see you. She's going to print a story about us tomorrow.'

'Oh, is she?'

'Yes. Alys Parry — she's the journalist — is going to say that Gary and Sarah are consulting a crystal healer and an astrologer, and I bet she will mention the paranormal evenings, or whatever Sarah calls them. It's going to make them — and potentially us — sound very flaky.' Jo hunted out her phone. 'So I need to tell them. Alys is going to email me the article this evening.'

'This sort of article is nothing we're not used to,' Hanni said, blowing gently across her mug of tea. 'I know Sarah will feel the same. Don't worry about it. It's more important that you don't just ignore this question of Teddy's.'

'I'm sorry I got upset.' Jo blew her nose. 'It's just that I really don't know how I feel yet.' She sipped the green tea and sighed. 'And I know this might be good for my chakras, but I'm going to make myself a coffee.' She carried on talking as she got to her feet and fired up the familiar old coffee machine. 'I'm not ignoring Teddy's question, but these other questions are just as real and just as serious. Someone killed Leah Ellerman by bashing her over the head. And this must have happened close to her house, because she was quickly bundled into the cellar, probably pushed down the chute from that door in the path, and then apparently forgotten for maybe a week.' Jo poured out her coffee, pausing as she stirred in the hot milk. 'What I can't understand is why no one reported her missing. Her sister says they weren't close, but she must have had friends, work colleagues. The builder who worked for her, a guy called Matty Sullivan, seems to be the only one who actually missed her.' Jo carried her coffee over to the café table and sat down. 'Plenty of people disliked Leah — and maybe will be better off now she's gone. Maybe they were just glad she wasn't around.'

'Couldn't it have been an accident? Then hastily covered up?'

'I don't think so, given the deliberate attempt to hide the body. It wasn't as if they just pushed it down those runners and left it at the bottom of the steps. You saw it yourself. It had been moved to the back wall and pushed under the shelves. Hanni, I've got to ask.' Jo looked across at her friend. 'Do you think Gary or Sarah had anything to do with Leah Ellerman's death? Or with hiding the body?'

Hanni looked shocked. 'No, neither of them could cold-bloodedly kill anyone.'

'What about in anger?' Jo pressed her friend. Privately, she felt there was a suppressed energy about Gary, which made her feel he might have a nasty temper, and Sarah was certainly not straightforward.

But Hanni remained firm. 'I've known Sarah for years. That's why, when she asked for my help with the supposed poltergeist activity, I couldn't refuse. Although I've always stayed out of their dabbling in the spirit world.'

'You know that Sarah has invited me to a so-called paranormal evening on Thursday night, don't you? I admit, I'm slightly terrified. What the hell is going to happen?'

Hanni spread her hands. 'Well, I've never been to one, but it's a sort of séance. Sarah has always claimed she can contact the spirit world. Did you know that she holds them in the back room of the pub? You have to go through there to get to the cellar where . . . well, where we saw the body.'

Before Jo could react, the door of the shop rattled. They heard the lock shake in the frame followed by a double rap on the glass, and stared at each other. Hanni took a breath and crossed to the door.

Irene Ellerman-James pushed her way into the shop, a scowl etched on her face. 'I know you're closed, but I'm looking for Hanni Light, which must be you, I suppose.' She squared herself in front of Hanni, jutting out her round chin. 'You found my sister, didn't you? I want you to tell me all the details, and don't hold anything back because, I assure you, I am not some psychological weakling who is going to crumble. I went to identify the body, and that's not for the faint-hearted.'

Hanni stood silently for a moment, her eyes large and reflective. 'What negative energy,' she said at last. She indicated the café area. 'I'm making tea. Come and sit down, and you can ask me anything you want.'

Irene shifted her gaze and recognized Jo. 'Oh, it's you. I saw you at the police station and again at the press conference. What have you got to do with all this?'

'Pleased to see you, too.' Jo remained seated at the café table. 'As I told you, I'm a friend of Hanni's,' she said. 'Sometimes I even work here. Come and sit down.' She indicated one of the mismatched but comfortable armchairs nearby, and unexpectedly, Irene plodded across and fell into it.

'Police stations and press interviews are more or less my whole life at the moment anyway,' she said, staring disconsolately at Jo. 'I suppose you're a friend of the Robarts, are you? You know my sister despised them, don't you? She saw them as a pair of deceiving charlatans. Leah called them out for selling snake oil and preying on gullible teenagers and old folk.'

Jo was glad that Hanni was at the counter and could at least pretend not to hear this. 'When was this?' she asked. 'What did Leah say?'

'Leah regularly told Sarah Robart what she thought of her. She couldn't stand anything fake and she thought their shenanigans brought the wrong sort of attention to the area.' Irene looked around the bookshop until her eyes fell on the glass shelves displaying crystals and books on Hanni's specialist subject. 'Looks like you're in the same business.' She nodded towards the cabinet as Hanni arrived with another herbal tea.

Hanni placed the mug on the table deliberately. 'You shouldn't make claims when you don't know anything. Now, I will answer your questions, but you will have to stop being rude about my business.'

Irene stared back, her big hands spread on the table. 'All right. Just tell me what you found. Exactly. In detail. Because the police are keeping me in the dark for whatever reason of their own, and I won't have it.'

Hanni embarked on recalling her discovery of the body while Jo sat uncharacteristically quiet. She had no intention of revealing that she had also seen Leah's body. This would almost certainly cause trouble for her friend and had to remain a secret between them. Instead, she read Alys Parry's article on her phone while Irene Ellerman-James listened to Hanni in focused silence. Jo noticed a slight hesitation on Hanni's part when it came to describing the cellar — it was the only part of the account she seemed to gloss over — and Jo made a mental note to tackle her about it later. It tweaked her earlier suspicions that Hanni was not being completely open with her.

'Do you have any idea how long she was down there?' Irene asked when Hanni finished.

Hanni shook her head.

'At least a week,' Jo answered, taking pity on the woman. A heavy silence fell and Jo returned her phone to her bag. 'Tell me why you're asking us this?' she asked. 'The police should respond to your questions. They can't really keep you in the dark.'

Irene gave a derisory snort. 'Don't you believe it.' But her anger had drained away while she had been listening to Hanni. Now she seemed to struggle to summon the energy to speak. 'Leah could have been dead two weeks, so how could I not know? Surely sisters are meant to have a connection? An instinct?' The round eyes pleaded with Hanni. 'I know we weren't close. Not in an obvious way, not living in each other's pockets. We had different interests, you see.'

'Not everyone knows when death happens to someone close. In fact, that's very rare,' Hanni said simply. 'It doesn't mean you didn't love her.'

Tears rolled unexpectedly out of Irene's large eyes and tracked down her tired make-up. 'The thing is,' Irene caught her breath on a sob, 'nobody knew. No one missed her for days. She had to be . . . found.' The word came out raggedly. 'Like a down-and-out or a nobody. My sister wasn't a nobody.' The woman's shoulders heaved. Jo found the tissues and pushed them towards her.

'As I'm the eldest, it falls to me now to do everything. To put things right,' Irene went on. As her tears dried, her anger revived. 'And the police are incompetent. Do you know they keep asking me if I called in sick for Leah? I mean, why would I? She's a grown woman, and I've never had anything to do with her job. It's another example of the police going down blind alleys.' She drew herself up to a straighter position and eyed them both. 'But I am grateful to you. At least you haven't treated me like I'm an idiot, who needs protecting. I need you to meet our brother, Duncan. There's only the three of us Ellermans and Leah was the youngest. Now, just two.' Her voice wavered, but she held their gaze. 'Will you come and meet him? He must be part of this. I want him to hear it too. Otherwise, we'll just continue with our heads in the sand, politely ignoring each other, and that would be wrong. I want you to come to my house and I will pin Duncan down. Will you do this last thing, if I arrange it?'

'Yes, we will,' Jo said quickly while Hanni was looking doubtful. 'We'll both be there. Just let us know when.'

Irene pulled herself out of the chair. Having gained their agreement, she was clearly keen to be on her way, but something had occurred to Jo so she followed her to the door. 'Did you say someone phoned in sick for Leah? To her office?'

'Apparently. They seem convinced it was me and I can assure you it wasn't.'

'That's odd.' Jo frowned. 'Do you know much about your sister's job? I know she worked for a business consultancy, but I'm finding it hard to work out what that actually means.'

Irene snorted. 'You wouldn't be the first to wonder. I know she made a lot of money at it, and it always provided the perfect excuse when she didn't want to do anything related to family life.' Perhaps recollecting that she wanted a favour from these two young women, she added in more appeasing tones, 'I'm sorry, but I've already told you, we keep our interests separate. All we Ellermans are like that. I do know that she managed a team in London and went down there pretty regularly. She never mentioned her clients, but it came out once that she was working with the local NHS Trust, because she knew their chief executive, who is a school governor at the same school as me.' She hitched up her bag on her shoulder and turned to go. 'I don't know if any of that helps. Probably not. I will be in contact with you about a date.'

Jo and Hanni watched the woman walk back to her Mercedes, which was parked at an angle on the cobbles. 'Why did you say we'd go to her house? I'm not sure what we're getting into,' Hanni said. 'And you can't work for her as well as Sarah, can you?'

'Well, no one is actually paying me, if you hadn't noticed,' Jo pointed out. 'But don't worry, I can keep the strands separate. And we have to go. To understand Leah, we have to understand the family. I'm convinced of it.'

'I'm not sure I want to understand Irene Ellerman-James.' Hanni shook her head slowly. 'Did you notice? She wasn't crying because she was sad. She was ashamed.'

CHAPTER SEVEN

Jo had expected the article in the *Standard* to generate some phone calls. She was not expecting one of them to be from Macy.

'I see you're blending your two businesses nicely,' he said in a deceptively bland tone.

'Ye-es, I admit, that wasn't really the plan,' Jo said. After she'd left the Rivermill the previous evening, she had called Sarah Robart about the article. Her response had been matter-of-fact, as Hanni had predicted.

'Well, we are talking to you and you're an astrologer,' Sarah had said. 'So, I can't see a problem.'

Hanni's attitude had been similar. 'I'm not embarrassed about what I do, Josephine,' she had said, after reading the draft on Jo's phone. 'I know the benefits of crystal healing and spiritual cleansing. I see the evidence every day. If this journalist wants to make out it's all nonsense, she hasn't done her research thoroughly.'

As a result, Jo had felt better about it herself and had managed a good night's sleep. When she read it again on the paper's website at 6 a.m., however, all her qualms returned.

Murder pub turns to spiritual healing and the stars. The headline, and some of the story, had been amplified by an editor overnight, and it now made her cringe when she read it. The article allowed the reader to choose whether Gary and Sarah were a gateway to the occult or stupidly gullible.

So, when Macy rang after breakfast, she was very aware of the potential damage to both her astrology business and the new PI work, which hadn't even got off the ground yet. She was sitting at her desk with the article open on her laptop and all her notes in front of her. Lela-May's chart lay untouched on the printer. 'This article wasn't my idea,' Jo said.

'What *was* your plan, then?' Macy was merciless. 'Because you must have given the journalist permission to use this stuff.'

'Alys Parry could have found out that information about me online. I only told her I was an astrologer,' she said. 'Maybe I should have made something up or told her I was working for Gary and Sarah as a PI. But I hadn't asked their permission.'

Macy said nothing to this, which was worse than one of his coruscating remarks. 'Anyway, my clients are OK with the article,' she went on. 'And so is Hanni.'

'It's not them I'm concerned about,' Macy said. 'I thought you wanted to keep your two businesses separate?'

'I do.' Jo felt wretched. She walked away from her unusually messy desk. 'But, look, it'll all blow over. There's really no need to worry—'

Macy tutted audibly. 'Look, your best bet is to throw everything you can behind the police investigation. Share everything you know with them. Because the sooner they resolve this murder case, the sooner it will be out of the local media and *then* it will blow over.'

'That's what I am doing,' Jo said impatiently, although Irene's low opinion of police competence came into her mind. If Macy was right, she had to hope desperately that Irene was wrong. 'Although, I don't know much, so I can't actually share anything with them,' she added. 'And they are certainly not sharing nicely with me.'

In a blatant attempt to change the subject, she asked if he didn't have his own cases to worry about. 'How is the Angry Cherub?' she asked, on her way downstairs to make coffee.

'For the last time, Jo, I'm not joking. Shut up about the fucking cherub. I've got to drive to Bournemouth today to appear in court, which is something I've successfully managed to avoid so far, and I'm really not in the mood to be entertained. And before I go, I've got work to do.'

Jo was left with silence as she entered the kitchen, her phone still to her ear. In the sink lay a bouquet of flowers, which she'd dumped into cold water the night before. Teddy had left them on her doorstep — she'd nearly fallen over them when letting herself and the cat in. She approached the red roses now as if they were an unexploded bomb and, with one finger, flicked over the note he had left with them. It said simply, *All my love, Teddy*.

There was nothing in this to help her make her decision, or even to know what to say to him. It just summed up his feelings. She bit her lip. How could he be so certain? Instead of arranging the flowers in a vase, she picked up her bag and hurried out of the flat. Like Macy said, there was work to do.

By 10 a.m., she found herself beside the canal cottages, having decided on her own version of a door-to-door enquiry. She planned to work through Sarah's list of the residents of Canalside Cottages. There were still two sets of people with whom she had not made any contact, and she needed to know what they thought of Leah and when they'd last seen her.

Standing on the towpath, Jo took a good long look at number five, where Leah herself had lived. It was the end cottage and the largest, with smart shutters at all the windows and a neat privet hedge behind the old blue brick wall at the front. Walking slowly around the house, Jo could see the shell of the sizeable extension being constructed on the ground floor at the back. She was struck by the fact that Leah would not see it finished, and yet the builders were still working on it. Through the empty window space, she could see an electrician on ladders fixing cabling for ceiling lights. She recognized Matty Sullivan, tousled head tilted back, hands on slim hips, standing on the doorstep talking to him. From his relaxed attitude, it was clear he was in charge. Jo mentally added Matty and the other workmen to her list. The garden of number five was the only one large enough to be bisected by the dusty path that ran behind the terrace of cottages. It was an L-shaped parcel of land, dropping down the hill, away from the canal. Peering down the garden, Jo could see a little copse with a caravan parked in it. A small brown dog lay outside, twitching an ear in Jo's general direction. She wondered if this was Matty's temporary abode. A stack of discarded kitchen tiles and some wooden panels lying nearby looked like they came from the building work.

All the cottages except Leah's had back doors into their little square gardens, which adjoined the path. Most consisted of lawns and shrubs, but one was particularly well-tended. It had neat rows of vegetables and, across the path, a bed of sunflowers nodding over multi-coloured dahlias and some tall bright blue flowers, which Jo couldn't name. This was Mr and Mrs Lilley's house, next door to Leah's. 'The last one standing', as Valerie Lilley had described it. Their house and garden were considerably smaller than the end of terrace, and Jo guessed that the couple must find the noise and dust of the building works intrusive. Not sufficient reason to kill anyone, though, she decided, allowing herself a small inner smile.

According to Sarah's list, the Hutchinson family lived at number three, but Jo could see no sign of life there, nor at number two, which Sarah had noted as being renovated. Against cottage number one, the note said: *Holiday Let, Tenant* and a big fat question mark. Naturally, Jo was drawn to it first.

Reaching the last gate along the narrow path behind the cottages, it struck Jo that it would not be easy to sneak in and out of these houses without the neighbours noticing. Anyone leaving number one had to take the path that ran behind the gardens of all the other houses, or the canal towpath at the front. Either way, they would be in full view of their neighbours. Leah's house had the most privacy, as she could access the lane directly, as could anyone coming and going from Matty's caravan. The white brick of the pub with the large green umbrellas in the beer garden was a prominent feature all the way along the terrace and from their front windows. Not an easy place for secrets, Jo concluded.

When she rang the bell at number one, she could hear the domestic hum of a vacuum cleaner through the open sash window. 'Is that the taxi for Lucia Hewitt?' a female voice called out, but Jo could see no one until she stepped back and an arm with bangles waved out of an upstairs window. It was followed by a woman's head, surrounded by a striking halo of untidy ginger hair. 'You're awfully early. I'm not quite ready, I'm afraid.'

'No, I'm not the taxi driver,' Jo shouted, vying for attention with the vacuum cleaner. 'Can you spare me five minutes? It's about your landlady, Leah Ellerman.'

The head and arm disappeared abruptly, the window slammed shut and a minute later the drone of the machine stopped. The sturdy narrow door to the cottage opened and a different woman appeared in the doorway: stouter, older, with wire-framed glasses on her square face and the vacuum cleaner in one hand. They recognized each other in the same moment. 'Oh, it's you,' the woman said.

'Maureen? You work here too?' Last time Jo had seen the cleaner, they had both been summarily dismissed from the pub by DS Watts.

'Oh, yes. I do number five, this one and number two, as well as the pub.'

The ginger-haired woman bobbed up behind her in the narrow hallway. 'You can come in but I'm actually leaving today, so you only just caught me.' The woman waved her in and Maureen stood back so that Jo could pass down the hallway.

'The police said to expect more questions, although I told them I won't be any help because I've been here less than a fortnight.' The ginger-haired woman hurried ahead down the hallway, past a pile of luggage in the kitchen doorway. 'My name is Lucia Hewitt, by the way, and as you probably know, I'm just renting this place as a retreat for a couple of weeks.'

'I should explain, I'm not with the police,' Jo said. 'I'm working for Sarah and Gary Robart from the pub across the canal. They are very upset about what's happened on their premises—'

'Aren't we all?' Maureen muttered from behind them as she dragged the vacuum cleaner into a room next to the back door.

Lucia waved Jo into the kitchen. 'I've said Maureen can start the cleaning because she's on a tight schedule, and I was expecting to be gone by now.' She lowered her voice theatrically. 'To be honest, she gets a bit anxious if she doesn't get done on time.' She grinned at Jo and held out her bangled arm. 'How do you do, anyway. I'm just waiting for the cab and getting a few last things together.'

Jo shook the woman's hand and introduced herself, blinking after being in the dark hallway. The kitchen filled the front of the house, facing the canal. Watery sunlight poured in from the two sash windows behind Lucia. The room had clearly been redesigned to take best advantage of the light, with a shining range on one side of the kitchen, a narrow island in the centre and light paint on the walls.

'Clever, isn't it? What they've done.' Lucia followed her gaze. 'It must have been unbelievably dingy, but they've pared it right down and kept to natural, using light materials. No storage, of course, but I don't care about that, do I? I'm only here for two weeks.' She gave a little giggle, which made her sound almost nervous.

'It must be horrible to find yourself in the middle of a murder inquiry when you're on holiday,' Jo said, with ready sympathy.

The woman gave a swift nod. 'Believe me, I'm more than ready to go home.'

To Jo's organized mind, she looked far from ready, judging by the jumble of bags piled on the stone flags by the door. She had a rapid, unconsidered way of speaking, the words tumbling out over each other. 'I mean, I didn't know the poor woman who died, but it makes me feel a bit creepy that I've been staying in her house when she was brutally murdered just over the canal.' There was a shine across Lucia's top lip and her eyes darted around, settling on Jo. 'Ohhh, wait a minute. Are you the astrologer who was in the paper? Maureen brought it in with her.' She dragged the local paper across the granite worktop and stared at it. 'It is you, isn't it? So, do you draw up horoscopes for people, or what?'

'Yes, I do, but that's not what I'm doing for Sarah and Gary Robart,' Jo said.

'I'm a Pisces,' Lucia interjected. 'So there's bound to be something fishy about me.' She laughed immoderately at her own joke. 'What sign are you?'

'Virgo,' Jo said, thinking that this interview was not going as expected.

Lucia's eyes dropped to the newspaper again. 'So, are you using astrology to find out what happened to Leah Ellerman? For instance, what sign was Leah? Do you know?' She perched on a stool and leaned her elbows on the worktop, looking at Jo intently. All thoughts of her imminent departure appeared to have left her mind.

'Actually, I do know. She was a Libran.'

'When is that? October, isn't it? And what are Librans like?'

'They are calm and diplomatic, with good taste and their own style, and they usually have a knack of getting their own way.' Jo decided to go with the flow of this conversation to see where it would lead. 'I can't draw up her birth chart because I don't know her birth details, but does this sound at all like Leah?'

'Oh, I can't tell you, because I don't know her,' Lucia said. 'But wait, Maureen will know. We can give this astrology thing a proper test. Hold on.' She jumped off the stool and poked her head around the door. 'Maureen, come and listen to this. Jo's an astrologer and she wants to know more about the owner's personality.'

'Well, that's not really why I'm here,' Jo began, but the cleaner was already in the doorway, cloth in hand, looking understandably bemused.

'Jo says Leah was calm and diplomatic, but she liked her own way. Is that right?' Lucia looked from one to the other. 'What else can you tell us, Jo? Come on, Maureen, you knew her for years, didn't you?'

'I've known Leah a long time, but I wouldn't say I knew her well,' Maureen said, still mystified. 'She was just my boss.'

'But did she have good taste? Was she stylish?' Lucia went on. 'Sorry to put you on the spot, but you're more likely to know than me.'

'Stylish?' Maureen gave a little laugh. 'Well, I'm hardly the person to ask. All my clothes are about twenty years old. Although, my daughter, Charlotte, always says that Leah dresses well. Charlotte's at university in Nottingham, studying marketing,' she added, and Jo found herself smiling and nodding, while at the same time aware that she had lost control of this conversation. 'So, she has an opinion on everything and would do much better than me with these questions. What were the other things? Calm and diplomatic?' Maureen consulted the ceiling lights. 'Yes, generally, and as for getting her own way, I'd say, yes, definitely.'

'That's very helpful, thank you.' Jo made an attempt to regain the upper hand.

'Pretty good,' Lucia broke in, clapping her hands. 'Now tell us something about us. What sign are you, Maureen?'

'Umm, Virgo,' Maureen said, one eye on the kitchen sink. 'Look, do you mind if I finish up in here? It's just that I've told Matty I'll be next door at eleven. No doubt his workers have made another mess he wants me to clear up.'

'Of course, go ahead.' Lucia waved airily and then returned to the subject in hand. 'Ah, so we have two earthy Virgos and a fishy Pisces. You two are obviously both more practical than me. I'm in my own world most of the time.'

Jo and Maureen refrained from stating the obvious as the cleaner took Lucia at her word and began to run the taps. 'Actually, I'm not acting as an astrologer in this case.' Jo made another attempt to steer the conversation. 'I'm acting as a private investigator for Sarah and Gary.' It felt good to say this out loud at last, and Jo wondered why she had not just come out with it before. 'So, what I really want to know is when you last saw Leah and what you thought of her.'

Lucia looked disappointed. 'Oh, well, I'm not going to be much help there either. I only met her once on the towpath, walking her dog. She's got a cute little sausage dog called Frankie, but I suppose you already know that. She was polite but distant, I would say. She didn't even give me the keys to this place—'

'No, that's my job.' Maureen had her back to them now, vigorously scrubbing the enamel draining board. 'One of the many.'

'That's true,' Lucia said. 'In fact, Maureen will be much more use to you than I will. Maureen, you must be able to tell Jo something about Leah Ellerman, having worked for her such a long time.'

Maureen rinsed her cloth. 'Matter of fact, I actually work for her sister, Irene, and have done for more than twenty years. Irene's the one that pays me, and Leah's the one that gives me most of the work, if you know what I mean. But I can't honestly say I *know* either of them.'

'It must have been a shock, hearing the news?' Jo said to Maureen's back.

'I couldn't believe it.' Maureen glanced over her shoulder at the two women, while continuing to sluice the sink. She shook her head as she wrung out her cloth. 'I'm still not sure I've taken it in. In fact, I have hardly slept since Sunday.'

'One thing that's bothering me is why no one reported her missing,' Jo said. 'Have either of you got any theories about that?' She directed her question at Lucia, who struck her as the sort of woman to have theories about most things, but it was the other woman who answered.

'That's almost the worst thing,' Maureen said. A citrussy chemical smell pervaded the room as she sprayed the taps vigorously. 'Because the truth is, I did notice she wasn't back from London, and now of course I wish I'd said something.' She stopped and turned to face the other two women, her eyes large and baffled behind her glasses. 'But you've got to understand that it wasn't unheard of for her to spend longer in London. Bless her, no one could say she wasn't a hard worker. So, if something needed finishing, she used to stay in town till it was done. That's what I always thought, anyway. And when she was here, she was either on her laptop all hours or handing out orders about the building work. I feel terrible now for not saying anything.'

'I met her sister, Irene, and even she had no idea her sister was missing,' Jo said sympathetically. 'They weren't close, apparently.'

'No, that's true, they weren't. Maureen started to pack away her cleaning materials into a large plastic carrier. 'But if anyone has reason for a guilty conscience, it's Matty Sullivan. He obviously suspected something bad had happened when he burst into the pub on Sunday with all that drama. But what did he do about it? Diddly squat, as usual.' She ran her eye over the items in the bag and added darkly, 'He was her little lapse of judgement, if you ask me.'

'A bad choice to be in charge of the building works?' Jo said innocently, although she was sure this was not what Maureen meant.

'What do you think?' The older woman shot her a knowing look but said no more.

Lucia was watching them both dreamily. 'It's very strange and sad, what's happened, but I hope you don't think too bad of me for trying my best to stay out of it. I'm here as a sort of retreat, so I don't want to get involved in any nastiness. That's why I'm going home early.'

'So, if this is a retreat,' Jo said, and paused, 'can I ask, what are you retreating from?'

'Work. Life. London. The daily commute. The air quality.' Lucia numbered them on her right hand, starting with her thumb. 'Do you want the full list?'

'Leah worked in London, too,' Jo said, aware she was clutching at straws.

'It's a big old city, you know,' Lucia said, with another giggle. 'Really, all I know about Leah Ellerman is that she has a nice dog and owns this place. Turns out, I'm the first person to rent it, you know. It's not the best start for a business venture, is it?'

'It's booked up for the rest of the year, though, and even number two has a waiting list and it's not ready yet,' Maureen chipped in. 'Credit where credit is due, Matty has transformed them — all due to Leah's vision, of course. You ought to have a look at next door. I can show you round any time. It's a little palace,' she said to Jo. 'Especially when you compare it to the Hutchinson's or the Lilley's, which are so cluttered and dark and old-fashioned.'

'I might just do that, thanks,' Jo said. She turned back to Lucia. 'Just as a matter of interest, what do you do in London?'

Lucia rolled her eyes. 'I'm a buyer for a department store. Sounds sort of glamorous, but it really isn't. Considering I've got a Masters in English Literature, you might think it's a bit of a waste.' When Jo made polite noises of disagreement, Lucia held up her long hands in a stop sign, rings and bangles on display. 'No, shush. Don't say it, I know it. Ideally, I'd like to just read every day and maybe do some painting, like I have these last two weeks. Maybe even write something. But I have to earn my money first.'

'Well, I understand about that,' Jo was saying feelingly when Lucia's phone pinged with a message.

'He's here. It's the taxi.' She pulled a white linen jacket off the back of the stool. 'So sorry, got to go. Maureen, I've loved our chats.' She threw air kisses at them both and made a dive for her bags.

It took all three women, in the end, to transfer Lucia and her assorted luggage to the cab, which was waiting in a layby in the lane. Just as she was about to get in the taxi, Maureen grabbed her arm and Jo heard her say, 'Don't forget.'

From the look on Lucia's face, it seemed she had forgotten, and Maureen pressed forward. 'You promised you'd look into an internship for Charlotte.' She pushed a folded piece of paper into Lucia's hand. 'That's my phone number, and I've already got yours, so I'll call you.'

Lucia slipped into the back seat and waved cheerfully as the taxi set off, with no apparent regrets to be heading home. Maureen didn't even stay long enough to see the cab move away, but hurried back along the path to number two.

'Who's leaving? Is that Miss Hewitt?' A young voice spoke up from behind Jo's shoulder as the taxi disappeared around the first bend.

'Yes, she's going home to London, apparently.' Jo turned to see a boy of about fourteen, arms folded over an orange Wolves sweatshirt.

'Can't blame her,' he grinned. 'Why would anyone want to come on holiday here, even without a murder?' He hoisted a large bag of potatoes from the path into his arms.

'I don't know, I think it's pretty,' Jo said, and the boy looked at her as if she was mad.

'Boring as hell,' he pointed out. He nodded down at the sack of spuds. 'Gotta go. This is part of the weekly shop and my dad's waiting.' As he crossed the lane, a tear in the side of the bag caused two potatoes to drop out onto the grass verge.

'Bugger,' the boy muttered. Jo ran forward to collect the rolling potatoes and caught up with him as he reached Leah's cottage. 'Oh, thanks. Sorry for swearing.'

'Can I give you a hand?' Jo asked, as he wrestled to wedge the sack against the garden wall so that no more potatoes could escape.

'If you could open the gate.' He nodded towards number three, which confirmed Jo's guess that he was one of the Hutchinson family. Gary had said that Gil Hutchinson had a daughter, Nora, and a son. This boy seemed a couple of years younger than the girl in the hoody, who she'd seen staring into her car and sitting moodily on the lock gate.

Jo held the gate as the front door swung open. A bespectacled man hurried out to take the heavy bag. Jo recognized him from the police station. 'I was coming back for that. I meant you to bring the lighter ones,' he said to his son.

'Careful, it's got a hole.' Jo managed to catch another potato that had escaped in the transfer.

The man registered her presence. 'Oh, thanks. Can I help you?' He frowned, and his glasses slipped down his nose. Jo saw that the layout of the property was different to the renovated houses, as the back door opened directly into the small, dark kitchen, which meant he was able to lean in and dump the sack of spuds onto the worktop. He returned to the doorstep to peer at Jo suspiciously.

'I'll go back for the other bags,' his son piped up, and was jogging back along the path, jingling his father's car keys, before he could argue.

'Unloading the shopping is even more of a pain while our car park is cordoned off.' He craned his neck to watch his son's progress and said, 'That's my son, Jacob, and I'm Gil Hutchinson. Are you something to do with the investigation?'

Jo explained her mission for the second time that day, feeling more comfortable with it this time.

'A private investigator?' Gil Hutchinson wiped sweaty strands of hair off his forehead. 'That's a novelty for little old Stokesly. We've got TV crews and journos, as well as the SOCO teams and police everywhere. Now a PI, too.' He nodded slowly. 'Well, I don't mind helping Gary out by answering a few questions, but I'll have to tell the police I've spoken to you.' He hovered on the doorstep, arms folded, glancing behind her frequently to see if Jacob was on his way back.

Jo thanked him. Then, realizing from his distracted expression that she probably wasn't going to have very long for questions, she asked how well he'd known Leah Ellerman and when he'd last seen her.

'I've given this some thought for the police, obviously,' Gil said. 'Firstly, as a landlady, Leah was fair and efficient, but I had hardly any contact with her personally, considering she lives next door but one. All our business is done by emails and bank transfer. As for when I last saw her, I'm pretty sure it was the first of June. I'd picked up Jacob from karate, and Nora — that's my daughter — was also in the car. Leah and I exchanged pleasantries through the car window, as I recall. About the weather, that sort of thing, I suppose.'

'I think I've seen your daughter,' Jo said. 'She was over by the pub on Sunday.'

'Yes, that would be Nora.' Gil's permanent frown deepened a notch. 'She likes to help out there, supposedly. Sarah is very good to her, although I'm not sure Nora appreciates that.' He sighed. 'They both get so bored at home, but then they tell me they hate school. How can you win?' He appealed to her with harassed grey eyes. 'And I'm on my own. I'm convinced Delia would know what to do — especially with Nora. That's my wife, who died three years ago. I've a bit more of a clue with Jacob, simply because he's a boy.'

'I'm sorry. Three years, that's not very long,' Jo said, and he gave her his full attention for the first time.

'No, it's not,' he agreed, and smiled. 'We all adapt differently. I sort of soldier on regardless, but Nora just seems desperate to bring her mother back, so I'm not sure she has really come to terms with it, even now. Jacob is only sad when he remembers. Boys are just so much more straightforward, aren't they?'

'My nephew has just decided he wants to leave school against my sister's better judgement. So not all boys are so easy-going,' Jo said. 'It will be interesting to see who wins that battle.'

'My money is on your nephew.' He grinned suddenly. 'As a parent, I feel oddly disempowered.' He broke off as Jacob swung through the gate with three carrier bags. The boy was almost as tall as his father, and came to stand beside him.

'Sorry, I'll leave you in peace in a minute,' Jo said. 'Just one more question — what did you think of Leah? I mean, to be honest, she doesn't seem very popular, and nobody noticed she was missing for two weeks. Didn't she have any friends?'

'I had nothing against Leah herself, but I didn't agree with her plans for the cottages,' Gil said thoughtfully. 'It means we have to move out in the autumn. I've started looking, but obviously, we need a three-bedroom place and there's not a lot out there.'

'And a games room,' Jacob put in. 'Big enough for a snooker table.' He turned to Jo. 'I think Leah had friends in London, because she was often away, but they never visited her here. So, when she went missing, maybe the London lot thought she was here and her family thought she was there.'

Handy for the murderer, Jo thought, but she smiled at his sensible reasoning. Encouraged, the boy went on. 'You really should talk to Nora. She hangs out with the neighbours more than I do and knows more about what's going on around here than any of us. She could tell you all the gossip, if she chooses. But she's at school. I'm on exam leave. I'm meant to be revising,' he said, breaking into a sudden grin like his father's. 'What else do you want to know? It's only fair,' he added. 'You helped with the potatoes.'

Jo laughed genuinely for the first time that day. 'I'm just trying to understand Leah Ellerman, so you've already helped a lot. And it would be great if you can think of a way to get your sister to talk to me. She sounds like a mine of information.'

Father and son exchanged knowing glances. 'Now that, we can't promise,' Gil said. 'She doesn't even talk to us most of the time.'

'Bribery is probably the best route,' Jacob suggested seriously. 'Offer to buy her a hot chocolate or a smoothie, and make it conditional on her telling you stuff. Even then I can't guarantee it.' He dug out his phone and flicked rapidly back through his photos. 'I can show you another side to Leah, though. I actually went to spend a day at her office in London. It was part of my work experience project last

Easter. It was a weird day, but she bought me lunch, so she can't be all bad.'

'No one is saying she's all bad, Jakey,' his father said patiently. 'Don't forget, the poor woman has died in horrible circumstances.'

'No, OK, OK!' Jacob held up one hand towards his father, and with the other, handed Jo his phone. There were four pictures of his day in London. In one, Leah was presenting in front of a group around a boardroom table, a presentation on a screen behind her. Nothing on the screen made any sense to Jo, but she looked hard at the image of Leah: smart and neat in a business suit with fair, bobbed hair. Although she was smiling for the photograph, she looked a little strained and her eyes remained serious. The other pictures were of Jacob's lunch, and, as he was in two of them, Leah had probably taken them. 'Seems like she gave you a good day,' she said.

'It was very generous of her,' Gil said.

'I got an A for my essay,' he grinned.

As Jo handed the phone back, a news notification flashed onto the screen: *Missing in Highland Storm*. But it wasn't the headline that grabbed Jo's attention, it was the headshot of a businessman below it. There was no mistaking the florid cheeks and discontented blue gaze — it was the Angry Cherub.

'Sorry, but could you tell me what that news bulletin is about?' Jo asked.

Jacob clicked on the headline and scanned the story quickly. 'It's a guy, Adrian Carmichael, the director of a law firm, who went hiking in Scotland. Near St Andrews, it says. He's been missing twenty-four hours, so the rescue people are searching for him. They think he might have fallen into the sea.' The young boy looked across at Jo, puzzled. 'Why? Do you know him?'

'Adrian Carmichael,' Jo repeated the name. 'No, I've never heard of him,' she said, honestly. 'I thought I recognized his photo, that's all, but I was mistaken.'

After that, she thanked them both and made her exit as soon as she could. She had warmed to the Hutchinsons far more than Lucia Hewitt, who she'd found altogether more strange. She was still walking along the towpath when she dialled Macy's number.

'Took you longer than I expected,' he said.

CHAPTER EIGHT

'I'll meet you,' Macy said, which meant he didn't want to talk in the office. They settled on Strensham services on the M5, which lay between Stokesly and the Macy and Wilson Agency in Birmingham. It was a lot closer to Jo, however, so she judged she had just enough time to pay her clients a brief visit.

There were no media people or police hanging around the pub this morning. Sarah had her own theory about that. She was in the front garden, dead-heading geraniums. 'They take down the tape and suddenly there's nothing to look at,' she said. 'So, it was actually the police cordon that was causing the problem.'

'I'm not sure I follow that logic,' Jo said. 'But, look, I was just popping in to see if you and Gary are OK.'

'OK? Give me a break,' Sarah snorted, tugging savagely at a scarlet bloom. 'When we're not hiding from the local press, we're bombarded with criticism about our crap security. Gary will be getting the same going-over from Paul right now.' She jerked her head towards the pub. 'Paul's the guy from the brewery,' she added. She pronounced his name to rhyme with 'owl'. 'He's Danish,' she explained, 'and I'm keeping out of his way.'

'No sign you can re-open yet, then?' Jo indicated the blackboard at the front door.

'No chance. Meanwhile, our margins are falling through the floor and the police are treating us like villains.' She turned unexpectedly and patted Jo's arm. 'Still, at least we know you're on our side.'

'Actually, I've just got one quick question.' Jo explained that she had visited the canal cottages earlier, and they both automatically turned towards the Victorian brick terrace, its reflection rippling warm red in the dark canal. Now that Jo had visited them, she found she could better distinguish between the houses. Similar flourishing baskets and white shutters were visible in the cottages at either end, supplied by Leah, she supposed. At the Hutchinsons', in the middle of the terrace, unmatched curtains and cluttered windowsills could be seen behind the ragged privet hedge, whereas the Lilleys' cottage had a neat and tidy front garden with no showy baskets.

'I met your cleaner, Maureen, again,' Jo said. 'She hinted that there might be something going on between Leah and Matty. I suppose it fits with his dramatic announcement on Sunday.'

'I bow to Maureen's long experience.' Sarah gave a humourless laugh. 'She knows all the gossip around here. But, let's say, I wouldn't be at all surprised. All year, I've seen Leah regularly popping in and out whenever he was working on the cottages, and at lunchtimes they often sat on the lock gates, sharing a sandwich. I'm sure the renovations don't require such in-depth conversations.' She threw a hand in the direction of the terrace. 'I mean, they are all the bloody same.'

'They didn't keep it quiet, then?'

'I didn't say that,' Sarah responded. 'Leah was like a clam about her private life. About most things, actually.' Her naturally rounded, relaxed features gained a new edge and her gaze sharpened. 'There's something I need to tell you.'

Here it comes, Jo thought, with a little rush of adrenalin, *I knew they were holding out on me.* Sarah turned to face her, palms stiffly by her side. 'Leah and I had the odd falling out, and it was always about our paranormal evenings. Basically, she didn't like me holding them. She came round here one Thursday night a few weeks ago, just before our regular session, and demanded we stop it.'

'Why? What did she have against them?'

Sarah rolled her eyes impatiently. 'She thought they lowered the tone of the area. She didn't actually say that, but behind all her holier-than-thou words, basically, she was worried that the reputation of the pub would devalue the cottages. She'd have liked a chic bistro pub — preferably with a Michelin star. Well, that's hardly me and Gary, is it?' Sarah grabbed at another geranium and Jo waited patiently. 'There were customers in the bar, so I took her into the back room to tell her "no" in private. She didn't like it. I don't think she was used to the word.' Sarah threw Jo a grim smile. 'Our little spiritual soirée went ahead, of course. I'd already arranged it, and I wasn't about to let people down. They rely on me. So, after that, Leah wrote to the brewery — talk about an overreaction. She really didn't care about the impact on us, provided she got her own way. And now, Paul has a copy of her email — along with the rest of his portfolio of relevant documents, no doubt,' she jerked her head towards the pub, 'which is one of the reasons I'm staying out of the meeting. So now you know,' she finished, with a smile that didn't touch her eyes. 'You said to be totally upfront with you, and anyway, as I said to Gary, it would come out sooner or later.'

Jo had plenty to reflect on as she drove up the M5 to meet Macy. She was still left with an uneasy feeling of not having heard the full story about what had happened at the New Navigation. And she had to decide what to make of Lucia Hewitt, who had denied any knowledge of Leah. There was something distinctly odd about the woman. About Leah herself, only young Jacob had anything really positive to say. His dad, Gil Hutchinson, like the other tenants, had hated her plans to turn the cottages into holiday lets. Of course, her position as landlady gave her power, which she clearly wasn't afraid to use, and as a VP of an international bank, she was probably accustomed to that, Jo decided, thinking of the pictures she'd seen online of the businesswoman at work.

And yet, a stronger image kept coming into her mind, as she took the exit towards the motorway services, of the red roses she'd abandoned in the sink that morning. She knew she had to talk to Teddy, although she wasn't yet sure what she was going to say, and instead, she was racing to meet her old boss and ex-lover, David Macy. She gave herself an honest look in the mirror before she left the car. *What am I doing here?* she asked herself, not for the first time.

Macy was, of course, already there, his elegant shape looking very formal in a dark suit and tie, his expression brooding. 'You only had to come five minutes up the road,' he complained, when he saw her hurrying across the coffee shop. 'Whereas I've had to drive out into the back of beyond. Surprised I wasn't delayed by cows crossing.'

'On the M5? Don't be silly. They have bridges.' Jo took a seat and picked up the coffee waiting for her. 'I was delayed by my client telling me things she should have told me three days ago. And now she's made her confession, I suspect it's still a half-truth. At best.'

He nodded at her approvingly. 'You are gaining the right amount of cynicism for the job.'

She took a few sips of cooling coffee, regarding him steadily. 'Come on, it is him, isn't it? The Angry Cherub? I saw his photo on a news bulletin and instantly recognized him: Adrian Carmichael, director of a law firm. They said he's gone missing on a Scottish mountain. Police and rescue teams are looking for him, it said.'

'Not anymore.' He was pale and, for once, badly shaven.

'What? They've found him?'

'No, they've called off the search. Coastguard, Mountain Rescue and RNLI, the lot. They were searching the water as well, because his backpack and camera were found on a clifftop with a steep drop to the sea.'

'What's happened to him? Do you know? I mean, were you expecting this?' She stared into his weary, impenetrable eyes. 'What the hell did he say to you in Cheltenham?'

'Let me start at the beginning,' he said, taking a minute to gather his thoughts. Jo waited patiently, watching the motorists and families queue at the counter. For some reason, their section of the café remained empty, and she wondered if she had strolled past a sign saying 'closed'. Or maybe she and Macy had created an invisible forcefield?

'I've known Adrian Carmichael for about twelve years,' Macy began. 'He's a director of the legal group now, but he was a jobbing solicitor in Coventry when I first started out. He quickly made partner, but carried on putting work my way. Still does, although the work is less about serving papers these days and more about character checks. It's good business,' he added.

Hard-headed Cancer the Crab looked directly at sensible, rational Virgo, and they understood each other perfectly. He went on, 'Adrian asked me to meet him in Cheltenham on Sunday, so I knew it was something different. He chose the day, the time and place to signal that this wasn't regular business.'

Jo thought back to the crowded restaurant, how the cherub had pleaded his case, the uneasiness she'd perceived between the two men, and then the sudden handshake. 'He had a proposition?'

Macy nodded, still taking his time. 'He wanted to know how to disappear. As what we do at Macy and Wilson is trace people, he figured I would know how someone could avoid being found.'

'He doesn't want to be found.' Jo tested out each word softly. 'What has he done wrong?'

'It's not like that,' Macy continued in the same even tone. 'He just wanted to escape from his life. He'd had enough of it and wanted a new one.'

'No one can have a new life,' Jo said, feeling suddenly very old. 'What about his home life? Wife? Partner? Kids?'

'His wife is already well set up with most of his assets in joint names. His kids are grown up and are not bothered about him. I doubt that myself.' He made a little sceptical moue. 'But that's what he said.'

'Why then? Debts?'

'No debts. I told you, I've known this guy for years. He is minted and not the flashy sort.'

'Lover?'

His enigmatic face stretched to a smile for the first time since they'd met up. 'You're getting too good at this. Yes, there is a lover — Kay. But let me come to her in good time.'

Outside the window, a family was picnicking on a bench in the sun. One of the boys was walking a Jack Russell-type dog on a lead around the scrubby grass. Leah Ellerman had a dog, Jo remembered suddenly. She must find out what had happened to it. Most likely it was the small brown dog she'd seen outside Matty's caravan. She filed this detail away for checking and brought her attention back to Macy, whose dark eyes had also drifted outside. There was something subtly different, something wistful about his expression. She felt as if something substantial had happened, but, as ever, he was not fully letting her in.

'You felt sorry for him, didn't you?' she asked eventually.

'I told him I'd have nothing to do with his disappearance. But I felt for him a bit, yes. Everyone deserves a second chance, don't they?'

'But this man's had tons of chances and he wants to throw them all away. He's rich and privileged and has a family.'

'Would it help to know his wife is also seeing someone else?'

'No, not really.' Jo glared out of the window at the innocent picnickers. 'Everyone has to face up to their responsibilities.'

'Agreed,' he said. 'Look, I'm sorry I got you involved in all this.' He reached across the table and unexpectedly took her hand. 'I didn't know what he was going to tell me at the

Hotel du Vin, and when he did explain his plan, I didn't realize he was on the brink of carrying it out. I suppose I thought there would be time to talk him out of it. So, when I saw the news reports yesterday . . .' He ran out of words, but his face was grave.

'I don't feel like I'm involved,' Jo said honestly. 'But he has put you in an impossible position.' She took her hand out from under his so she could cover her eyes. Somehow, it felt like a lot to process. 'You'd better tell me about the lover, Kay,' she said.

'Kay knows nothing. He was insistent about that.' She heard him sigh. 'He knew it was risky. Particularly getting out of the country. He was using his uncle's passport. The man's in a care home and Adrian just took it—'

'Nice,' Jo commented.

'Also, driving to the airport was fraught with risk. He'd hired a car in his uncle's name, and I think he had some sort of plan to make himself look older, but the airport is riddled with CCTV and police, customs, etc. So, he knew there was a chance he could be caught.' Macy paused. 'I don't actually know where he is right now.'

'Good,' Jo said. She had placed her hands on the table again. 'So, just let me get this clear. His wife and kids and family — and his lover — all believe he is dead, that he has fallen down a cliff while on a hike. Or that it's possibly even suicide?'

'Yes. It's a shit situation,' he acknowledged. 'Though if he gets away and gets access to his funds abroad, which he has stashed away in an overseas account—'

'Of course he has. I wouldn't expect him to go wanting.'

Macy ignored her sarcasm and ploughed on. 'I think in a few weeks, he may contact Kay and give her the choice of joining him. He wanted them to be together, but he didn't want to implicate her.'

'He implicated you, though.' Jo sighed in frustration. 'You could go to the police and tell them what you know. That's what you'd tell me to do.' She watched him shake his head implacably.

'I can't do that,' he said. After that, they sat in silence and watched the family pack up their picnic and straggle towards the car park. Jo rubbed her eyes again. Suddenly the red roses in the sink didn't seem such a massive issue. Even the problems of her own case seemed more manageable.

'I'm glad you told me,' she said, after a while.

'Thanks. You are the only person I could even think of telling.' He seemed to relax a little and pushed himself away from the table. 'The best thing I can hope for now is that I never hear anything else about Adrian Carmichael for the rest of our lives.'

When they got to their feet, she noticed his well-tailored suit and how well he wore it. 'Are you on your way to court today?'

'No, the trial is in Bournemouth and I hoped I might be driving down there this morning. The sooner the better for me — I just want to get it over with. But they called me to say there's been a delay. A juror has gone sick. So, now it will probably be tomorrow.'

'Bournemouth?' she repeated, and looked at him curiously.

'Yes, it's our case.' He threw her a tired smile. 'The one we worked on together at the end of last year. The prosecution want me there as a witness because of the surveillance work we did.'

'But that's brilliant news,' Jo said, unable to keep the enthusiasm out of her voice. 'You get to see that woman brought to justice and do your bit.'

Macy walked by her side past the little kiosks and shops towards the entrance, still looking gloomy. 'If you say so, but it's not something any private investigator rushes to do. To stand in a witness box and announce their job to the world. Well, it's far from private, is it? So, it goes against the grain. The only good thing is, it's a long way from my patch.'

'Well, I think you're doing the right thing,' she told him as they stepped out into the still air together. Jo had lost track of time and was surprised to see it was already past 2 p.m.

'You didn't get chance to tell me what's on your mind,' Macy said as her car came into view. 'I know there is something. Is it about the dead body in the cellar? Or something else?'

'It's just . . . I'm mulling over a decision I've got to make,' she said. 'Honestly, compared to what you've just told me, it pales into insignificance.'

His body still felt tense when she hugged him. 'When it becomes significant again,' he said, 'call me.'

CHAPTER NINE

Jo's phone had been on silent for most of the morning, so she only saw the list of missed calls and voicemails when she had parked near her flat: Teddy, then Hanni, plus three calls from the same unrecognized number. She listened to the messages while walking down Fleece Alley.

Teddy: *'Hi, it's me. Did you get the flowers? I was worried the cat would eat them. Andy asked me if we would babysit Lela-May tonight so he and Nikki can go out. They haven't been anywhere together since the baby and they want to see a movie. So I said yes. Hope that's OK. Give me a call. I'm on the course til two and giving lessons between three and five.'*

Hanni: *'Josephine, we've had a strange invitation from that rude woman who came to the shop. What are you going to say? By the way, I'm getting some new business, thanks to that article in the local paper. I'm grateful to the gods of unintended consequences.'*

Unrecognized: *'Hello, this is Irene Ellerman leaving a message for Jo Hughes. I've arranged for my brother to come over tomorrow. He has to make arrangements to be away from his business, so it's not been easy and I hope you can make it. Morning is preferable. Please call me back on the landline.'* This was followed by two other calls from this number at half-hour intervals, with no messages.

Hanni was right — Irene Ellerman was unlikeable, but she was also very keen to see them again, it seemed. Did she imagine that people could just drop everything simply to meet her elusive brother? All the same, Jo reasoned, climbing the steps to her flat, that is exactly what she was going to do. The opportunity to find out more about Leah Ellerman's family life was too good to miss. And she hoped to persuade Hanni to do the same.

The conversation with Macy had been sobering. Seeing the scope of his problems had helped put hers into perspective. She felt it was also something to do with the way he'd opened up to her, which made her feel able to cope with anything. Whatever the reason, she felt much clearer about her own plans. She tidied up her workroom and ate a hastily made cheese roll. Then, over a second coffee, with Halifax settled on the best armchair, she called Teddy and left a message, graciously accepting the invitation to his brother's. After a chat with Hanni, which was necessarily brief because her friend was in sole charge at the Rivermill, Jo called Irene Ellerman on her home number, as instructed.

She half-expected the phone to be answered by a butler or some other member of staff, but it was unmistakably Irene's voice that barked down the line at her. Jo thanked her and accepted her second invitation of the day.

'Good, because Duncan needs to hear your version of events — and from your friend who found Leah. I refuse to let him stay in his remote little Cotswold idyll any longer, pretending the world is made up of, what does he call it — random acts of kindness? No, it's made of cruelty and sheer nastiness, jealousy and revenge. That's how this . . . this tragedy came about.' She had to stop to take a breath. 'It *is* a tragedy,' she added, a little defensively.

'Of course it is.' Jo was listening closely. 'Your sister has died too early and needlessly—'

'Yes, she did, and Duncan needs to be by my side now that Leah is gone. The trouble with us Ellermans is, we are all too independent. It's a trait our parents drummed into us — self-reliance. But I accept we may have taken it too far. I literally had no idea what Leah was up to, and I think she conveniently forgot that I am still managing the estate. She only ever showed me the sketchiest outline of her plans for the cottages, and Duncan always says he was even less in the picture—' She broke off abruptly and cleared her throat. 'Well, anyway, I'm sure you've got better things to do than listen to me venting so, all being well, I'll see you at Stokes Manor at eleven a.m., yes?'

'Yes, and Hanni will be there too. Do you mind if I ask you something about Leah first? It's about her private life.'

'Private life?' Irene repeated. 'How would I know about that? She was still single, if that's what you mean.'

'Did you realize she was seeing Matty Sullivan?' Jo broke in, matching the other woman's bluntness. 'He's the builder who is doing up the cottages for Leah. He's living in a caravan on her land.' And looking after her dog, too, she added silently to herself. Did Irene even know her sister had a dog? Let alone a boyfriend?

'Good God, is he? Well, I don't know why I'm surprised. What you never ask, you never get told, I suppose. Look, I must go to meet the solicitors shortly. It's about the will. All I want to say is, don't hold anything back when you meet Duncan tomorrow. He needs to know the ugly truth and he needs to hear it from someone else, not me. It's the only thing that will get him out of his cocoon of denial.'

Jo didn't know what to make of Irene Ellerman; the woman seemed to have been oddly galvanized by her younger sister's death. There was a whole host of things she didn't understand about this family and its links with the claustrophobic canal-side community, but right now, she had other priorities.

She pulled Lela-May's birth chart off the printer and began her interpretation, a systematic process which she found absorbing. She hoped to take the completed chart with her that evening, but she also knew it would take as long as it needed. She was examining the position of the Midheaven and its implications for the baby's future career when the doorbell rang.

A woman in a neat dark suit, slim and unsmiling, was waiting expectantly outside. 'Are you Jo Hughes? The astrologer? You were mentioned in the local paper.'

Recalling Hanni's message, Jo entertained hopes that this might be a potential new client. 'Yes, that's me. How can I help?'

The woman took out her phone and scrolled down until she found the small photograph of Jo that had accompanied the article. She scrutinized it, glancing back to Jo, and, apparently satisfied, she held out a delicate hand. 'I've tracked you down. It wasn't too difficult. All your details are listed on the local Mind, Body, Spirit site,' she said. 'I'm Meena Sanyal. I worked with Leah Ellerman. I wonder if you could spare me a few minutes? I'm only up from London for the day.'

'You'd better come in.' Jo led the way. Inwardly, she was writing an email to get her address taken off the website. It would not do for a local PI to be so visible. Outwardly, she politely said, 'So, you work for StadtBank? I was intending to call them.'

'That would have saved me a lot of trouble,' Meena Sanyal said. 'Although you might have talked to someone who just fobbed you off or who didn't really know Leah. So it's probably just as well I came.'

Jo showed her into the living room, where the woman sat gracefully on one of the dining room chairs and, when offered, said she would prefer tea with a generous amount of milk. Jo found a teapot and teacups from the back of a cupboard, dusted them off and set them out with a milk jug and sugar bowl on a tray. Something told her that Meena Sanyal would approve of this formality.

'This is very hospitable, thank you,' she said, when Jo returned with a full tray, including ginger biscuits. 'I hope you don't mind my coming to your door like this? I heard about your involvement from the landlady of the New Navigation, Mrs Robart. She assured me you wouldn't mind. I'm pretending to be Sherlock Holmes for a day to get answers to a few questions that are bothering me about Leah's death.'

'You are not the only one. Maybe we can share some information.' Jo poured out the tea and passed a cup to the woman opposite her. Meena Sanyal was maybe a little older than herself, business-smart and self-possessed, and with a certain look that could cut glass. 'I'm guessing you really knew Leah,' Jo went on easily, 'and I'm keen to understand her. She is still a bit of a mystery to me, to be honest.'

'You are working as a private eye for Mr and Mrs Robart? I must say you are not what I'd expect from a private detective.'

'Well, you're not much like Sherlock Holmes,' Jo responded. Meena smiled, and it instantly enlivened her intense face. 'What are these questions that are bothering you?'

'What actually happened to Leah, of course. I have worked with her for twelve years as her executive assistant. It's a fancy title for a PA,' she added, seeing Jo's expression. 'So, yes, I certainly did know Leah, and I'm not just going to sit on my hands and let people make false assumptions. I've been closely following everything published about her since I heard the dreadful news.' She swallowed and set her cup down. Her eyes rested on her clasped hands as she recalled finding out about Leah's death. 'The director called me into his office to tell me, one to one, on Monday morning. I suppose he must have known that Leah and I were close as we'd worked together so long. Later that day, the police came to the office to interview us, but I can't find out much about their investigation or what's happened since. Then yesterday, I saw the article on the local paper's site, so I took today off to do my own detective work.' She looked up with a brighter expression.

'I can see you miss her,' Jo said. She felt oddly relieved to finally meet someone who'd seemed to like Leah Ellerman. 'The police are taking it seriously. I went to their press conference yesterday. They are doing door-to-door enquiries and seem to be focusing on the local community.'

'I know they will be doing their best, but . . .' Meena struggled for the right words. 'I mean, they are just a handful of local bobbies in a country village. How can they understand someone as complex as Leah?' She smiled suddenly at Jo. 'This is a bit of a breakthrough, though, now that I have managed to find you. Thank goodness for that article. So that we don't duplicate effort, would you object to telling me what you have found out?'

'I'll tell you what I can,' Jo said. 'I've been talking to the other people who live along the canal to find out when they last saw Leah. Sarah and Gary had fallen out with her. They claim the pub is haunted and they run regular paranormal evenings. I can't work out if they are just trying to raise the profile of the pub or if there is something weirder going on. Leah objected to them, but I don't really understand why. I suppose I'm trying to build a picture of her.' Jo decided it was time for Meena to share what she knew. 'What was she like at work?'

'She never mentioned much about the pub to me — although I knew she didn't like the landlords. She thought they were flaky and brought down the area. Leah was a landowner, after all. At work, she was efficient, competent, brilliant at her job, didn't take any prisoners. I respected her.'

'Yes, but . . .' Jo hesitated. 'Did you like her? It's an odd thing, but I have hardly found anyone who wholeheartedly liked her.'

'I admired her, and yes, I did like her too. Otherwise, why would I be here on my day off? She was very good to me, very loyal, and took life seriously.'

Jo conceded this with a smile. 'You implied something had been missed,' she prompted. 'What questions should the police be asking?'

Meena responded eagerly. 'Well, nobody seems to be investigating her sister, who called in sick for Leah on Monday the seventh of June, and again later in the week. I didn't take the first call, but of course, I made a note. I thought it was unusual, out of character. Leah is one of those strong women who are rarely sick, and even when she occasionally did get a tummy bug or something, she'd be phoning me every morning to check things or move appointments. Which I would have already done, of course,' she added, drily.

'Of course.' They exchanged another smile. Jo said, 'You do know that she was almost certainly dead when those calls were made? So, the person who phoned in sick for her is important.'

Meena nodded soberly. 'Indeed. Even at the time, I suspected something wasn't right, especially when I took the second call from Irene myself. She told me Leah couldn't speak, that she had tonsillitis and was on antibiotics.'

'Irene maintains she didn't make those calls,' Jo said.

Meena sat back, concerned. 'But I spoke to her myself, and she even told me which type of antibiotics Leah was taking.' She met Jo's eyes. 'I decided I'd like to meet Irene, having heard so much about her over the years. I found her number in Leah's contacts, but the woman won't take my calls. I've told the police all about my suspicions, but I don't think they are following it up.' Meena shot Jo a meaningful look. 'The Ellermans are an important family around here, aren't they?'

'Well, yes, but I don't think the police are bothered about that one way or the other. It is still very early in the inquiry.' Jo paused and, realizing that the police did not need her to defend them, changed tack. 'In fact, I've been invited to Irene's house tomorrow to meet her and her brother—'

'To Stokes Manor? To meet Duncan?' Meena raised well-groomed eyebrows. 'I can give you some background on him. He's the archetypal "difficult middle child" in the family and has inherited his father's furniture business. But it's Irene who manages most of the estate, including the manor house and the land that goes with it. Even the land that she didn't inherit, such as Leah's canal cottages, she acts like she owns.'

'This is according to Leah, of course,' Jo pointed out.

'Yes, granted, I only have Leah's perspective on the family. But I have witnessed Irene's controlling behaviour for

103

myself over the years. Irene was a tyrant about Christmas, for example. They all had to gather at her house come what may, arriving and leaving at the times she decreed and bringing particular food. Leah would be desperately constructing little parcels from sugared almonds on the twenty-third of December because everyone had to have a "table present". And she was always having to fit in the family "do" around work demands.' Meena paused. 'And then there's the financials.'

'Go on,' Jo said.

'Irene used to insist that Leah and Duncan chip in to help her with maintenance on the manor house, saying it was part of the family legacy, because it's Grade Two listed, you know. Although, neither of them has any offspring, so any "family legacy" is clearly going to Irene's own kids. But still, Leah had to find a few thousand for roof repairs about two years ago, whereas Irene never paid a penny towards Leah's maintenance for her cottages. This was the sort of thing Leah would confide in me,' Meena said more softly. 'I don't think she told another soul and, it goes without saying, neither did I. But now things are different.'

'Leah sounds like quite a feisty woman,' Jo observed. 'A senior leader at StadtBank, yes?'

'Yes, she was a VP and managed a whole raft of high-profile customer accounts. She was next in line for a board role and had been marked out in the succession plan.'

'So, why didn't she stand up to her sister?'

Meena sighed and spread her hands. 'Now that, I don't know. Pure family dynamics, maybe? I mean, Irene was the big sister and you can never really comprehend what goes on in families, can you?'

'That's true.' Jo's mind flitted briefly to the Scarboroughs. If she did ever marry Teddy, she would be marrying his family, too, even if she didn't take his name. This gave her an unexpected qualm.

'Can you do something for me?' Meena asked. 'When you see Irene tomorrow, can you confront her? Ask her about the phone calls.'

Jo agreed, a little reluctantly. 'I will, if I can, but I know the police have already questioned her about them, because she mentioned it to me.'

'I know we should leave it all to them, but . . .' She threw Jo a sidelong look of guilt. 'Honestly? I came here because I was a little nosey, too. I wanted to finally see Leah's cottages and get a sense of her life here. She'd told me all about it — the renovations and the Lilleys and the Hutchinsons, who are the next to be affected. Leah knew it would hit them hard. That's why she has given them plenty of notice. Did you know the previous tenant from number one was a single mum who had twin boys, who were only toddlers? Leah helped her find another place to live. Helped her out financially, I mean.'

'No, I didn't know that. What about Matty Sullivan? Did Leah mention him?'

'I saw him today when I had lunch at the pub. I went across and had a little walk along the towpath. He was inspecting some work on number two.' Meena gave a knowing look. 'I guessed what was going on between them, but Leah and I never spoke about it. If you're asking what I think of him? Not nearly good enough for her,' she smiled. 'But I'd probably say that about anyone.' Meena drained her teacup and consulted her fitness watch. 'Thank you, that was very refreshing. I have to go and catch my train now. I must admit, I've quite enjoyed playing detective for the day.'

'And I'm really glad you came, Sherlock,' Jo smiled as she showed her guest out. 'I feel I've seen another side of Leah.'

'I'm glad too. The best results require effort, don't you find? And will you tell me what happens at your meeting with Irene and Duncan?' Meena produced an old-fashioned business card from her handbag. 'These are my work and personal numbers.' Jo pocketed it and assured her she would call. 'And I want to know what you make of Matty Sullivan,' Meena added. 'He's on-site now, you know. He said he was expecting delivery of some tiles to number two by six o'clock. I'm just saying . . .'

Jo laughed. 'I'll see what I can do,' she said.

After she'd waved Meena off, she felt buoyed up by the woman's focused energy and made a quick calculation of timings. She and Teddy were due to be at his brother's at 7.30 p.m., so ideally, she should be at Teddy's half an hour earlier. It didn't give her long, but Matty was on her list. As Meena said, the best results required effort.

CHAPTER TEN

There was a heaviness to the evening, as if the air hadn't shifted all day. The glassy strip of water between the pub and the cottages seemed almost solid. She peered over the bridge parapet at the drop down to the pub and water level. Voices carried from the beer garden to the lane, and she saw a few of the outdoor tables were taken and a holiday barge was moored nearby. Clearly, Sarah and Gary had been allowed to re-open for business. Their little car park was almost full, with a delivery van half-blocking the entrance, so Jo had parked in the layby down the lane, where Alys Parry had caught up with her two days ago.

Ever since she had noticed that Alys was pregnant, the journalist was inexplicably linked in Jo's mind with the nagging question she had been harbouring for almost two days: what did she really feel about Teddy's desire to settle down and have children? Did she want to be part of that plan? Could she still be a successful independent career woman, as Alys appeared to be? Could she still be herself? As she was about to spend the evening with Teddy, she knew she couldn't dodge it any longer, and she leaned on the warm, rounded bricks to order her thoughts.

Her attention was caught by a quick-moving figure in black, clearing tables in the pub garden. It was Nora, 'helping out' again. As the girl was only fifteen, Sarah must be pushing the boundaries of the law in allowing it. Although that seemed to be par for the course with Sarah, Jo reflected. She remembered how the young girl had stared into her car on Sunday, and how her father and brother had exchanged telling looks when Nora's name was mentioned.

'She knows more about what's going on around here than any of us,' Jacob had said. Jo mentally added Nora and Alys Parry to the list of people she needed to talk to, and shifted her gaze to the windows of number two Canalside Cottages, where she hoped to track down Matty Sullivan.

The row of cottages had a quiet, closed-up look this evening. There was no answer to her ring on the doorbell of the second cottage, and when she peered in through the front windows, she saw an empty kitchen identical to that in number one. Only the decoration remained to be completed. Glancing anxiously at her watch, she walked around the back of the cottages.

All building work on Leah's house had ended for the day. Or maybe for good? To her left, down the slope of the garden, she saw Matty's caravan and a drift of smoke shadowed against its off-white frame. A small barbecue, which stood on some rough slabs nearby, was lit, and the faint smell of grilled fish reached her on the air, reminding her that she'd only eaten a cheese sandwich since an early breakfast.

She opened the wooden gate and picked her way down the steep grassy path towards the caravan. When she was closer, she called out Matty's name, but there was no response so she trod cautiously on. The smell of sardines was tantalising by now, and surely an indication that the owner was close by. She rapped on the door of the caravan, glancing warily around her. She half-expected Leah's dog to rush out, and, having once been attacked by a guard dog, she was nervous of them. Although the dog she had seen outside Matty's van had been a little sausage dog, she still felt tense, as if she was being observed. She turned on the narrow steps and called out once more. The silent row of houses loomed on the ridge of the towpath and the leafy, rustling copse surrounded the back of the van.

Furtively, she pushed down the metal door handle. With a click, it gave and she opened it carefully. She was met with a combined smell of damp and toast as the door opened directly into the kitchen area. A buttery knife and crumbs littered the little table, which faced the sink and cooker. The light was dimmed by orange curtains across the windows, and, at the back, another patterned curtain was half-drawn to screen the rumpled double bed. A large TV was positioned opposite a bench seat, blocking another window.

Almost as soon as she stepped inside, Jo regretted it. She had no reason to be there and no idea what she was looking for. She started to back out, while still hastily scanning around her. In the worn, well-used narrow space, one thing struck her as incongruous — a shop label dangling from a new coat which lay across the bench seat. The heavy-duty hooded outdoor coat was similar to the one she had seen on Leah's body, and in several photographs on Len Martell's computer screen. She had been struck then by the contrast in the size and style compared to the rest of Leah's clothes. She had been sure it was a man's coat, and she wondered if she was looking at its replacement.

She almost fell backwards out of the van, slipping on the metal steps and righting herself by grabbing the door frame. It seemed like her mission to meet Matty had failed, as she now had to hurry back to her car to be in time to meet Teddy. Even the discovery of the coat seemed rather lame, as the police would certainly know by now if Leah had been wearing Matty's coat and would be following this up. One thing was for sure, they were not likely to share any results with her. Alys Parry might be more willing to swap information like this, though, she thought.

She paced up the hill back to the towpath, resisting the temptation to peer into the cottages as she passed. To reach her car, she had to walk alongside the lock, after which the path dropped steeply to the lower water level, then cross the humpback bridge to return past the pub. She wished she had chosen somewhere closer to park, and hoped she wouldn't be delayed by Sarah or Gary — or anyone else, for that matter.

Scurrying down the steep path by the lock, she heard a shout ahead of her. A young female voice repeating, 'No, no, no,' followed by angry, incomprehensible words. Anger or fear? Jo couldn't tell. A man's bass voice carried back to her, rumbling and distorted by the brick tunnel of the bridge. Beyond its shadowy arch, she could see nothing of the path ahead. She glanced across to the pub garden on the opposite side of the canal, where the customers were too remote and preoccupied to have heard. Nora could no longer be seen darting between the tables.

'I won't!' A girl's voice echoed back, higher-pitched now and fierce. Of course, it could be just a couple arguing. She knew that, but she quickened her pace towards them. She ducked her head when she reached the short, dark tunnel, and the narrow stony path forced her to slow down. The arc of daylight ahead revealed only the empty towpath. *Maybe the couple were on the bridge above her head?* Her own footsteps resounded off the curved brick walls. There was a warning shout. A male voice, she noted, which was followed by a swift gathering sound like a train on a track.

She whipped round as a force struck her on the back of the legs and sent her sprawling onto the coal-like grit of the towpath. There was a gravelly rush and something weighty and metallic rattled past, toppling over her, and she scrunched up, hands protecting her head. The speed of it almost dragged her with it as a metal wheel flew past her ear. It hit the water and she felt the shock as cold, dirty water hit her mouth and face.

Her feet scrabbled backwards to stop herself from falling in after it, spattering stones into the canal. The back of her head connected with brick and she flailed, grasping at slimy paving to haul herself away from the water. Other hands grabbed her shoulders and pulled her back towards the tunnel wall. The hands tightened on her shoulders, dragging her onto the path. She lay over her knees, spitting out water and watching blood pool from her left leg.

'You're all right, you're all right,' a man's voice kept repeating. He pulled her round so she could feel the bridge wall at her back. She was shaking and her thoughts broke up like prayers. Squatting next to her, the man released his grip and dragged over a heavy cardboard box, which lay on the path. He propped her feet on it, pulled off his T-shirt and, working purposefully, leaned over her and bunched it onto the cut on her leg. 'Hold that there,' he said, adding, 'it's reasonably clean.'

Jo obeyed, able to add pressure to the wound while feeling like she wasn't really present. Her rescuer watched intently and then suddenly broke into a grin, showing white, even teeth. 'You should take more care if you're going to go jogging along canals.'

Jo tried to thank him and ask what had happened, but her voice didn't respond to instructions. As he spoke, she gradually recognized him as Matty Sullivan. She tried hard to concentrate on his words, which came to her through a fog of faintness.

'Stupid bloody delivery guy left a full trolley stacked with tiles at the top of the path with no brake on. I was on the road—' he pointed above their heads — 'signing off the order and saw it start to roll. I'd seen you jog under the bridge and it just picked up speed, heading straight for you. Lucky you dived out of the way, or . . .' He pulled a face.

Jo could see the metal sides of the square trolley sticking out of the canal and realized her leg was resting on one of the boxes of tiles. Most of the others had sunk, she assumed.

'The wheels hit my leg,' she said, and felt pleased with herself for producing a sentence.

'Then you almost went in with it,' he said. 'We're going to A&E next. You might need stitches in that cut, and at the very least, a tetanus jab.' Matty Sullivan got to his feet. 'Will you be all right on your own a minute while I fetch my van? Keep pressing down on it.'

'I'll be here till you get back,' Jo said weakly. She knew her normal faculties were returning when she clocked his bare back above his jeans as he returned up the path. However, when he came back and tried to help her to stand up, the green of the hedgerow and the grey grit of the towpath tilted horribly, and the climb up towards his van was a dizzy ordeal.

'This is really very good of you,' Jo heard herself say, when propped up in the passenger seat.

Matty grinned across at her. 'Just call me your guardian angel,' he said, and started the engine. Jo's head was teeming with questions, but for the next hour or so, she needed all her attention to avoid throwing up. She was aware of swaying tarmac and traffic, a hospital smell in a noisy corridor and finally feeling grateful to be seated on a hard chair in a waiting room.

CHAPTER ELEVEN

For the second time in a week, Jo woke up on her sofa. The cat was sitting on the arm, staring down at her as if assessing the extent of her injuries. She did the same, pushing off the wool blanket and easing herself into a sitting position. She had to sit very still for a minute as the familiar room rocked a little. She felt the tender spot at the back of her head and noticed she was barefoot, but still wearing the T-shirt and skirt she'd worn the day before, and her hair smelled disgustingly of mud. She wriggled her toes gingerly and examined the dressing on her left leg. The cut was only superficial, although still sore, as were the bruises on her upper arms. But she knew, as Matty had said, it could have been a lot worse.

Halifax jumped off the sofa and walked meaningfully towards the kitchen. Jo, too, began to turn her attention to the day ahead. The main issues were logistical ones. The priority was to get washed, including her tangled and smelly hair, and find clean clothes. Being so grimy injured her Virgo soul.

She also had to consider how to get to her 11 a.m. appointment at Stokes Manor, when she clearly was not going to be able to drive just yet. Taxi? Bus? Lift? It would have to be one of these options, because she was certainly not going to miss it.

She found a bottle of water by the sofa, probably left for her after she had been covered by the blanket. She remembered categorically refusing to climb any more stairs and lying down fully clothed on the sofa, but other parts of the evening remained hazy. She limped to the kitchen, where Halifax was already eating, demonstrating that he was capable of looking after himself for the moment. She made herself a coffee, which she drank with some painkillers. After that, a hot shower was the priority.

It took her an hour to wash and dry herself. She was carefully wrapping her sore head in a towel when the solution to her second challenge rang at her doorbell. She pulled on some loose clothes to cover her injuries and made her slow and tentative way downstairs and down the hall. Hanni was waiting patiently outside, her face full of concern.

'How are you, Josephine?' Hanni studied her closely.

'A lot cleaner than I was an hour ago.' She grinned and opened the door wide.

'I've come to make us breakfast and take us to the Ellermans, if you are up to going?' Hanni announced, heading straight for the kitchen. 'How about pancakes with maple syrup?' She began to unpack a string bag.

'Sounds wonderful.' Jo propped herself against the fridge and watched in awe. 'I can make coffee,' she offered.

Hanni was already whisking the batter. 'Just stay there and tell me everything that happened,' she said.

Jo gave a faithful account, recalling additional details as she went along. 'I definitely heard two people arguing ahead of me on the towpath — a young girl and a man's voice — but Matty said there was no one there. I ran to see what was going on, and when I was under the bridge, a metal trolley full of tiles came hurtling down from the lane, straight at me. I dodged, but it still hit me, and I probably would have gone in the canal if Matty Sullivan hadn't dragged me back onto the path.' She massaged her shoulders at the memory.

Hanni frowned at the butter melting in the pan. 'What about the idiot who let go of the trolley, which could have killed you? What happened to him? Shouldn't he be called to account in some way?'

'Yes, I need to talk to Matty properly — and thank him, of course. He must know more, but I couldn't take it all in last night. I saw the delivery lorry, though. It was parked at the pub when I arrived, so maybe Gary or Sarah might know who he is. Nora was working at the pub too. I thought it was her I heard shouting. I thought she was in trouble.'

'You'll have to find out. You can't rely on this Matty Sullivan's word for what happened,' Hanni said, as she flipped the pancake onto a plate. 'First, pancakes are served. I will carry them in for you.'

'Matty was good to me, though.' Jo hobbled to the table behind her friend. 'He described himself as my guardian angel.'

Hanni set down the plate and the syrup. 'Angels don't normally advertise,' she said. 'I'll be back in a minute.'

Jo continued to puzzle over the whole experience while she ate steadily. When Hanni arrived with more pancakes, another question was bothering her. 'Did you say you were going to take us to the Ellermans? This is gorgeous, by the way.' She looked up over her plate. 'Thank you. You are a definite angel. I'm less sure about Matty.'

'You look better,' Hanni said, pushing a coffee towards her and tucking into her own pancakes. 'And yes, I did. I've borrowed Mum's ancient flatbed truck. It's not glamorous and hasn't been used for years. In fact, I'm not sure how you're going to get into it. But I knew you'd still want to go to meet Irene and Duncan Ellerman, if possible.'

'I'll get in, don't worry.' Jo grinned at her friend over her hot coffee. 'I feel more human now than at any point in the last twelve hours. But I didn't even know you could drive.'

'Well, obviously, I prefer to cycle.' Hanni sipped her mountain herb tea. 'And the truck and I are not made for each other, as my feet don't fully reach the pedals and it took ages to get it started. I thought it had seized up!' Jo had begun to laugh and Hanni waved a dismissive hand. 'Don't worry, it will all come back to me. Driving, I mean.' She started to clear up the plates. 'We'd better get going soon, as it might take a bit longer. The truck isn't very speedy.'

Following her friend into the kitchen, Jo noticed that Teddy's red roses had finally been moved from the sink and lay on top of the microwave oven, looking a little battered. Hanni washed up without mentioning them.

'One other question,' Jo said, taking up the tea towel to dry the dishes. 'How did you know what happened to me? I know I'm a bit hazy about the timeline after the accident, but I don't think I messaged you, did I?'

Hanni shook her head, drying her hands and picking up her patchwork jacket. 'David called me after he left you asleep on the sofa.'

Jo felt the colour rise in her cheeks. She had forgotten that Macy had Hanni's number.

'I wanted to come round there and then, but he said you were sound asleep and you'd be fine until the morning. It was a good job he rang, because it gave me time to get the wretched truck out of the garage.'

Jo stopped gaping and hugged her friend. 'You and Macy are both amazing.'

'He's a good soul, and I'm glad you called him from the hospital,' Hanni said. 'Now, we have to go, as it's going to take you a while to get down the steps. Then, once you're at the gate, I will go and fetch the truck, so you just have to walk down the alley.'

On the short walk along Fleece Alley, Jo found that her memory of the last twelve hours was not as patchy as she had first thought. In fact, she had, by now, pieced together pretty much the whole evening, from the time she had parked in the layby near the pub to climbing painfully up the steps to her flat, leaning on David Macy. She recalled a difficult conversation with Teddy, in which she'd told him not to come to the hospital. Her insistence had made some heads turn in A&E, but it had been effective, as Teddy had not appeared. After a shorter and more simple call, Macy had turned up in time to drive her home. At some point, Macy had told her he was in court today, and would call her when he was free. She couldn't remember thanking him.

She heard the truck before she saw it and shuffled out onto King Street, which was busy with shoppers. The long, scratched side of the vehicle came to rest at an acute angle to the kerb and Hanni's triangular face peered worriedly at Jo across the cab. 'Do you need a hand? Shall I get out? I daren't switch the engine off, though.'

'I'm OK.' Jo wrenched the door open and hauled herself inelegantly into the cab with the help of Hanni, who dragged her across the seat. Hanni then let out the clutch ferociously and drove off with breathless tension. Jo decided it was best not to speak, and settled down to fully enjoy their arrival at Stokes Manor.

Hanni took the winding drive between ancient deciduous trees at a pace. A branch bashed off the cab roof at one point and both women instinctively ducked and then laughed at each other. When Hanni brought the vehicle to an abrupt halt two centimetres away from an ornamental cherry tree, with two wheels on the close-cut front lawn, she turned to Jo with a mix of triumph and trepidation. 'I just hope I can start it again,' she muttered grimly, and wiped the sweat from under her fringe.

The biscuit-coloured manor house sat slightly lower than its long lawn, a faded wisteria looping under the first-floor windows on the left. With its soft yellow stone and diamond-paned windows, black-framed in old-fashioned Cotswold style, it was, in many ways, like other small, gracious country houses Jo had seen since she'd moved to the five valleys. However, a three-storey tower jutting out from the right corner of the house, its top tier stooping slightly over the purple-slated roof, marked this one out as different. The narrow tower, with its curling outdoor staircase, leading up to a crenelated turret, added to the sense of remoteness from the bustling market town and even the villages nearby.

'Are you admiring our folly?' A soft voice greeted them from behind. Jo turned to see a white-haired man in gardening clothes. 'It's my observatory,' he said, pointing a slightly shaky hand towards the top of the tower, where they could just make out the nozzle of a telescope. 'Howard Ellerman-James. Irene's husband,' he added, holding out his hand, and Jo introduced herself and Hanni. He nodded politely, but was keen to tell them about a meteor shower he'd been watching in the early hours. 'We are lucky to have very dark skies here, you see.'

Hanni made a polite response. Jo started to tell him about her other job, because, as an astrologer, she also liked observing the night skies. Sensing her enthusiasm, he said, 'You should ask Irene to invite you back for dinner some time and you can come up and have a look. I expect you're here to see her, aren't you? She is at home.' He waved towards the manor house door. 'I'd fetch her for you, but I'm in the middle of cleaning the steps.' He pointed to the worn, sandy-coloured staircase clinging to the old stone tower. He waved vaguely, picked up the bucket at his feet and pottered away in the direction of his observatory.

Jo and Hanni exchanged glances and Jo pressed the ancient doorbell, which was set into the Cotswold stone beside the studded and barred front door. Hanni glanced behind her at the truck as if half-expecting it to self-destruct. Jo noticed that the only other car on the pinkish gravel was an old Audi convertible with worn leather seats and the top down.

Irene Ellerman pulled the door open and glared at them. 'Good, you've come. He's here, so all is going well so far.' She lowered her voice with suppressed excitement. 'You've brought the ammunition and I'm ready to fire the bullets.' She turned on her flat heels and marched down the panelled hall.

'What?' Hanni murmured, looking askance. Jo could only shrug and follow, limping awkwardly. She caught her foot on bare threads in the carpet and steadied herself with a hand on the delicate, twisted wooden banisters.

'We're in the morning room,' Irene Ellerman said, from in front. Her broad back was clad in a high-coloured floral shirt with a clashing scarf patterned with berries. She turned to them briefly with a conspiratorial smile before she leaned on the curved iron handle and the door swung inwards.

A spare, long-limbed man stood looking out over the back lawn. He was in no hurry to turn when Irene entered, but he came over to offer them both a handshake. His palms were surprisingly rough and dry, but then, he was a carpenter, Jo remembered. She had seen his picture on his website, looking distinctly younger, showing off a carved table and matching chairs in a workshop. Although the photograph was clearly old, she supposed he was making the point that he was a hands-on director as well as the owner of the company. Jo assessed his age as late forties. Due to his slight build and sandy hair, she could see the family resemblance with Leah.

Irene made brief introductions and he responded with an affable smile. 'Lovely to meet you,' he said, in a quiet, educated voice. 'I'm only sorry it has to be in such strange and sad circumstances.' He pulled out two chairs beside a French-polished rectangular table.

A tiny connection with a memory fizzed in Jo's brain. She would follow it up later. Right now, she had to concentrate on sitting down as gracefully as she could. She and Hanni murmured their appropriate responses and all eyes turned to Irene, who was clearing away the papers that she and Duncan had been studying.

'Coffee and shortbread biscuits will be along shortly,' Irene said, stacking the papers on the sideboard next to a bronze deer ornament and a black-and-white framed family photograph. Jo itched to get a closer look at it and hoped the arrival of coffee would provide an opportunity.

Duncan was too well-mannered to allow a pause to become awkward, so he turned to Hanni, who was closest to him, and asked, smiling, where she was from. 'Light is a Cotswold name, isn't it?'

When she told him she'd been born in Slad, he knew the farm, and so within a minute or two they were deeply engrossed in a conversation about the current farmer and the stock he kept. Jo was happy to sit back, observe and rest her sore leg. Eventually, however, he prompted his sister gently. 'Well, Irene, aren't you going to explain why you've introduced us? I'm sure these young women have jobs to get back to.'

Irene sent him a vengeful look, as if he had managed to gain an advantage in some strange game. She positioned herself at the head of the table, her fists closed on the back of the mahogany chair that stood before her. 'I'm coming to that,' she said.

'Well, do get on with it,' he responded easily. 'From all you've said so far, it sounds like we're gathered for a game of Cluedo.'

'Don't be ridiculous. It's not at all like that,' she snapped, and then compressed her lips. After a pause, she repeated more calmly, 'Not at all. It's serious, very serious. I want you to hear firsthand the account these women have to give. As you know, our sister, Leah, was found in the cellar of a pub. We need to understand what happened and what could have led up to this — this shocking end to her life.' She fixed all three of them with a stony look. 'It's just you and I now, Duncan, and we need to act as one. So—' she turned to Jo and Hanni — 'would you mind describing what you found?'

Hanni, speaking quietly as she generally did, gave her now-practised account of finding Leah Ellerman's body. Duncan listened intently, his hands clasped in front of him, but asked no questions. Jo was surprised he didn't want to know more about the spiritual cleansing, as this was unfamiliar to most people. His only question came at the end, after he'd thanked Hanni. He turned to Jo and asked about her involvement.

'Hanni called me because we're friends and I've worked as a private investigator for some years. In fact, I've just set up on my own.'

'And she thought this would be good business for you?' He softened the sharp question with a charming smile.

'It was more because I needed some advice,' Hanni broke in. 'The landlord and landlady of the pub are my friends, and they were thrown into shock at the news of a body found on their premises. They didn't know what to do straight away, and neither did I,' she admitted.

Duncan nodded. 'I see. Well, thank you for coming to explain all that. It must have been a horrific experience for both of you.'

'It's horrific for *us*,' Irene burst out. 'It's our sister. What on earth had she done to get herself into this situation? Why would anyone want to bludgeon her over the head in a frenzied assault? It's not like she was mugged, Duncan,' she added, taking a patronising tone. 'All of her belongings were still with her. And then her attacker hid the body somewhere she'd be sure to be found.' She looked at Jo. 'Seeing as you have got a sort of professional role in this, can you tell us what exactly you've found out so far?'

Jo thought about her answer, and then looked straight at both the Ellermans. 'Well, I'm pretty sure your sister was having an affair with Matty Sullivan, the builder who is working on the cottage renovations.' She watched Duncan closely, but he simply looked pained, as if he would rather be somewhere else.

'You've already told me this,' Irene muttered. 'Go on.'

'OK. Well, it seems Leah was not very popular with her tenants, because she was turning the cottages into holiday lets.'

'Show me a landlord who's popular with his tenants.' Duncan gave another wolfish smile.

'It's hardly a motive to kill someone, is it?' Irene dismissed this brusquely.

'Maybe there is no motive in this case,' Duncan said smoothly. 'Maybe this was just senseless violence or a crime of passion? What do we know about this builder chap?' He looked at his sister expectantly.

'He was after her money, of course. Leah had assets, with which she was funding the renovations,' Irene said. 'Isn't that what they say? Follow the money?'

'I'd be careful of taking that tack, if I were you.' Duncan's eyes drifted to the pile of papers on the sideboard. 'You are the only one with kids to inherit all this, you know.'

'And you know that they are not in the least interested,' she snapped back. 'Both are overseas. I mean, could they get much further away? Tom is working in Japan, for heaven's sake, and my daughter is busy saving the planet in Ethiopia.' Irene paused, seeming to remember Jo and Hanni were also in the room. 'You must understand that although we are not a showy family and we don't do emotions well, it doesn't mean we don't care about each other.'

Given what Meena had told Jo about Irene's 'tyranni-cal' family Christmases, there was something about this bold statement that didn't quite ring true, Jo felt. To her surprise, Hanni said softly, 'I believe you care for each other, but the vibrations I am picking up are of conflict and estrangement.'

'What are you getting at?' Irene frowned. 'I've already told you we don't live in each other's pockets—'

'I suppose we're each of us very different,' Duncan said, breaking his watchful silence. 'We have different interests, even. Irene manages what's left of the estate and I've got the business to run. That's how our parents envisaged it. They left it as a sort of template in their wills, and we have simply followed it.'

Once again, Irene shot him a surprised look. She was not the sort of woman who liked surprises, Jo guessed. 'And what was Leah's template?' Jo asked.

'Oh, she did all right, don't you worry,' Irene said. 'She was the one to go to university, so she was always going to do well. Whereas I got married young and Duncan had to learn the business.'

'And she was left the cottages,' he added, in his calm, ameliorating tone.

'She was happy with the settlement?' Jo asked, but she never received her answer, because she was interrupted by the arrival of coffee and biscuits.

'Ah, Maureen, thank you. Leave them on the table, please,' Irene's voice became warmer.

Jo turned at the name and recognized the sturdy, capa-ble cleaner from the pub and cottages. 'We'll have to stop meeting like this,' Maureen said, catching Jo's eye as she placed the tray down.

'Indeed,' Jo agreed with a smile. While the coffee and biscuits were being handed around, she got to her feet to view the family photograph. 'May I see?' she asked, edging closer to the sideboard.

'Of course,' Irene said, shrugging, as Maureen bustled out and Duncan and Hanni chatted over the coffee. The framed photograph was a little dusty and the colour was faded, but it showed the Ellerman family of five: Irene, Duncan and Leah, and their parents, posing outside the manor house. Judging from their clothes and the children's ages, Jo reckoned it was taken in the early 1980s.

'Not long after they bought the house.' Duncan had moved quietly to stand beside her. In the picture, Leah was a babe in arms, Irene a mutinous-looking pre-adolescent in a too-short summer dress, and Duncan a very young, willowy boy, gazing past the camera. 'Irene has lived here most of her life. She and Howard moved in with the parents after their wedding. And here they have stayed,' he added, with a sidelong glance at his sister.

'Why would anyone want to live anywhere else?' Irene demanded defensively. 'Anyway, Mother and Father needed some looking after by then.'

It was mainly due to Duncan that the conversation moved away from Leah and Irene after that. He talked about his business and showed them pictures of some ash sculptures he was creating for a local stately home. It was also Duncan who noticed Jo was limping when they got up to leave and offered his arm as they walked down the hallway. He didn't ask awkward questions about the accident, for which Jo was grateful. Irene, who appeared to have lost interest in them once they'd delivered her 'ammunition', followed behind. It was hard to tell from her expression whether the gathering had achieved what she'd wanted.

'It's a beautiful house,' Jo remarked, as they made slow progress on the gravel drive.

'Beautiful and ruinously expensive,' Duncan sighed. 'The heating bill alone is crippling, because it's not on the mains. Irene has to arrange for oil to be delivered.'

'If your parents only bought it in the eighties,' Jo said, thinking back to the framed photograph, 'then it hasn't been in the family all that long?'

Duncan laughed lightly. 'That is forever for us. Our family doesn't go back hundreds of years like some around here. We don't have a coat of arms with pennants and lions courant or whatever. My father, Harold, was an immigrant from occupied Holland. His mother brought him here as a baby during the war, while his father, my grandfather, stayed and was active in the resistance. My father and mother met in London, and they built the business together. Affordable, well-made furniture was exactly what people needed after the war, and the proceeds bought this house.' Duncan's voice faded as the figure of Howard Ellerman-James appeared, descending uncertainly from the bottom steps of the tower. They acknowledged each other briefly as the older man passed them on his way to refill the bucket from an outdoor tap. 'That's my brother-in-law, Howard,' he said. 'Don't let him fool you, he's not as old — or as daft — as he looks.' He threw a sardonic glance at the other man's back. 'His great hobby is astronomy. He's written books about it. Well, he wrote a pamphlet once, as we used to say.' He chuckled to himself.

'We?'

Duncan shot her a rueful glance. 'Me and Leah. Because Howard opts out of anything remotely difficult, it means that Irene must shoulder the whole burden of the estate. So, if she's a bit abrupt sometimes—' He was brought up short when Hanni hoisted herself into the cab of the ancient rusty truck. 'Good Lord, is this your transportation?' He stepped back in alarm as Jo hauled herself into the passenger seat and Hanni searched for reverse gear. In the wing mirror, Jo could see him standing away, arms folded. Behind him, Irene and her husband exchanged a few words before he trudged back towards the tower.

'Duncan is an old-fashioned sort of chap, isn't he?' Jo commented, as they shot backwards. Hanni said nothing, but took the bends in the drive at a terrifying pace. A small, flat, transparent stone slid noisily across the dashboard and Jo picked it up. 'What is it?'

'It's selenite, a protective crystal,' Hanni said, hugging the steering wheel. 'I felt we needed some purifying energy after that place . . . and those people. Did you notice that all the paintings in the hall were slightly crooked and thick with dust? They must have been like that for months, years even. Why are they so frightened to change anything?'

'It doesn't say much for Maureen, who seems to clean half of Stokesly,' Jo laughed. She was feeling light-hearted as the pain in her leg had eased.

'I'm adding her to the list of people I need to interview.'

'I hope you got all your questions answered today, because don't expect me to go back there.' Hanni floored the accelerator and the old truck thundered onto the main road. 'Or have anything more to do with that strange rude woman.'

'I did, I suppose,' Jo mused. 'But inevitably, I now have more questions. And I don't know what that was all about, really. One thing was pretty obvious, though. For all he's a nice affable chap, Duncan made sure I knew that his sister had the strongest motive for killing Leah. Why would he do that?'

CHAPTER TWELVE

'I'll pick you up at six o'clock to take you to Sarah's paranormal evening,' Hanni shouted over the thumping of the truck engine as Jo half-fell, half-scrambled out onto the pavement at King Street.

'I thought you didn't want anything to do with it?'

'I don't,' Hanni said. 'But I know you need to be there, so I will attend too, just this once. Now, I've got to go. I told Chloe I'd be back at the shop at lunchtime. Can you get home OK?'

'Yes, and thanks,' Jo said, waving. Once back at her flat, with coffee in hand and chocolate biscuits for sustenance, her first call was to Macy. She'd had a missed call from him, one from Teddy and one from the pub.

'I've got to be quick,' he said, as soon as he picked up. 'The judge has called a short break, but apparently, I need to stay close by. How are you feeling? I left you fast asleep.'

'I'm doing OK, thanks. The leg's getting better. Hanni came over and made breakfast, and then she drove us over to a meeting with the Ellerman family.' She paused to consider for a second. 'I don't know how much attention the police are giving them, but I am pretty sure they are the main beneficiaries from Leah's death, so they have to be top suspects.'

'Hang on a minute, you said Hanni *drove*?'

'Well, after a fashion,' Jo laughed. 'But I was very grateful, and I'm even more grateful that she is coming to this horrible séance thing with me tonight.'

Macy groaned. 'Rather you than me. Are you sure you're OK? Do you need to get to the doctors or anything?'

'No, I should be all right. They said I can take this dressing off in a day or two. You know, it could have been a lot worse. In fact, I've been wondering if it was intended to be a lot worse.' She could hear echoey voices in the background at Macy's end, but she followed her train of thought aloud. 'I mean, don't you think it's odd that there were no witnesses to the accident? Where did this mysterious delivery driver disappear to? Was it really his fault? I've only got Matty Sullivan's word for that. And what about those two people I heard arguing — a girl and a man? What happened to them? So, I've been thinking, what if it was deliberate?'

'Aren't you giving yourself delusions of grandeur?' Macy said. 'Why would anyone want to take you out? You keep telling me you don't know anything.'

'Yes, but maybe it's something I don't know I know,' Jo said.

'You've lost me now. Look, I've got to go—'

'Wait. Any news on the Angry Cherub?' she asked quickly, before he could ring off. There was a short silence, then Macy said, 'I'll be in touch.'

Jo frowned at the phone for a second after the call ended, and then, taking a deep breath, she clicked on Teddy's number. When he didn't pick up, she felt a guilty mixture of relief and disappointment. She left her message and then hobbled to the kitchen to make more coffee. While she was there, she finally cut the roses and was arranging them in fresh water when Teddy called her back.

'How are you, Jo?' was his first question, but his voice lacked its usual warmth. Jo gave him more or less the same update she'd given Macy, leaving out her speculation that she had been targeted.

'Well, good, but why on earth didn't you want me to pick you up from the hospital?' Teddy demanded. 'I just don't understand it.'

Jo sighed. 'I don't really know. I suppose I thought you'd ask lots of questions and I just wanted to sleep. Anyway, you were babysitting.'

'Don't be silly, I could have arranged something. And why did you tell me not to come to the flat?'

Jo stared at the roses miserably. 'I'm sorry. I suppose we need to talk, don't we? But not tonight. I can't do tonight.'

They fixed up, in rather too-polite terms, to meet the next evening after he had finished work. Jo returned to her makeshift desk in the living room, feeling sad and confused about almost everything and still a little shaken up. Work, as ever, proved to be a solace, the normality that soothed her Virgo soul and made her feel useful.

She made a new list and started to draw circles around some of the names, which led directly to her calling the New Navigation. She had lots of questions for Matty and she guessed that Sarah would have his number. While the phone rang out, she studied the list of people she needed to see: Nora Hutchinson, Maureen Toomey and Alys Parry were at the top, and she had also promised to call Meena to report back on her meeting with the Ellermans. Just as her call was answered, she added another name to the list: Duncan Ellerman.

Sarah had heard all about her accident, presumably from Matty, and she sounded concerned. 'Gary and I have been worried about you. I tried to call a few times, but I thought you must be sleeping. We didn't even know anything was happening until the delivery driver came running back to his van. How are you?'

So, at least this much fitted with Matty's story, Jo thought. 'I need to thank Matty properly, and I thought you might have his number. It was very good of him to take me to the hospital, but now I need to find out what actually happened. What did the delivery driver have to say?'

'The driver? He just said there'd been an accident with the trolley and someone nearly went in the canal. We didn't realize it was you, of course. He said he'd offered to call an ambulance, but Matty told him he had it all under control and he was taking you to A&E. Matty said you had a bad gash on one leg.'

'Oh, it's not too bad. But someone has got to be responsible for the accident. Surely someone at the pub must have seen something?'

Sarah said she would ask Gary. 'The volunteers who look after the canal have dredged out the trolley and most of the boxes today,' she added helpfully. 'Matty is bound to know more about the delivery firm. He's been asking after you. I said you might be over later, but I understand if you're not feeling up to our little social evening with the spirits.'

Jo promised that she and Hanni would be there, although she didn't feel as cheery as she sounded. Before she rang off, she asked if Sarah had heard anything more from the police about the investigation.

'Diane Watts was over here yesterday morning, making us go through our stock procedures, cleaning regimes and more questions about security. It was like another inspection from the brewery.'

'He gave you a clean bill of health, did he? Paul, the brewery man? I saw you were fully open again.'

'Oh yes, thank God,' Sarah said. 'It's probably more of a temporary reprieve than a full tick in the box, but it's better than we expected. Of course, we are making money for them, too,' she added. 'And the additional publicity doesn't seem to have affected trade too badly. It might even have helped.'

'That's what Alys Parry predicted. She's the journalist from the *Standard*.'

'I know Alys. She was round here as soon as the police left, acting as if there is some huge secret that she is going to ferret out, which they have missed. You'll see her tonight, in fact.'

'She's coming to the séance?'

'The paranormal evening, you mean. Oh yes, Alys is a regular. At first, she was a sceptic, and came with her journalist head on, hoping to write up a really cynical article. But now, well, let's say, she has another view. It happens,' she added knowingly.

Jo still felt anxious about the evening ahead, but at least it was good news that Alys would be there. She was sure she could manage a quiet conversation with her. 'One more thing before you go,' Jo added. 'Will Maureen be there tonight? I could do with a chat with her, too.'

'You've got to be kidding,' Sarah said. 'She hates our gatherings almost as much as Leah did. Anyway, she only works for us three mornings a week. She's got another job in the afternoons, at the old people's home at Stokes Avon.'

'Oh, yes, I remember,' Jo said absently. On her notepad, she linked the circles between Maureen and the Ellerman family, frowning. But the questions about her accident were uppermost in her mind, and when Sarah gave her Matty's number, she called him next. Judging by the sound of drilling in the background, he was clearly on-site when he answered.

He moved away quickly, the noise growing fainter as he asked how she was doing. 'At the hospital they were concerned because you'd bashed your head,' he said. 'I suppose they were worried about concussion.'

'Oh, I just felt a bit woozy,' Jo said, 'but my leg's already feeling better. The main problem is that I'm a bit hazy about the whole thing. Did you see what happened?'

There was a pause and then Matty said, 'Yes, I saw the delivery van pull up at the pub, so I went up to meet the guy. He unloaded the trolley full of tiles and I counted them while he waited on the bridge. I was signing off the order when I saw the trolley start to roll.'

'Wasn't there someone else on the path?' Jo asked.

'No, nobody.'

'There were at least two people on the path ahead of me,' Jo insisted. 'A man and a girl. I heard them.' In the background, a man's voice called out to Matty and he shouted to him to hold on. 'Wait a minute,' he said to Jo. He kept the call open while he dealt with a question about measurements. Jo waited patiently, listening to the birdsong, which made her feel like she was back by the pub at the canal-side.

'OK, I'm back with you now, and I'm sitting on the bench by the canal where the guys can't pester me,' he said. 'Go on, you said you saw someone on the towpath.'

'No, I didn't see anyone. I heard them.'

Matty sighed. 'Well, all I can say is, the only other person I saw was the idiot delivery driver. He's a regular, so I can help track him down, if you want to.'

'Good. How well do you know him?'

Matty blew out a sigh. 'Well, we're not buddies, if that's what you mean. He's just done a few deliveries to the site. We've been here a good few months now, so you get to recognize people. Why?'

Jo wasn't ready to confide in Matty her vague suspicion that the attack might have been deliberate. She didn't want to sound paranoid, so, instead, she changed the subject. 'I suppose you must have got to know Leah pretty well during that time,' she said. 'It must have been hard hearing the news about what had happened to her — especially when you suspected something was wrong,' she said. When this was greeted with silence, she added, 'I was at the pub on Sunday when the police arrived. My friend Hanni found Leah's body.'

There was a short silence while Matty appeared to digest this information, and yet Jo was pretty sure he had known who she was when he'd been ministering to her injuries, which meant he must have recognized her from the gathering at the pub. Eventually, he said, 'Yes, it's still difficult, and you can't help blaming yourself for not doing something sooner. Leah was more than a client to me.'

'So, you and Leah were close?'

There was another pause and she felt he was choosing his words carefully. 'Depends what you mean. I've worked for her for about a year, and I'm living on her land. I've even inherited her dog, Frankie, who now seems to have moved in with me. I expect the Ellermans won't approve of that either.' He adopted a mock-official voice. 'The dog is part of the estate and should be disposed of according to the most profit.'

'What else did they not approve of?'

'Well, they didn't know most of it,' Matty said, 'but they would have disapproved if they had known. When I say "they", I mean Irene Ellerman, really.' His voice became brisk. 'Look, I'd better get back to the lads on-site. I want to check where they're up to before they all bugger off.'

'I can imagine Irene being disapproving,' Jo said. 'OK, look, thanks again, and I'm sorry about the ruined T-shirt.'

'You can reimburse me if you like. It was three quid from Primark.' Jo laughed, and he added, 'Don't forget, I'm your guardian angel.'

She ended the call and stared at the phone. Maybe he had come to her rescue, she thought, but angel he was not. She'd never heard of angels telling lies, and Matty Sullivan had definitely lied to her.

She found herself staring thoughtfully at the list of names on her notepad and puzzling over her meeting at Stokes Manor that morning. She still felt that Leah Ellerman remained remote and inscrutable, but without understanding her, she could never discover what happened to her. There was, however, one woman who might shed some light on the unlikeable and opaque Ellerman family, if she was prepared to open up. After she'd finished her calls, Jo called a taxi to pick her up on King Street in twenty minutes and limped out.

Stokes Avon Home for Elderly Residents was created from former Victorian alms houses, which now made up a single impressive red-brick building set back a little from a busy country road, where cars swept past at speed between woods and fields. Jo made an extravagant decision and asked the chatty cab driver to wait for her. If Maureen was working, she wouldn't have long to speak, so Jo knew she would have to be quick and focused.

There was a small unoccupied office just inside the entrance and a book where she was meant to sign in. But, as there was no one around, Jo wandered in and spoke to the first member of staff she met. A small man manoeuvring a heavy tea trolley pointed her towards a conservatory at the end of the corridor. 'I just saw Maureen down there.'

Jo passed a series of private rooms, glimpsing patients in bed or propped up on chairs, usually watching TV. She wondered queasily if this lay in store for her own parents, and made a private pledge to go and see them as soon as she could drive. As she passed the door of one of the rooms, she recognized Maureen struggling to half-lift, half-steer, a tall, ungainly man from his seat to an upright position. Seeing the woman tackling this alone, Jo instinctively stepped forward and Maureen spotted her. 'What are *you* doing here?' she panted, red-faced.

'Can I help?' Jo asked from the doorway. 'Or get someone?'

'No point.' Maureen had managed to shift the man onto a walker and was checking his hold was firm enough. 'There is hardly anyone experienced here. Who are you here to visit?'

'I came to find you. I can see you're busy, but is there any way we could have a quick chat?'

'As long as it *is* quick.' Maureen stood back, hands on her hips, making a rapid calculation. 'Give me a few minutes to move this gentleman and I'll see you outside the conservatory.' She pointed towards the end of the corridor and Jo made her way along to the small area where five or six residents sat in armchairs. One was knitting, but the rest were dozing. The room was stifling, although the door to the garden was open.

'What have you done to your leg?' Maureen asked from behind her as Jo limped towards the garden door. Some of the residents watched with interest, but most stayed asleep as Maureen led the way out to a bench just outside the conservatory.

'Oh, it's a long story and will wait for another time. It's nothing serious, thank goodness. Sorry for interrupting the job,' Jo nodded back towards the main building. 'It looks like hard work.'

'We're not supposed to tackle lifts alone,' Maureen said honestly, 'but sometimes you've no choice.' She positioned herself at the far end of the bench, where she could watch the conservatory door. 'I suppose there are worse places. We do our best for the poor buggers but I'll be honest with you, I wouldn't want to end up here. I've told Charlotte to shoot me first.'

Her flat, square face looked so serious, Jo wasn't sure if this was a joke, so she moved on quickly by asking how long she'd worked there.

'About four years. This job helps to pay Charlotte's rent at university.' She folded her arms over her uniform shirt. 'The cleaning alone would never have been enough. The books and subscriptions they have to buy for a marketing degree, you wouldn't believe.' She craned her neck so she could see further into the conservatory. 'It's not exactly the norm for the staff to have visitors, you know,' she added. 'If my boss comes along, I'm going to say you're a relative of Jennifer's. She's the lady doing the knitting. So, what can I do for you? I suppose it's about your visit to the manor house this morning?' The beginnings of a grin crept onto Maureen's dour face. 'They're a bit eccentric, the Ellermans, aren't they?'

'You've known them years, I suppose?'

'I've worked for Irene ever since her parents died. They had worked the other old dear to death. I got the job, but I told Irene there was no way I was going to live in. I said, "I'm a single mum with a flat of my own." It might only be on the estate in Charwell, but I had no intention of being at their beck and call twenty-four-seven.'

Jo nodded sympathetically. 'And what did Irene say?'

'She wasn't happy, but she gave me a trial and here I am, fifteen years later. And, OK, Charwell is not Stokes Manor, but it's not far from here, so this job is really handy. I do three mornings a week for Irene either at the manor house or at the cottages, depending on what's needed. The cleaning job for Sarah Robart came out of that. She just tapped me on the shoulder one day, and it seemed rude to refuse.' She finished with a shrug.

'You don't like working for Sarah?'

'The job's all right as long as she keeps out of my way. She acts like she is some sort of clairvoyant, saying she can see spirits around you, and I can't be doing with that.' She gave a little shake and continued stoically. 'I'm not the type to be taken in by all that hoodoo, but there are some people who are.' When Jo looked quizzical, she went on, 'I've got a daughter, you remember, who wasn't always a little angel. She had her issues when she was in her teens, I can tell you. Got involved with drugs and all sorts just from going around with the wrong people. I can see that girl, Nora, going the same way if she keeps hanging around that pub. Charlatans like Sarah take advantage of people when they're vulnerable, and that's not right.'

'Leah didn't approve either, did she?'

'No, she didn't. Leah was no fool. She had her standards and expected people to meet them.' Maureen glanced at her watch. 'Now, what did you want to know about the Ellermans? Because I don't have all that long.'

'What about Irene and Howard? He seems a lot older than her. How do they get on?'

'Yes, he is a good ten or more years older, but he was quite a catch for her in his day. Hard to believe now, I know,' she said. 'They seem to get along all right to me.'

Aware of the cabbie's meter ticking, Jo switched her focus to Irene and Duncan. Maureen admitted that he'd had a better relationship with Leah. 'Irene could never get close to those two, and couldn't understand them either. But what could she do?' Maureen turned down her lips philosophically. 'You can't make people like you. Money helps, mind you,' she added pensively.

'And do they have a lot of money?' Jo asked. 'Duncan said this morning that the manor house is ruinously expensive.'

The woman opposite her considered this question. 'It depends,' she said eventually. 'To me, I would class them as rich, but I suppose when you're brought up like that, with boarding schools and skiing twice a year and Saturday gymkhanas and what have you, your expectations are different. They think they are poor. They are not poor.'

Jo nodded to show she understood perfectly. Maureen went on, 'Monied people have a different idea of family, don't they? The Ellermans hardly saw each other, except on big occasions like Christmas, and then it was all for show with no heart in it. I don't envy them,' she added. 'I think of them when me and Charlotte are curled up on the sofa with a box of chocs and catch-up TV. They've got it all wrong, you know, the Ellermans and their like.' She gave a self-amused chuckle and jerked her head towards the elderly people in the conservatory. 'I'd better get back to the old dears in a sec. Some do pay attention, you know. They're not daft. I've got to start taking them in to tea.'

'OK, just quickly then — I'm asking everyone the same questions, so I've got to ask you too. What did you think of Leah? Did you like her?'

'She was more straightforward than her sister. As long as you got the work done, she didn't bother you. In my job, you have to learn what people like. Irene likes to know everything, so she always asks me lots of questions. A bit like you,' she added drily. 'Leah liked to be in control of things, which made her much easier to handle, and she didn't want any chit-chat, which was fine with me. I understood that she had a lot going on, what with holding down her London job and managing the building works. She tried to stay out of her sister's way, but she was fond of Duncan. Matty was her weak point. He could do no wrong for her and that was a mistake.'

'And the last time you saw her?'

'Tuesday morning, first of June, but we hardly spoke, which was normal. She was working in her study while I cleaned the house. As much as you can do, that is, when half of it is a building site and covered in plaster dust.' She looked up as one of the elderly women came to the doorway and peered out at them. Maureen called for her to go back indoors and Jo got to her feet, recognizing it was time to leave. Maureen showed Jo an alternative way out, through a gate in the garden wall, pointing out there was less chance that the manager would see her.

'And if they do, I'm Jennifer's great niece,' Jo smiled. She thanked Maureen, who looked nonplussed and said, 'I haven't done anything.'

Before she slipped through the gate, Jo hesitated. Feeling apprehensive about the so-called paranormal evening with Sarah, she couldn't resist asking, 'When you said that Sarah can see spirits around you, what did you mean?'

Maureen grunted. 'She says she can. But you wouldn't catch me going to one of her séances. People shouldn't dabble with evil. It's dangerous. If you ask me, that's why Sarah gets a kick out of it.'

CHAPTER THIRTEEN

'Welcome to our soirée for the spirits.' Sarah's greeting to Jo and Hanni when they arrived at the New Navigation a couple of hours later did not make Jo feel any less apprehensive. 'Come through into the back room when you are ready. We'll be starting in ten minutes.' She beamed and swept past them in a long, layered outfit, bestowing a wave or two at the early evening customers.

'The séances certainly don't seem to deter business,' Jo remarked to Hanni as Gary waved at them cheerfully from across the bar. The old-fashioned lounge was already lively, and she noticed he had another barman in to assist tonight — a strong, silent type with a buzz cut and multiple piercings, who was serving Alys and Matty.

The couple were shoulder-to-shoulder at the bar. Matty was half a head shorter than Alys, but their faces were close as they exchanged a laughing remark. The instant Matty spotted Jo, he stood back to give her a warm welcome and asked how she was. 'Still limping a bit, I see.'

'A bit, but I smell a lot better,' Jo replied. She introduced Hanni, and Alys turned to her straight away. 'So, you're another newcomer to the spirits' soirée?'

'I am.' Hanni looked so unenthusiastic that Alys laughed.

'It's nothing to worry about, you know. Absolutely nothing happens most of the time. We just sit around looking at each other like a bunch of dopes.'

'You change your tune regularly on this subject,' Matty broke in teasingly. 'Sometimes you are the great sceptic, but then, once, you admitted that Sarah told you something that nobody could have known — except your grandad, who has been dead for twelve years.'

'Once,' Alys admitted. 'Just once, in all the months I've been attending these things in the vague hope of discovering something I can write up for the paper. And, as time goes on, I wonder if that was just a lucky guess of Sarah's . . .' She turned to Matty and he made a disbelieving face.

Jo asked Matty if he'd managed to track down the man who delivered the tiles and he shook his head. 'Probably fears he will be sued, so he's keeping a low profile.' When Jo didn't smile, he went on, 'Look, I'll call the company and find out. If you come over to the site tomorrow, I'll have his contact details for you.' He picked up the beer he'd ordered for himself and the tonic water for Alys and led the way into the back room.

As Alys turned to follow him, Jo impulsively reached out and caught her arm. 'Do you have time for a chat later? I thought we might be able to share some information about the case and . . . well, actually, there are a few things I just wanted to ask you. Is that OK?'

Alys regarded her curiously for a second and then nodded. 'Sure, if there's time afterwards.'

A 'soirée of the spirits' made the evening sound almost sophisticated and elegant. It didn't sound like the sort of evening where the doors would be locked from the inside and the keys collected, so that no one could leave. This was the second unexpected occurrence to alarm Jo. The first was when Sarah confiscated their phones as soon as she and Hanni took their seats at the round table.

'It's a perfectly normal precaution,' she smiled, as she tripped around the table behind their seats with a wicker basket. 'If you pop them in here, Gary will keep them safe behind the bar and you can just collect them on the way out.'

Everyone dutifully dropped their phones into the basket, except for Valerie Lilley, sitting on Jo's left, who said she didn't have hers with her. Sarah accepted this and took her haul off to Gary. While she was briefly out of the room, Jo found it impossible to make eye contact with any of the people sitting around the silk-covered table. Although she knew almost all of them, without Sarah's formidable presence, the group fidgeted and looked away sheepishly, as if they might be called upon to explain why they were there. The large round table was covered with a maroon cloth, its texture like thick silk. Valerie Lilley, sitting next to Jo, commented on it when Sarah re-entered the room. 'This is new, isn't it, Sarah?' Valerie rubbed the texture beneath her fingers. 'The old one had symbols — zodiac signs and the like — didn't it?'

'We don't need symbols,' Sarah pronounced in a rich, gravelly voice. She turned the key in the adjoining door. 'It works better than a *Do Not Disturb* notice,' she said, seeing Jo's startled look. 'Perhaps you could check the outside door behind you, Jo?'

Jo did as she was asked, trying to forget that the last time she had passed through the door had been after seeing Leah's body. She confirmed that the door to the path that ran along the outside of the pub was indeed locked, with no visible key. Sarah nodded and resumed her seat directly opposite, facing the two main doors with the cellar door to her right.

'I see the building work is still going on,' Valerie Lilley was saying. 'And I heard that the Ellermans are going to continue with Leah's plans. Have you heard anything, Matty?'

'Don't ask me, I'm only the builder,' he replied quickly. 'As long as someone is paying me, that's all I care about.'

Across the table, Jo observed Matty shift uncomfortably. Sarah, sitting directly opposite her, seemed absorbed in shuffling a pack of tarot cards. Alys was placed on the other side of Hanni, with Matty next to her. Beside Sarah, Jo recognized Nora Hutchinson, the teenager from number three Canalside

Cottages. With her dark hair tucked into a black hoodie, she sat silently, her narrow hands resting on the tablecloth. Next to her was the only person who was a stranger to Jo — a girl of around Nora's age, but very different in appearance. She was fair with a fat, unformed face, lurid with make-up, and lively eyes, which roamed the room expectantly.

'We've not met before, have we?' Jo said chattily, catching her eye.

'I'm Tegan, Nora's friend,' the girl responded readily, but Sarah cut across her.

'We don't need to introduce ourselves. We will be talking to the spirits, not to each other. And they will recognize us instantly. Now, let's begin our welcome to the spirits.'

Jo wiped her sweaty palms discreetly on her cotton trousers and placed them on the table as the others had. She felt her own tension mirrored by the others seated at the table as Sarah leaned forward and lit a candle in a globe-shaped bowl. On a little nod, Matty stood up and switched off the wall lights. His long shadow rippled around the room as he regained his seat.

Hanni had placed the clear, flat selenite crystal between herself and Jo, who was sure Sarah had noticed, but had refrained from comment. Jo licked her dry lips and felt her attention ratchet up to its highest pitch. That morning, she had circled the names of some of the people seated around this table. Now she rested her eyes on them, feeling a chill grip in her stomach as she grappled with the reality that one of them could have murdered Leah Ellerman not very far from this room, then hid her body in the cellar below it.

Sarah was speaking in a monotone, eyes half-closed, reminding them all to rest their palms on the table, to make any spirits welcome and to focus on what they wanted or needed to manifest. 'As usual, I will draw three cards from the pack to guide us all, including any visiting spirits.' Sarah tapped the tarot pack at her elbow. 'This gives us an indication of who is in the room with us tonight and what they want to communicate.'

The cards meant nothing to Jo, but she heard a small gasp as the third card was turned up. It showed a woman resting on a tomb with ominous swords suspended above her.

'That's the ten of swords,' Tegan spoke first, moving her hands to her face as she spoke. 'It means treachery and ruin, or . . . or—'

'The most feared card in the pack,' Valerie Lilley breathed. 'It's never come up before. It could be because of Leah.'

'Oh, for God's sake.' This was a mutter from Matty, whose eyes were firmly closed. Jo could see his fingertips digging into the cloth, rucking it up under his large hands.

'Hands back on the table.' Sarah was firm but her eyes remained fixed on the dark air above Jo's head. 'Remember, we do not interpret the cards in the usual way here.'

Without moving her palms, Nora pointed with her index finger towards the middle card, which showed a woman pouring water. 'That's her card,' she said quietly. 'It's my mother's card. It means she's here.'

'Let us listen now,' Sarah spoke again more softly. 'Let us listen and feel for what the spirits are telling us. Their messages may come to us privately and, if they do, there is no need to share them.'

In the tense, shadowed light, the air seemed fractured with small sounds: the creak of a bentwood chair, breathing, and the spit and crackle of the candle. Jo could see Nora's head moving back and forth. Tegan sneaked a concerned look at her friend and kept her eyes firmly open, Jo noticed, as did Alys Parry.

'That door to the cellar is locked as well, isn't it?' Matty demanded suddenly. His chair grated on the stone flags as he shifted backwards. 'We didn't check that one.'

'We stay still and calm and know that all will be well,' Sarah intoned. She didn't look at Matty, but Jo saw her hand close firmly on his wrist, and although he was strong enough to resist her, he stayed put.

'My Richard's not with us tonight,' Valerie sighed. 'I can feel it. There are no familiar spirits.'

She might have said more, but Sarah's voice brought them all to attention. 'Hello, Spirit,' she said. 'We have entirely female spirits with us this evening.' Her voice had dropped an octave. 'And some of these are newcomers. We welcome you,' she murmured to the charged, flickering air. 'What do you want to tell us?'

Jo could hear her heart pounding, although her brain was busy employing all her sensible reasoning to calm herself down and stay vigilant. The uneasy quiet extended into minutes and the candlelight swooped around the room.

'Who is here?' Matty asked, sitting very upright, shoulders tense.

'A spirit wants to say something about the first card,' Sarah said eventually.

'The first card is the three of swords,' Tegan said. 'It means conflict and broken hearts.'

Watching the participants very closely, Jo noticed the smallest glance pass between Matty and Alys. She also detected an impatient sigh from Sarah, who began a quiet chant, repeating thanks and asking for blessings and messages. Nora's shoulders and head had dropped and Jo began to feel concerned for the girl. Seeing the teenager apparently mesmerized, Jo's patience with the whole proceeding suddenly evaporated. She had an urge to tell Sarah to snap out of it, switch on some lights and bring some common sense back into the room, but she didn't want to shock the poor girl any further. Sarah was still speaking monotonously when there was a sudden loud bang from the cellar door behind Nora. Jo's whole body jumped in the hard wooden chair. Her eyes fixed on the door as the dull thud repeated from inside the cellar.

'Who's that?' Matty was on his feet.

'No! No!' Nora leapt up, crashing her chair to the floor and spinning round to stare at the plain wooden door. Tegan shrieked and jumped to her feet, making a grab for her friend. 'What is it? What is it?'

Sarah moved to calm the young girls and was speaking to them in a normal reassuring voice when a third bang resounded around the room. Valerie Lilley snatched at Jo's hand, but Jo was already on her feet. As was Alys Parry, who was nearer to the cellar door. She was already pulling at the handle when Jo reached it.

'It's definitely coming from down there,' Alys said. 'We need a torch. Get me a torch, Matty.'

'Switch the fucking lights on, someone,' Matty shouted.

'It's important we all stay calm.' Sarah used her strong voice just as Alys wrenched open the cellar door and Hanni switched on the room light.

Jo and Alys stared down the steep stone steps, which Jo remembered very well. She also remembered seeing a light switch when racing out of the place. Now she reached around the door frame to flick it on. Instantly, the damp floor and spare trestle tables were illuminated on the level below, as well as the shelves, under which Leah's body had lain. Alys started to descend.

'Stop!' Sarah shouted. She brought the flat of her hand onto the table with a commanding crash. 'If anyone is going down there, it's me. But no one needs to do anything just yet. You can see for yourselves, we're not in any danger. We cannot be in disarray like this while the session is still open. Please return to your seats.'

'I want to see what made that noise,' Alys said.

'You can. You can come down with me in a minute, if you insist,' Sarah said. 'But first, we need to close the session properly. Believe me, that's where the real danger lies.'

The two teenagers were still hugging each other, and Jo, seeing their white faces, caught Alys's arm. 'We'd better go back.'

Sarah led the girls back to their seats and resumed her own place behind the cards. Jo, with Alys following reluctantly, returned to the table. Jo watched all seven participants as Sarah intoned a ritual closing chant, adding words of protection for those assembled. She saw that Matty was still tense and sweating, and as Sarah came to the end, he reached out a hand. Only two cards remained upturned on the table beside the pack.

'Leah's card,' he said. 'The ten of swords. It's gone.'

CHAPTER FOURTEEN

Jo wasn't the only one eager to get out of the room and back to normality. As soon as the lights were on, people began to disperse, talking in low voices. Sarah called for Gary to get some soft drinks for the two girls, and she and Valerie walked with them to a quiet corner of the main bar, which was convivial, well-lit and blessedly ordinary.

'Are they OK?' Jo asked quietly as she passed Sarah.

'Yes, they're fine, but I'm going to call Nora's dad. I don't think he likes her being here, but he ought to know she's had a shock.' Sarah looked a little sheepish. 'It's a shame we were interrupted. It's not the sort of thing that normally happens. You'll have to come another time to experience a proper evening with the spirits.'

Not in a million years, Jo felt like replying, but she merely said something non-committal and hurried off to seek out Alys. She was sitting beside Matty with her coat on while he downed a whisky. His face had the tight, grey look of someone who hadn't slept for nights, but Alys remained bright-eyed and curious.

'What was all that about?' Jo said.

'It was no ghost, that's for sure,' Alys said, while Matty stared into his glass and said nothing.

'Sarah was very keen we didn't go into the cellar,' Jo said. 'I decided against it because of those two kids, who were already freaked out, and we didn't know what we were going to find.'

'There's no point now.' Alys signalled towards the bar with her eyes and they both watched Sarah and Gary share a muttered exchange before Sarah left the bar, presumably to make her call. Not for the first time, Jo realized there was a lot she didn't know about her clients.

'Are you thinking you've backed the wrong horse by representing those two?' Alys said astutely. Jo gave a philosophical shrug. 'You think they staged it all, don't you?'

'They just wouldn't do that,' Matty said, his colour returning now he had finished his drink. 'I know Sarah has a gift. You just haven't seen her at her best.'

Jo caught sight of Hanni heading over with the truck keys in her hand, clearly determined on an exit. Jo started to explain about the lift, but Alys was quick to understand the situation.

'Tell your friend I'll give you a lift home,' she offered. 'You live in Stroud, don't you? That's where I'm going, so it will save her a journey and you can ask me whatever you want on the way back. I'll see you in the car park in a few minutes.'

Hanni didn't need much persuading. 'I won't be sorry to return that beast to the garage,' she said, regarding the truck balefully.

'You can go back to cycling tomorrow,' Jo said. 'But thanks for today — especially for coming tonight.'

'Actually, it wasn't as bad as I'd expected.' Before Jo could ask what she meant, she added quickly, 'Jo, there is something I need to tell you.'

They were standing by the gate of the pub and Jo shifted so she could see her friend's face under the lantern that hung above it. *Finally*, she thought, and waited.

'You remember when you saw the body? Tell me again exactly what you saw.'

Jo recounted seeing the body tied in the plastic wrapping, strangely flat and oozing onto the flagstones with the single white hand sticking out from under the coat sleeve.

'And on top of the body?'

'I could see she was wearing a parka-type coat, which I think might have been a man's coat. And the body was rolled under a shelf, like an old carpet. Piled on top of that shelf was a load of linen, like sheets or folded white tablecloths. At least, I assumed they were tablecloths, because there was a stack of dismantled tables against the back wall.'

Hanni's almond-shaped eyes came up to meet hers. 'That's what I feared. When I found it, there was another cloth on top of the plastic. It was the dark one covered in symbols that Sarah uses for her paranormal evenings.' She regarded Jo steadily. 'Are you sure you didn't see it?'

When Jo shook her head slowly, Hanni sighed. 'It means that Gary must have moved it before he called the police.'

'If so, he tampered with the crime scene and lied about it, which is an offence,' Jo murmured. Instinctively, they stepped out of the pool of light. The night air had deepened and cooled, and Jo shivered. 'You'll have to tell the police,' she said.

'I should have told them as soon as I suspected. When you didn't mention the cloth covered in the zodiac signs, I knew then, really. I don't want to admit that you saw the body after me, as that will get all of us into trouble.' Hanni chewed her bottom lip.

'Just say you realized tonight when Sarah produced a new tablecloth for the séance.'

'They'll be round here to search the place again, which will be very difficult for Sarah and Gary. Don't you think I should warn them first? They're my friends.'

'And my clients. But I still think you have to go to the police first,' Jo said. When her friend still looked doubtful, she added, 'Look, let's sleep on it and talk in the morning.'

Hanni heaved a sigh. 'I'm sorry I got involved with all this. It was against my instincts from the start, and now I've got you into it too.'

'Don't worry about me,' Jo said. 'But don't keep anything else from me, will you?'

Hanni shook her head and hoisted herself into the cab of the truck. The coughing thump of the engine and screech of the gearbox echoed around the dark waterway as she drove off. Most of the cars had already left and Jo hoped that Alys's wasn't one of them.

She waited with her hands in her pockets, looking along the side of the pub, and could just make out the recess that led to the back door and, beside it, the lean-to shed which covered the woodpile. It seemed to Jo that Leah must have been murdered close by. She lifted her gaze to the patch of tarmac in deep shadow behind the pub's car park, where Leah and the other canal-side residents parked their cars. There, presumably, Leah's murder had taken place — maybe an argument, which had turned violent, or someone lying in wait, anticipating when she would cross the bridge to her car. It didn't make any sense to bring her body here if she'd been murdered elsewhere, as the body had not been well hidden.

The metal covering of the outside cellar door, set into the path, caught the light as Jo shifted position slightly. She envisaged Leah's murderer dragging or somehow carrying the body from the car park to this trapdoor. The people who knew this route best, and had access at all times, were Sarah and Gary. But why leave the body where it was sure to be found?

'You coming with me, then?' The tap on her shoulder startled Jo and Alys apologized. 'I'm not surprised, mind you,' the journalist laughed. 'It's been a night of shocks.'

'What did you make of the banging from the cellar?' Jo asked as they walked towards the car together.

'It's what I've always suspected about Sarah and Gary. They are eighty per cent genuine and twenty per cent . . . well, fake sounds a bit harsh, but let's say they give the ghosts some human assistance. Sarah definitely believes that she can communicate with the spirit world — or whatever you want to call it. She believes the paranormal evenings are doing good — almost like therapy for people, you know.'

'Hmm, well, it seemed to go a bit wrong tonight,' Jo said, as she climbed awkwardly into Alys's low-profile sports car.

'That's the problem,' Alys agreed. 'When you mess with people's heads, you can't predict the outcome.'

'Those two girls shouldn't have been there.'

'I've seen them there before; they are two of her regulars. They usually love being a bit spooked, but tonight it was too close to Leah's death — in both senses.' She pointed the car into the lane and accelerated around the dark bends expertly.

'I'm guessing you know these lanes pretty well,' Jo said, as they sped along a straight stretch of country road. She couldn't wait to return to driving herself, as it felt a lot safer, and decided that tomorrow she would take off the dressing and give driving a go. Outwardly, she asked politely, 'If you suspect some of what Sarah does is fake, why on earth do you attend?'

'Those sessions, and the ghost nights at the pub when they invite in the crazy ghost hunters with all their weird technical equipment, have a sort of fascination for me,' Alys admitted. 'I always feel I might get a story out of it, because my readers are grabbed by this stuff, too. Also,' she added after a pause, 'Matty likes to go. His mother and father have both passed on, you know, and he lost a brother, too.'

'Are you and Matty together?' There was something about the privacy of the car at night that made it easier for her to ask. But Alys's reply was clear and definite.

'No, not anymore. He's been seeing Leah for months. So, that's another loss for him, if you like,' she added thoughtfully. She went on in the same even tone. 'Once I found out, I finished it with him. I'm not having any man cheat on me.'

'You're still close, though.' Jo made a quick calculation. Although no expert, she guessed Alys was about six months pregnant. This fitted with Sarah's estimate that Matty and Leah had been together 'all year'.

Alys was looking across at her. 'I know what you're thinking, and the answer is between me and my baby. No one else needs to know.'

'Of course, sorry. I didn't mean to be nosey,' Jo said quickly. She glanced automatically at the wedding band and diamond, currently resting on the steering wheel.

'They're my mum's,' Alys smiled. 'She died when I was eight, so I've got a lot of sympathy with Nora.'

'I'm sorry,' Jo said again, and they lapsed into silence. She was longing to ask how Alys felt about pregnancy and motherhood but, for once in her life, she couldn't find the right questions. Everything she wanted to ask sounded too personal, even for someone as comfortable in their own skin as Alys appeared to be. She had to content herself with giving directions to King Street, and they talked idly about the case they were both involved in.

'I'm finding out more about the Ellermans,' Jo said, when Alys asked about her progress. 'I'm convinced they are key to finding out about Leah, who remains a mystery to me. I only know she was a driven, successful and self-sufficient Libran who didn't seem to need friends or family much.'

'We all need friends,' Alys said, as she brought the car to a halt at the kerb. 'Was that all you wanted to ask me?'

'No, I wanted to ask about the baby. Nothing private. I mean, it's entirely your business about the father. I get that, but . . .' Jo floundered, wondering why she found this so hard, and tried again. 'I mean, are you happy about it? It will change you, won't it? Do you feel ready?'

'Oh, lots of questions.' Alys let out a sigh. 'I could say, yes, yes and no. But I think you're then going to ask me *how* will it change me? And of course, I haven't a clue. And no, I don't feel ready, but, well, here I am.' She waved an arm vaguely around herself. 'Sorry. That's a bit inadequate, isn't it?' she added, staring through the windscreen.

'No, not at all,' Jo said hurriedly. 'That's really helpful, thank you. And thank you for the lift.' Suddenly, she was desperate to leave, in case Alys wanted to know why she was asking. But, as she waved Alys off, standing on the pavement, she felt oddly disappointed with herself. For once, she felt she had wimped out. She limped down Fleece Alley, determined to do two things tomorrow. The first was to drive her own car. The second was to drive it to see Duncan Ellerman. These things she felt certain she could do.

She had not told either Alys or Hanni about her visit to the Stokes Avon Home for Elderly Residents. On her way home in the cab, she'd realized why the friendly driver had seemed familiar. He was the same driver who had picked up Lucia Hewitt and all her various items of luggage from Canalside Cottages. Fortunately, he'd been equally chatty on the way back. He'd been quite happy to tell her that he had not taken Lucia to the station, as Jo had expected, but to an address in Great Yelding, a village in the Cotswolds. The cabbie was specific about the address, as were the results from Jo's phone when she looked up Duncan Ellerman's carpentry business. Tomorrow, she looked forward to surprising Duncan and Lucia.

CHAPTER FIFTEEN

However, Friday started with a phone call that instantly derailed Jo's plans.

'Jo, we're being arrested. Me and Gary. He's talking to a solicitor now, but we're allowed one phone call each, so I'm calling you.'

Jo had never imagined Sarah as the panicky type. The woman had always seemed so calm, whatever she was faced with, but this morning she was clearly feeling harassed. 'What should we do? Can you do something to help us?' She paused as if she had more to say, but only one word came out. 'Please.'

Jo had grabbed the phone from the shower to take the call. She now sat on the side of the bath in a towel. 'What's the charge? They can't arrest you without charging you.'

There was a confused mix of voices around Sarah, and then she returned to the phone. 'Sorry, I shouldn't have said "arrested". Detective Sergeant Watts is here and she says we're just being taken in for questioning, but they need us to go with them right now. We've had to call Paul to see if he'll look after the pub again.'

'OK, just answer their questions, and maybe, yes, consult a solicitor.' Jo thought for a second. 'They must have given you some reason?' She wondered if Hanni had already

152

contacted the police about the evidence-tampering, but felt sure her friend would have told her first.

'It's about Leah, of course,' Sarah dropped her voice, and Jo had the impression she had moved somewhere more private. She sounded more like her usual self. 'That complaint she made to the brewery, and then coming round here causing a scene. Paul had to show Leah's emails to the police, he said.' She groaned. 'Oh, this is the end of the road for us running the pub, Jo. He is going to hang us out to dry in his report to the brewery.'

'That's nothing new – there must be something else. Look, I'll come to the station and see if I can find out what's behind this,' Jo promised. Sarah seemed satisfied with this offer, although Jo had no idea exactly what she was going to achieve by being there. In fact, as Macy had said a few days ago, the most useful thing she could do for them was to find out who had killed Leah Ellerman. That alone would take the pressure off — assuming, of course, that Sarah and Gary were innocent. If only she could be certain, Jo sighed, as she peeled the dressing off her injured leg. She could put more weight on it today, which was just as well, because she was determined to get back in her car. She would have to drive if she was going to seek out Duncan Ellerman and Lucia Hewitt and find out what was going on there.

Today was also the day on which she finally had to tell Teddy her answer to his sort-of proposal. Although her conversation with Alys in the car last night had been useful in many ways, she hadn't felt able to talk about her own private dilemma, and felt no closer to knowing what she was going to say to Teddy. She turned over her decision in her mind during her breakfast of coffee and toast, but thinking didn't seem to help, so she called Hanni and told her the news about Sarah and Gary.

'In a way, it makes it easier to tell the police what you know about the tablecloth,' she said.

'I'm not sure about that. It's only going to make things worse for them. But I know I have to do it.' Jo envisaged her friend pacing around the Rivermill, tidying books that were already perfectly in order. 'I'll have to wait until Chloe comes in. Then I will go to the police station,' she said. 'I'd rather talk to them in person.'

'I'll probably see you there,' Jo answered. 'Ask for DS Diane Watts. She still seems to be dealing with the case.'

When Jo ran into the station about half an hour later, in a heavy shower, she virtually collided with DS Watts in the lobby. The detective sergeant didn't seem at all surprised to see her, and granted her precisely five minutes with one of her clients. Jo chose Sarah, and was shown into a small, grubby interview room where Sarah was sitting at the bare table, doing her best to look indifferent.

Jo didn't bother sitting down. 'We've got to be quick,' she said. 'Tell me what I can do to help.'

'I could do with a cigarette,' Sarah said, 'but I expect that's out of the question.' She caught Jo's serious expression and made a face. 'Look, it's good that you're here. We do appreciate it, because everyone else is turning on us, Jo. Apparently, Gil Hutchinson has made a complaint about last night, because Nora is young and sensitive and should not have been taking part.' She rolled her eyes at Jo. 'She's been coming for months, and he has been turning a blind eye because it suits him.'

'Well, those girls were too young to be there,' Jo said reasonably. 'I felt sorry for Nora.'

'Then I suggest you talk to her,' Sarah shot back. 'Let the girl speak for herself. Yes, last night didn't go well. She and Tegan had an abreaction, but that was just one night. It was unfortunate, yes, but you need to ask Nora about all the weekends she's spent with us, all the Sunday roasts she's had in the kitchen and, yes, the comfort she gets from some contact with her mother.'

'But, be honest, you and Gary are not above using a bit of fakery, are you?' Jo said.

Sarah met her eyes, steadily shaking her head. 'I believe in what I do,' she said. 'My gift brings people a bit of hope and the sessions provide a refuge.'

'Hanni knows Gary tampered with the crime scene,' Jo said, very conscious of her granted time ticking by. 'She knows he moved the tablecloth from the body, and she will have to tell the police. She's coming here today.'

Sarah closed her eyes briefly, opened them again, and said, 'So be it. And so much for you helping us.'

'I am trying to,' Jo said. 'Neither Hanni nor I believe you had anything to do with Leah's death, but if I'm going to really be of use, we've got to help the police find out the truth.'

'The truth is rarely simple,' Sarah said. 'And you can be as sceptical as you want, but the truth is exactly what I am about, too.' A uniformed PC peered in through the doorway, holding up his wrist to show his watch. 'Go and talk to Nora, like I said, and also to Matty. He's not as stupid as he makes out. And tell me what's happening at the pub,' she called, as Jo was shepherded out.

Rather than being shown back to the lobby, however, Jo was hurried along a corridor, passing windows into the open-plan offices, where people were working on phones and screens. The PC leaned in at the end door, and Jo saw DS Watts look up from her desk in the corner then stride towards them.

'I've got a suggestion,' she said directly to Jo. 'Shall we go for a coffee? It means I can get out of this place for a bit — no offence, Charlie,' she added to the uniformed PC, who was still loitering. Without waiting for an answer, the detective picked up her jacket from the back of her chair and led the way out.

Jo followed amiably, although it meant postponing her trip to see Duncan Ellerman. Not that she had a great deal of choice, she reminded herself, as she tried to keep pace with Diane Watts along the high street. But, on the plus side, she approved of the coffee shop the detective chose.

It was a sparse place with hard, wooden tables and chairs, but the coffee was excellent. Diane Watts brought their flat whites over to where Jo was perched on one of the high stools, as far away as she could get from any other customers. DS Watts nodded approvingly and got straight to the point. 'Your friend, Hanni Light, arrived while you were with Sarah Robart. She's with DC Williams now. What is she telling him?'

Jo explained about the cloth used for the paranormal sessions without revealing that she had also seen the body. She fervently hoped Hanni would stick to this story and her hands became a little sweaty at the thought. Diane Watts watched her closely while adding generous amounts of sugar to her coffee. Her dark hair was longer these days and even more unruly. Jo unconsciously put a hand up to her own curly locks, which could never be relied upon to look smooth and tidy. In fact, the two women silhouetted in the window looked a little alike. Both were in their late thirties, with dark hair and eyes. DS Watts looked tired and unkempt, but her eyes were sharp.

'I thought it was time we reminded ourselves that we're on the same side,' she said into the little silence following Jo's explanation.

'I know we are,' Jo said quickly. 'I haven't been in touch because I really haven't known what the heck is going on.'

'And I'm not in a position to enlighten you about our inquiry. Obviously.' DS Watts paused to stir her coffee. 'But I will tell you what I can, if you will share what you have found out, working from the inside, so to speak.'

'All right,' Jo said, maintaining her natural reserve, although she had never thought of herself as 'working from the inside'. 'I don't have any evidence yet. Just theories. But I think you can rule some people out.'

'Such as Gary and Sarah Robart?' Diane Watts looked disappointed. 'I expected you to say that, but we've got enough evidence to hold them. The body was found on their premises, after all, and Miss Ellerman had complained about their paranormal activities.'

'Which are not illegal and no money changes hands,' Jo pointed out.

'I'm sure the bar profits benefit,' Diane Watts said drily. 'And we've had a complaint this morning from the father of a teenager who attended last night's session. She's very distressed, apparently.' She paused briefly, glancing up. 'I understand you were there?'

Jo nodded and said, 'Gil Hutchinson's complaint has nothing to do with Leah Ellerman's death.'

'Possibly not. But maybe it justifies Leah's complaints. You do know that the brewery has also asked them to stop these so-called paranormal evenings? They are concerned it will damage their reputation.'

'Again, not a crime.'

'No, but it shows that the Robarts are inclined to over-step boundaries, disregard rules.' The detective considered her plain, unadorned hands on her coffee cup for a moment. 'Obviously, this is to go no further, but you should know that Gary threatened Leah with physical violence. There were witnesses.'

'Matty Sullivan?' Jo's guess was rewarded by the slightest inclination of DS Watts' chin. 'He's always around when something bad happens,' Jo added. Privately, she concluded that prospects for Sarah and Gary were even bleaker than she'd expected.

'You may have your suspicions about Matty Sullivan, but don't forget, he has no motive,' the detective said. 'Leah Ellerman had provided most of his work for the last six months — and promised a further three months, at least. And they were in a relationship.'

Jo said nothing. Her mind went to the list with the circled names, lying on her kitchen worktop. 'I'm convinced the family are key,' she said eventually. 'What do you know about Irene Ellerman-James, her husband, Howard, and her brother, Duncan?'

'They're a very well-known and well-connected local family, and we've interviewed all of them. There was nothing to justify any follow-up.' DS Watts spoke briskly. 'And, needless to say, no previous criminal activity.'

'But Leah was the only member of the family making any money. And Leah had no kids, so—'

'Of course, Irene and Duncan are the main benefactors in the will, but there's nothing out of the ordinary about that.' Diane Watts shook her head. 'No, they've too much to lose. Despite what you say, Duncan Ellerman's furniture business — OK, it's not on the scale of his father's success — but it's surviving. And Irene is very much a local figure. She's president of the Golden Valley WI, a school governor, she is on a number of charity committees locally, and she's on the board and a benefactor of the outdoor museum at Stokes Avon. As for Howard, he is something of a recluse, I understand.' She paused again and changed tack. 'But tell me some of your theories. Don't worry about evidence — you can leave that to us. What have you got on the Ellermans?'

Jo hesitated. In truth, she had not much more than circled names on her list. Maybe it was time to admit she needed some help. 'I was planning to see Duncan Ellerman today. I met him and Irene yesterday, and he didn't give much away, but I sensed he and Leah were close. Maybe he knows more than he says. Plus, as I said, there is a clear motive.'

'In my experience, it's never as cut and dried as that,' Diane Watts said, which seemed to bring further speculation on the Ellermans to a close.

'Can I ask you some things now?' Jo said, before they could reach the end of their coffees. 'Can you tell me what you've found out about what actually happened to Leah? I mean, how exactly she died and when?'

Diane Watts gave her a calculating look. 'On the basis that we are working towards the same end, and that what I tell you is strictly between you and me.' Jo nodded avidly and the detective went on, clearly weighing her words. 'She was bludgeoned to death in the private car park, her own land as it turns out, but only a matter of metres from the back door of the pub. As for timing, we have narrowed it down to forty-eight hours around the third of June. As it almost certainly took place in the hours of darkness, that means the night of the second of June or early hours of the following day.'

'About ten days before the body was found,' Jo said.

'It could have been an opportunistic attack, but as nothing was stolen except the car, it was more likely an argument which got out of hand. We have a good impression of the weapon. It looks something like a rounders bat, but it hasn't yet been found. Neither has her car, a grey Hyundai Tucson, 2015 plate.'

'That's odd, isn't it?' Jo said. 'To take the car but leave the body?'

The other woman gave a cynical smile, implying 'odd' was the norm for her.

'The best evidence, as ever, is from the disposal of the body,' DS Watts said. 'The car park, the cellar and the plastic wrapping have given us plenty of traces of blood and fabric. The plastic is identical to that used on the building site at Leah's cottage and was cut from a roll left outside. So, we have built up a pretty clear picture of what happened, but we have multiple DNA samples involving numerous suspects.'

'So, you have got a sort of shortlist and you've just got to narrow it down?'

'Have we identified a likely perpetrator, you mean?' Diane Watts gave a heavy sigh. 'Privately, I agree with you about the Robarts, but our interviews will test what more they know. We have seen everyone who was on and around the scene in the critical ten-day period. You'd be surprised how many, actually,' she added drily. 'Sullivan's sub-contractors have taken some tracking down, and then there are Leah's own contacts, her work colleagues and friends—' Her phone rang and she broke off in the middle of the list.

Although her answers were monosyllabic, Jo sensed the other woman's tension ratcheting up. She waited on tenterhooks herself as DS Watts gave the name of the coffee shop. It seemed her informal interview was about to end abruptly. 'Got to go. DC Williams is picking me up outside,' she said.

Jo knew better than to ask what had happened. The police car was drawing up as they stepped out onto the pavement. As Jo was about to walk away, DS Watts turned to her. 'You'd better get in,' she said. 'Irene Ellerman's body has been found at the manor house.'

CHAPTER SIXTEEN

'Same confidential basis, you understand,' DS Watts rapped out as the blue light bounced off the shop windows on King Street and police car sirens blared around them.

'Yes, OK. But why?' Jo, strapped into the back seat and watching the familiar buildings flash past, felt her heart race as if she was guilty of something. 'Why do you want me here?'

'I was about to ask the exact same thing,' DC Williams said from behind the steering wheel.

'Duncan Ellerman called it in,' DS Watts said.

'That explains everything.' Williams' heavy sarcasm was clearly wasted on DS Watts, who shot a look at Jo, like someone conceding a hand of poker. 'He's at Stokes Manor now. So, come on, Dom, get a shift on,' she added, with a sideways grin towards the back seat.

There were already two police cars, a plain white van and an ambulance in the neat, gravelled semi-circle in front of the biscuit-yellow stone manor house. Two of the uniformed police were hastily erecting a tent around a large shapeless heap on the gravel close to the base of the tower. There was a taped routeway in place, leading towards the unmoving form. Jo's eyes were drawn to it and her mouth went dry.

'Stay by the car,' DS Watts said to Jo, as she and DC Williams headed to the van. They emerged less than a minute later, clad in white SOCO suits, and trudged along the gravel to the body. Jo watched as a uniformed colleague briefed them and she wished she could hear what was being said. Instead, she had to make the most of what she could observe.

A breeze with a faint chill rustled the neat yew hedge behind the corpse and lifted a piece of thin, colourful fabric to waft fruitlessly from the chest. Jo recognized the bright berry pattern on the scarf, and this brought home to her that she was, indeed, looking at Irene Ellerman's dead body. It was the last she saw of her, as the white walls of the tent were quickly erected. She leaned back against the warm metal of the car and took a few breaths.

Duncan Ellerman stood by the front door of the manor house, where his sister had lived all her life. He had one thin arm folded across his stomach and the other reached up to his mouth. His white, lined face seemed to have sunk inwards since Jo had last seen him, and his jaw twitched. He appeared mesmerized by the activity, and when one of the PCs tried to encourage him to go indoors, he refused. Beside him was the man Jo recognized as Irene's husband. In contrast, Howard Ellerman-James' face was expressionless and wide-eyed. Jo glanced to the top of the tower, where his telescope could still be seen.

'What happened?' Jo asked one of the uniformed PCs who came up to move the car.

'Fell to her death,' the woman said briefly. 'Slipped down the outside steps of the tower.' They both looked at the soft, curved brickwork and the portion of curling staircase which was in view, with its narrow, wedge-shaped stone steps.

'An accident?' Jo murmured.

The PC shrugged. 'You've got to consider all the possibilities at this stage.' The officer looked across at Jo. 'You're with Detective Sergeant Watts, aren't you? I saw you arrive. Stay well back from the scene, won't you?'

'I will. Were they the only people here?' she asked, keeping her eyes on Irene's brother and husband.

'No, there's also a gardener, a sort of handyman and a cleaner. We'll take them all in for questioning — or do it here, whichever the sergeant wants. Don't think we'll get much from the husband, though. He's got dementia, poor chap.'

'That's tough.' Jo dropped her gaze from the two men and stared at the gravel beneath her feet for a second. She wondered how she could have missed this in her brief conversation with Howard, and why Irene had kept it from people. And yet, she also understood: it was all of a piece with Irene's pride and her sensitivity about the family name. Hadn't Hanni said that Irene was more ashamed than sad at Leah's death?

She shifted so that the PC could move the squad car out of the way of the SOCO team and their equipment. Jo realized that more vehicles had arrived and, scanning the churned-up driveway, noticed a transit van parked near the house, which looked decidedly familiar. In fact, she had been in it herself earlier in the week. Leaning against the door of the white van was Matty Sullivan, arms folded and grim-faced. As he seemed to be alone, she walked quietly up to him. 'What are you doing here?'

Matty spun round, clasping a hand to his chest. 'Fuck me! You could have given me a heart attack.' He blinked at her. 'I could ask you the same thing.'

'I'm helping with inquiries,' Jo said. 'At least I think I am. And you must be "the sort-of handyman" the police officer mentioned.'

'Thanks very much,' he muttered. 'This is a terrible thing, isn't it? My God, what a shock. Apparently, the steps were slippy after the rain.' He seemed to become more energized as he spoke. 'She must have walked up and down them hundreds of times, but it only takes a moment to lose concentration, doesn't it? As you well know.'

'Yes, I do. Strange how these bad accidents keep happening when you're around.'

He snapped his eyes to hers. 'That's not a very nice thing to say.'

'Well, what are you doing here?' Jo repeated. 'I didn't think you even knew Irene. You work for Leah.'

'Not anymore, I don't. You must have worked that one out. Irene has taken over the contract. She doesn't want to come to the site, though, so I have to come all the way out here to meet her.' He turned back to the wide front drive of the elegant manor house, scattered with vehicles, officers in uniforms and white suits carrying tripods and cameras, and, at the base of the tower, the bleak tent. DC Dom Williams was talking seriously to Duncan and Howard. 'God knows what will happen now,' Matty went on. They saw the PC who had spoken to Jo earlier making her way over to them with DS Watts following, and he sighed. 'Here we go. More fucking questions, I suppose.'

He allowed himself to be led indoors by the efficient PC, but Diane Watts detained Jo with a light hand on her arm. 'I need to ask you something,' she said. 'Why did you want to see Duncan Ellerman today?'

'Do you know Lucia Hewitt?'

DS Watts frowned. 'The holiday tenant at number one? She had a sound alibi for the critical forty-eight hours, so we let her go home.'

'She didn't go home, though,' Jo said. 'The taxi that was meant to take her to the station took her to Duncan's address in Great Yelding. So, I was going to see them both. Turns out, he's here.'

'I thought you'd told me everything,' the detective said, but she rapidly cut off Jo's excuses. 'Look, at least I know now. I want to talk to you some more, but it can wait till tomorrow. Meanwhile, I'll arrange for someone to take you back.'

'Could they drop me at the New Navigation?' Jo asked, remembering her promise to her clients.

'You can go where you want,' Diane Watts said irritably. 'But don't leave the area or you might find yourself brought back in a police car. I will be in touch.'

If Jo had been hoping for plaudits, she had to be satisfied with this dismissal instead.

CHAPTER SEVENTEEN

The evening air was heavy and humid with the threat of more rain, and the water was static, throwing back a perfect reflection of the cottages with the trees behind them. A twig hit the strip of water and floated aimlessly. Jo, standing on the humpback bridge, traced the arc of its fall and saw Nora Hutchinson sitting against the wall of the far bridge, preparing to throw another. She was well camouflaged in a green and black sweatshirt and dark jogging bottoms. Instead of going across to the pub, Jo took the path down towards the cottages, past their front windows and came to a halt in front of the girl.

'How are you doing?' Jo asked. This was greeted with nothing more than a non-committal shrug from the girl sitting on the path. 'Is it OK if I sit here?' Jo pointed to a stubby milestone post nearby. Nora didn't reply, so Jo sat quietly and the girl hugged her knees closer.

'It was horrible last night at the séance, wasn't it?' Jo remarked after a while.

'It's not a séance,' Nora said, and then turned her face away as if she wished she'd not spoken.

'Sorry,' Jo said. 'I've not been to anything like that before so I didn't know what to expect. I was shit scared, to be honest.'

Nora said nothing, but her arms relaxed a little around her knees.

'Did you know what to expect?' Jo asked.

The girl nodded. 'Mm-hmm.'

'You're braver than me,' Jo said. 'I won't be doing that again, I can assure you.' Another silence fell and she watched the sparse customers in the pub garden, sitting under the umbrellas chatting or fetching drinks from the bar.

'Have you seen Sarah?' Nora asked suddenly. Jo was stretching her sore leg, testing it out in the hope of improvements. When she nodded, the girl asked, 'How is she?'

'She was worried about the pub,' Jo said. 'That's why I came over.'

Nora tilted her white face towards Jo. 'The pub's OK, you can tell her. Business is quiet but steady. Paul is not exactly hilarious, but he's doing fine.'

Jo smiled. 'That's good.' She examined the bruise on her other leg, which was blooming into a range of colours.

'Did you do that when you fell in the canal and Matty rescued you?'

'Yep. Were you there?' Ever since the séance, Jo had been certain that it was Nora's shouts she'd heard echoing under the bridge. 'I still don't really know what happened.'

'I didn't see you fall, but I saw Matty talking to the delivery guy on the bridge,' Nora said.

'I thought I heard you call out, on the towpath, ahead of me,' Jo said. 'But it doesn't make sense, because I'd seen you working at the pub.'

Nora was silent for a full minute. They watched as a narrow boat put-putted past them, nosing its way through the still water. Then Nora sighed. 'Dad came and fetched me. It was embarrassing. He made me walk out in front of Sarah, Gary, Maureen and that new barman, Mark. All because he doesn't like Sarah. He thinks she's a bad influence, but he's so wrong.'

'You argued with your dad? So, that's what I heard. It's starting to make sense now.' They sat in silence for a while, watching the barge navigate the lock gates. A man stayed on the boat, steering, and a woman jumped off to open the sluices. A collie dog tried to follow both of them, racing back and forth, and Nora watched, mildly entertained.

'Sarah also said I should talk to you,' Jo said at last. 'That's another reason why I'm here.'

Nora looked up, startled. 'What about?'

'So, I can understand why you go to the paranormal evenings. I assumed you were scared, but that was probably because I was scared.'

The girl watched the barge as it sank from view and the dog barked from the bank. 'Why?' When Jo didn't immediately answer, she went on, 'I mean, what does it matter how I feel?'

Jo sighed. 'Everything matters at the moment, because I'm trying to make sense of what happened to Leah.'

'Are you helping Sarah and Gary?'

'As much as I can,' Jo said honestly, 'but it's hard to know what to do for the best.'

Nora thought for a moment and then said, 'I like going because it makes me feel closer to Mum. Dad doesn't understand. He thinks that we all need to be doing things all the time. Like karate or after-school club or football, but I really just want to stay at home. That's why I like it over there.' She indicated the pub garden.

'It's always there, isn't it?' Jo said, looking at the square white building with the tables and umbrellas set out behind it.

And Sarah is too, she thought to herself. It was obvious the teenager was concerned about Sarah, and the older woman seemed to look out for Nora as well.

'I think Sarah and Gary might be back later,' Jo offered, after another pause. 'The police won't keep them overnight.' She looked at her watch. 'I've got to go and meet my boyfriend. I can't be late. But thank you for explaining a few things. It's helped quite a bit.'

Nora's doubtful expression was similar to Maureen's when Jo had thanked her before leaving the old people's home and Maureen had said, 'I haven't done anything.' Nora looked as if she was thinking the same thing. But characteristically, she didn't waste words. 'See you about,' was all she said as Jo waved on her way back towards the bridge.

Jo hadn't lied. Some answers had started to slot into place, but it was like an old-fashioned puzzle in which pushing one wooden piece satisfyingly into its groove immediately dislodged another. As she trudged back towards the pub, trying to regroup her various theories, she felt afraid that the whole thing would come apart in her hands any moment.

An hour later found her sipping a cold glass of wine under one of the umbrellas that she and Nora had been gazing at. In fact, she had a strong feeling that the girl might still be watching, which made her more than a little self-conscious. She had been intending to catch a cab home, have a shower and put on fresh clothes and some make-up before going out again to meet Teddy. However, her slow trek along the towpath had made her realize that she was not going to have time, and her injuries meant that rushing was not an option. Instead, she called him and asked if he could come and meet her at the New Navigation.

In a mirror in the ladies, she repaired her make-up with what she had on her, and told herself that her loose pants looked 'floaty' and her T-shirt was 'summery'. She brushed her hair fiercely into tidiness and bought herself a glass of white wine. Only then did she find a table outdoors, facing the pub so she could see Teddy arriving, and call Macy.

'Good timing,' he said to her. 'I'm just driving back from Bournemouth.'

'How did it go? Did you get a thorough grilling from the defence?'

'Oh, that seemed to go OK,' he said airily. 'It was more difficult trying to get an opinion from our side on the likely outcome. But they are nearing the end of the trial, so we should know soon anyway. How's it going there?'

'Leah Ellerman's sister has died. She fell down an outside staircase at her house in Stokesly. In fact, I don't know if she fell, was pushed or whether it was suicide, even. I was at the scene with the police, and I must admit, I don't envy their job.'

Macy agreed wholeheartedly for once.

'You sound more cheerful,' Jo commented, sipping her wine and keeping an eagle eye on the door into the bar.

'Well, the trial is still going, but they don't need me anymore, thank God. The effort of wearing a suit and tie every day is too much for me.' When she laughed, he went on, 'But the main thing is that I've heard nothing more from your Angry Cherub. So, that's a load off my mind.'

'You've still got the dilemma of whether you should tell the police what you know.'

'Thanks for pointing that out,' he said drily. 'But you know what, I made my decision during all the hours of waiting around at court over the last two days. If he appears to have got away as he planned it and nobody is hurt and no one worse off, I am not going to interfere with that. He's a grown man and he knew what he was doing. What do they say? Least said, soonest mended.'

'OK, if you say so.' Jo looked up and saw Teddy walking out of the bar with two large glasses of wine. Her stomach turned over as she forced a smile. 'Macy, look, I've got to go. Talk tomorrow.'

'Are you OK?' he was saying as she ended the call.

Teddy looked more handsome than ever, she decided, as she watched him walk towards her table. He was clearly brimming with some news. She felt her breathing slow down with trepidation, as if to put off the moment when she had to tell him what she'd decided.

'You'll never guess,' he announced, after he had greeted her with a kiss. 'You know the Ellerman family you were asking about the other day? I heard today that the elder sister has died — an accident at home, they're saying on the local news. That means both sisters have died within a week or so. That's bizarre, isn't it? And terribly sad, of course,' he added.

'I know,' she said.

'You know? Oh, is that why you were asking about them?' He looked concerned. 'You're not involved in any way, are you?'

'Yes, a bit. You know that Leah died here? Hanni found the body and she asked me if I could advise the landlord and landlady of the pub, because they didn't know what to do.'

Teddy's blue eyes were perplexed. 'And you took it on? Is this in your new PI role? But I thought you'd barely even finished your training.'

'I have qualified,' she corrected him gently. 'But yes, this is my first case.'

'And are you able to — to advise the publicans?'

'Yes, although right now they are at the police station, assisting with inquiries.'

Teddy's sandy eyebrows shot up. 'That doesn't sound good.' She admitted it wasn't. He took a sip of wine and looked around the beer garden and out at the canal, with the pretty cottages on the opposite bank. 'So, that's why you wanted me to meet you here? Although it's a nice enough place in its own right.'

Jo agreed it was. He asked about her injuries and how she was feeling. She reassured him she was fine, inquired politely about his day at the golf course and started the second glass of wine.

'It's a bit disconcerting to think that a murder took place here,' Teddy said, staring around him. 'Especially when it looks so idyllic.'

'You really wouldn't believe how different it is below the pretty surface,' Jo said. 'Everybody lives within a mile of each other and everyone knows everything about everyone else. It's positively claustrophobic,' she added with a shudder. She felt suddenly very tired and full of self-doubt. How could she act as some sort of 'insider' for the police when she couldn't make decisions about her own life? Her legs were sore, her head was aching and she just wanted to go home. To be fair to Teddy, she knew she had to address his question about their future. 'I know you didn't come here to talk about my case,' she said. 'That's not the reason we're meeting up. You asked me to think about what I wanted for us, for our future—'

'Jo! Jo, you're here.' Over Teddy's shoulder, Jo saw Alys tramping across the grass in heels, white-faced. The words that Jo had planned to say seemed to constrict her throat. Feeling desperate, she tried to send out mute signals to Alys that this was not the moment to interrupt, but the journalist was clearly distressed. 'You need to see this . . .' She held her phone screen out to Jo, her hand shaking.

'I can't talk now, Alys,' Jo said, but her words faltered when her eyes rested on the screen. The message read: *Leave the pub, forget Leah and go back to your life, bitch, or you won't have one.*

Teddy strained forward to read it. 'What the—? You should take this to the police.'

'Have you got something similar?' Alys demanded of Jo. 'Or is it just me?'

While Teddy watched, arms folded, Jo turned over her phone and scrutinized it briefly. 'No, nothing. But Teddy's right. You have to show it to the police,' she said.

'Don't worry, I'm going to.' Alys looked from Jo to Teddy and back again. 'Oh, look, I'm sorry for interrupting your evening. It's just that I've had these sorts of things before, on social media, related to various stories. But never a personal message on my phone. It was a shock.' She reached out to hold the back of a chair, her face drained of colour.

Teddy was on his feet instantly, solicitously pulling out a chair, and looking concerned. 'Look, sit down for a minute. Can I get you a drink? Maybe a coffee or something?'

'No, I'm fine,' Alys said, but her voice was strained. 'Actually, I might just sit for a sec,' she added, a little breathlessly. 'Are you sure you don't mind?'

Both Teddy and Jo reassured her and she dropped to the spare wicker chair with relief.

'So, what is this horrible threat about?' Teddy looked at Jo, baffled. 'And why would either of you get such a thing? I trust you are going to tell the police?'

'I assume it's about the Ellermans,' Jo said. 'Alys is a journalist on the local paper. She's been covering the story.'

'It's the biggest local murder story for years,' Alys explained, gradually recovering her colour and her voice. 'Particularly now that Irene Ellerman, Leah's elder sister, has died in unexplained circumstances. You must know the Ellermans?' She looked curiously at Teddy. 'You're a Scarborough, aren't you? Aren't you Andy's brother?'

Teddy admitted it. Jo, torn between concern for Alys and a desire for her to be elsewhere, listened helplessly while she quizzed Teddy on what he knew about the Ellermans.

'My mum knows them more than me,' he said. 'She and Irene Ellerman are both on the board at Stokes Avon outdoor museum. They are always raising money locally, so I know Irene will be missed. She's an overall good egg. I don't know Leah at all, I'm afraid.'

'She works in London, so that might be why,' Jo supplied. 'But she lived just over there.' She pointed to Leah's house across the darkening, serene strip of water. 'You know, it's getting late,' she added. 'Maybe we should be making tracks . . .'

Teddy looked hard at Alys. 'How are you feeling now? Are you driving home? Are you sure I can't get you a drink?'

She drew a shaky breath. 'Actually, a coffee would be good — if you're sure that's OK?'

When Teddy was on his way to the bar, Jo turned to her. 'Who do you think sent the death threat?'

'Unknown contact, of course, but I'm sure the police can trace it easily enough. And I'm not going to be scared off.' She placed a protective hand on her stomach. 'I'm sticking with the story, although I'll have to tell my editor and he might not like it.'

Jo shook her head in sympathy. 'I suppose just about anyone can send these nasty things now. But it's still horrible. Will you tell anyone else?'

Alys's clear blue eyes met hers and then dropped down to her well-manicured, plum-coloured nails. 'Well, probably Matty,' she said.

They exchanged a look, but Jo didn't comment. Instead, she said quickly, 'Listen, I really do need to talk to Teddy tonight, you know.'

Alys looked stricken. 'Of course, I'm so sorry—'

Teddy was walking towards them with three coffees and Jo felt unexpected tears at the back of her eyes. It was so like him to look after Alys, despite the unwelcome interruption, and she was struck with a sudden sense of loss, even while he was still here in front of her, chatting genially and handing out the coffees. She was going to miss him.

The journalist was as good as her word and gulped down the hot coffee, saying she had to get home — although Jo noticed her eyes straying in the direction of Leah's cottage as she spoke, and guessed her mind was on the caravan parked out at the back.

'Well, thank you, but I've really got to go.' Alys got to her feet, leaving her coffee half-finished. She was apologizing for the interruption when Jo's phone pinged, and she automatically covered it with her hand. It was a transparently guilty gesture, and Alys continued talking rapidly to cover it up. 'Thank you for the coffee and the background about the Ellermans. You're right, of course, Irene will be missed around here,' she said, smiling at Teddy. 'She gave to a lot of charities. Not just money, either, but her time and energy. Her death is a complete shock. The police are not ruling out suicide, even, or an accident . . .' Alys tailed off as Jo's face paled. She turned her phone towards them.

'I think I've just had my first-ever death threat,' she said.

CHAPTER EIGHTEEN

Teddy insisted they both report their complaints to the police immediately and, naturally, offered to drive them straight to the station. But, as Alys was going anyway, she said she would give Jo a lift, and this seemed the most logical solution.

'Look, I need to see a . . . a friend in the bar before I go,' she said, with a meaningful glance at Jo. 'So, I'll leave you in peace. Jo, just come and give me a nod when you're ready. Thanks for the coffee,' she added, setting down her cup and hurrying indoors.

'I still can't understand why either of you would get a death threat.' Teddy looked bemused as he watched her go. 'It must be even worse for Alys, being pregnant. And yet she seems very laid back about it.'

'She's a journalist,' Jo shrugged, as if that explained everything. She leaned across the table towards him. 'Listen, we were talking about something more important before Alys arrived.' He became very still and she impulsively took his hand. 'Forget about the death threats,' she said. 'I promise I will tell the police, but I have something to say first.'

Teddy straightened his shoulders, his face shadowed now in the dusk. 'All right, go on,' he said.

Oddly, now that Alys had finally left and Jo had claimed her moment to speak, faced with Teddy's straight gaze across the table, she struggled to find her words. 'The trouble with me is that I don't want things to change,' she said eventually, and then found that she couldn't say anything else.

Only a minute or two went by before Jo finally found her words and her courage, but in that time the muted chatter of the beer garden seemed to have died away, and the chilled air off the canal reached them. She took a deep breath. 'But I know things have got to change and you want something different.' Her voice wavered and she bit her lip, feeling she was not handling this at all well.

'It's all right,' he sighed. The details of his face were lost to her in the gloom. 'I've sort of worked it out. If you wanted us to settle down together, get a house, have some kids, you'd know it. And I'd know it, too. We wouldn't be "meeting to discuss it".'

'Wouldn't we?' Sometimes Jo felt more mystified by Teddy than any number of murders.

He shook his head. 'I'm right, aren't I?'

'I want you to understand that it is just about timing for me. It's not about you, Teddy, I — I . . .' she faltered again, but ploughed on. 'It's just that I'm not ready for babies yet.'

'I know. But seeing Andy and how nuts he and Nikki are about Lela-May has made me realize I don't want to hang around, and . . . well, I don't want to mention the age thing, but . . .'

Jo gave his warm hand a squeeze and let go. 'I feel that too,' she said, 'but I can't fake what I don't feel. I've never been any good at that.' She took another breath. 'So, I have been thinking about your question, while I know you think I've been avoiding it.' She met his eyes. 'The answer is "not yet" for me. We seem to be at different stages,' she sighed, 'so I understand if you want to move on.'

'I do, Jo.' Teddy sat back and met her eyes levelly.

A short, separated silence fell, and when they spoke again, it was about the phone messages — as if it was easier to talk about death threats. 'I really think you need to get to the police — or at least phone them. I'd feel happier if you and Alys went straight away,' he said, and eventually, Jo agreed, although privately she found it hard to take them seriously. She and Teddy returned across the garden, side by side but some distance apart. Alys wasn't immediately visible among the people in the bar, but Jo assured him she would find her and walked with him to his car.

They spoke some quiet words and hugged, and he made her promise to message him when she was home. She waved once in the dark as Teddy's Audi left the pub car park, then stood and watched the red tail-lights meander down the lane. Being alone in the summery darkness, she felt an odd, sad sense of release, and she had no desire to return to the crowded bar to search for Alys. She could see the journalist's sports car parked by the fence, but she didn't want any more to drink, and she couldn't face going over to Matty's caravan and interrupting them. In fact, she didn't really want to find Alys. She didn't want any company. All she wanted to do was to go home. And so, she started walking.

Although she was already limping, and maybe crying a little, she carried on walking out onto the lane over the bridge. It was about five miles to Stroud, so, realistically, she couldn't walk home. At some point she would have to order a cab or cadge a lift, but she just hadn't reached that point yet. She planned to text Alys — and Teddy — to say she was safe. But, for now, she wanted to be on her own.

She passed the backs of the cottages, the end ones in darkness, and kept on down the lane. Matty's caravan was at the far end of the cottages, and from where she was, Jo couldn't see if there were lights on, but she was sure she was right about Alys's whereabouts. Hadn't she more or less told Jo that was where she was going?

She didn't think about anything much as she walked. Occasionally, her mind drifted back to her case: she wondered why Sarah and Gary had not yet been released as DS Watts had indicated they would be; she puzzled about the death threat, but was not as worried about it as Teddy had been. She was pretty confident it would turn out to be a local crackpot, who had been following the story in Alys's paper. Neither of these things troubled her very much, and she didn't want to think about Teddy — nor even Macy — so she focused simply on putting one sore leg in front of the other in the direction of home.

Maybe it was the alcohol wearing off, or maybe her injuries made the going too difficult, but, after about twenty minutes or so, she began to consider calling a cab. The logistics of this occupied her for the next few minutes. She decided that she would get a taxi to meet her in ten minutes at the Co-op, which lay at the junction with the main road to Stroud.

As she brought the phone to her ear to make the call, the light on the screen reflected another flicker of blue-white at the side of the road. It seemed high up and tucked into a hedge, and at first, she thought it was some litter, caught up in the scrubby trees beside the lane. Then she caught some movement, a pale blueish light bobbing up against something white and flat. She caught her breath as she realized it was the side of a face. She stepped abruptly back into the shadows, although her steady tramping down the lane would surely have been both seen and heard by anyone nearby.

She peered through the leaves, twigs spiking her face. Her breath came quick and shallow in her chest while she forced the rest of her to be still. Shifting only her gaze, trying to get a fix on the pale light through the thick hedgerow, she could see the small white triangle she'd glimpsed, resolve itself into a man's face. A man, who was talking into a phone. Because he was clearly absorbed, she began to hope he hadn't noticed her. His muttered words were so low, she couldn't make them out, but it was clear from his gestures that a rapid dialogue was going on. Straining her eyes, she gradually realized that the man was standing in a layby with a shoulder hunched away from her, the phone nestled by his ear. He was a slim shape with a strong build. She couldn't see a vehicle.

Maybe this was someone calling a cab, she reasoned, just as she had been about to do. Or making some other innocent call. And yet the hidden location, the low, muttering voice and something covert about his stance had all Jo's warning senses on alert. A minute or two extended into more minutes and she still didn't dare move. She knew that, logically, she had just as much of a right to be on this lane at half past ten at night as he had, but she was fundamentally too scared to move.

He finished his call and stepped back into the shadows, but Jo could still just make out his shape. She was beginning to wonder if she could retreat up the lane and hurry back to the pub, maybe even reclaim her lift with Alys. Or if she could get a fix on the courage to brazen it out by walking past with a loud step, pretending she'd not seen him.

Swooping up the lane towards her were headlights, flicking first through a fence onto the field opposite as the car rounded a bend, then the beam lit up the tarmac of the lane. She pressed herself even further back as the car drew to a halt at the layby just in front of her, engine running. The man in the shadows ran forward to the driver's window. There was a very brief exchange, first of words, then a small dark package was passed through the window. Jo saw the phone light glint on something shiny like black plastic. Something was handed over, a white hand glimpsed briefly, and then the car drew off swiftly, passing Jo. But in that single moment, when the man with the phone had been forced to come out of hiding, she had recognized Matty Sullivan.

The car swept past her — a BMW M3 in black with a 2020 numberplate. She memorized it but still didn't move. She waited maybe ten minutes, but saw no further sign of Matty and no other movements from the layby. She guessed he must have moved back when the car passed her. But had he seen her?

Maybe there was a path down the back of these woods which led to the caravan, she wondered, as she craned her neck around in the dark. She could hear her heart beating as she agonized over whether — and when — to move. Eventually, she had to emerge, still uncertain, halting at every sound and scrabbling through the spikey hedge, until she stood on the lane again. This time, though, she turned back to the pub. It would be closing soon, but at least she could call a cab from there. She had walked for maybe half a mile up the hill when another car engine and headlights swept towards her. She recognized the sporty shape and knew it was Alys. The driver couldn't fail to pick her out in the headlights and came to a halt.

'Jo, I've been worried to death about you,' she shouted, leaning across to the open passenger window. 'Where did you get to? Get in, for heaven's sake. Are you OK?'

Jo clambered in. Alys switched on the interior light and glanced across as she drove down the hill. 'You look shit.'

'Thanks.'

'Did something happen with Teddy? I looked everywhere for you.'

'Well, yes and no. Look, I don't want to go into it now. Thanks for the lift and everything, but I really just want to go home.'

'Sure,' Alys said. 'It's a bit late to go to the police station anyway. I'd already given up on that idea. Can't see what difference it will make if we go in the morning. Or I may even just call them from work.'

Jo did not feel up to any sort of conversation, but Alys wasn't the type who was comfortable with long silences. She began to talk about Irene's death and how they were covering it in the paper. 'Irene fell from the tower at their manor house, did you know? I've seen some archive pictures of the tower; it's like an ancient stone folly stuck onto the corner of the house. Her husband used it as an observatory, apparently, but God knows what she was doing up there.'

Jo didn't want to admit she'd been present at the scene, so she murmured something neutral. Alys continued to speculate aloud as she drove down the deserted high street. 'It looks like accidental death as the most likely verdict, but obviously there is all sorts of speculation, because it happened so soon after her sister's murder,' she said. 'There is even the possibility of suicide — especially if she had a guilty conscience. What do you think?'

Jo shook her head tiredly. 'At least Diane Watts is leading on it, so she is bound to make all those connections with her sister's death.' As the little car turned left into King Street, Jo realized she was running out of time for the one pressing question she knew she had to ask — although part of her was dreading the answer. 'Alys, can I ask you something?'

'Go on,' the journalist said, although her tone was noticeably more wary.

'Did you see Matty tonight?'

Alys made a point of staring out at the darkened shop fronts and pulled up on the street directly outside the bank. 'This is where you live, isn't it?'

'Yes, thank you. I'm really grateful, honestly. I just want to go to bed and sleep for a week,' Jo said. She held her hand on the passenger door. 'So, you didn't say — did you see Matty after you left me and Teddy?'

Alys nodded. 'Yes, briefly. Why?'

Jo looked across at her. 'I thought I saw him, that's all. On the lane. About five minutes before you drove up.'

Alys shook her head resolutely. 'No, absolutely not. You couldn't have. He was in his caravan. I can swear to it.'

'I'm sure it was him,' Jo said, her heart sinking further with each word. 'When did you leave him?'

Alys's laugh chimed harshly in the dark car. 'What is this? A late-night interrogation? I was with him in the caravan, having a cup of tea if you must know, until five or ten minutes before I left the pub and picked you up.'

'OK, that's good,' Jo said, trying to sound cheerful. 'Thanks for telling me.' *A lie*, she added to herself, as she made her way slowly back towards her flat.

CHAPTER NINETEEN

Jo's phone rang out, loud in the dead of the night. She reached out a clumsy hand, which knocked it onto the floor beside the bed. Still with her eyes half-closed, she felt about until her fingers fastened on it. The screen showed Macy's contact picture, wearing sunglasses in a bar somewhere. Her first half-awake thought was, *Good job Teddy's not here.*

'Jo, can you talk?' His low, urgent voice cut through what remained of her sleepiness. 'I'm sorry, it's two fifteen a.m.'

'What's wrong?' She sat up against the pillows.

'I've got a problem.' His voice was wide awake but quiet. 'When I got home tonight, Adrian Carmichael's lover, Kay Denby, was camped on my doorstep.'

'Your doorstep?' Jo brushed her hair out of her eyes and felt the grittiness of last night's mascara. 'How the hell did she find you?'

'Fuck knows. Apparently, she turned up at the office today, giving another name. Rowanna gave her short shrift, of course, and they would never give out my address, but she warned me that a female had called in, looking for me. I never thought for one minute that it was Kay.'

Jo was fully awake now. 'She knows you know the Angry Cherub is not dead.'

'Yes. So, this changes everything,' Macy said. She could hear him pacing up and down. 'I will have to go to the police now and tell them what I know.'

'What did you say to her?'

'I lied, of course. I said I didn't know anything — and, God, I wish I didn't,' he groaned. 'I wish Carmichael had never involved me in this. I didn't like lying to her, and she didn't believe me.'

'She obviously suspects he is not dead, or she would not have come to you at all. That means Carmichael must have discussed his plans with her.' Jo spoke her thoughts aloud to the familiar shadows in her bedroom. 'So, that's why you've got to go to the police.'

'Exactly. And, yes, he must have told Kay he had confided in me,' he said. 'I've only just managed to persuade her to get back into her car. She was begging me to tell her where he is.'

'But you don't know where he is, do you?'

He repeated that he didn't, and she believed him. There was a shared silence on the phone, and then Jo went on, 'He obviously lied to you, so you don't know who else he has told, and if anyone goes to the police—' She broke off as other scenarios presented themselves. 'Or, worse, if *she* goes to the police, you will lose your license, at the very least.'

'What with Carmichael's disappearing act and this bloody court case, I may as well give up my job anyway,' he said bitterly. 'Why not just stick my mug on Facebook as your friendly PI?'

'That would be OK. No one looks at Facebook anymore,' Jo responded, and he laughed briefly. 'Where are you?' she asked impulsively.

'What do you mean? I'm at home, of course. I just said.'

'Yes, but where is that? This Kay Denby might be able to trace you, but I haven't a clue.'

'Don't you?' He sounded surprised. 'I still live in Coventry — on the outskirts these days.'

'On your own?'

'Of course I'm on my own. I'm calling you in the middle of the night, aren't I? Why?'

Jo shook her head at herself in the dark. 'Sorry, I don't know why I asked.'

'And I'm sorry to call at this hour,' he said, more gently. 'It's just that you're the only person I can talk to. Look, I'll go to the police station first thing. If I tell the local lot, I've got a chance of explaining myself.'

'I'm going to the police tomorrow, too,' Jo said. She explained about the threat on her phone.

'A death threat is a badge of honour, of sorts, I suppose,' he said.

Jo felt slightly disappointed with this response. 'Why? Have you had them?'

'Numberless times,' he said. 'But right now, I'm going to bed. I suggest you check your doors are well and truly locked, and I'll call you in the morning.'

* * *

Jo and Macy kept their local police forces busy the next morning. Jo returned to the police station in Stroud to be greeted by DC Dom Williams, who asked her if she wanted her loyalty card stamped. She dutifully reported the message on her phone, and learned that Alys had already phoned hers in. Although, according to DC Williams, she was not going to get off that lightly.

'We still need to see her, so she is due in later,' he explained, then held out his palm. 'We will also need your phone, please. It shouldn't take long. You can hopefully pick it up this evening, but obviously we need to try to trace the sender.' Jo handed it over reluctantly. She signed a form, which seemed to offer her no reassurance at all that her data would be safe, but it seemed she had little choice.

She tried to find out more about the inquiry on Irene Ellerman, but DC Williams would only confirm that it was being treated as 'suspicious', and Diane Watts didn't seem to be around. Before she left the station, however, she did at least manage to establish that Sarah and Gary had been released without charge and were back at the pub. She decided to go and see them that evening, by which time, she hoped to have more concrete news for them.

* * *

After a sleepless night, Macy drove to Coventry station to report what he knew about Adrian Carmichael's disappearance. At least he could talk to officers he'd worked with for years, and he had to hope that would stand in his favour. On his way, he called into Kay Denby's office to tell her what he was about to do.

She worked for a mobile phone company with a highly conspicuous building in the centre of the city. Even the furniture inside was brightly coloured, Macy discovered, as he waited for her on a tangerine sofa in what was meant to be a soundproof booth with deep purple walls. When she arrived, although well-dressed and possessing a certain gravitas, he could see she was as sleep deprived as he was, despite a good covering of make-up.

'I knew you knew,' she said to him as she sat down, not bothering with any pleasantries. 'Just tell me where he is.'

'I genuinely don't know.' Macy folded his hands on the table and looked at her levelly. 'Look, I should probably have said all this last night, but I needed time to think. I never asked to be the recipient of Adrian's plans. He chose me because he wanted my help, which I wasn't prepared to give. Consequently, I had no idea when he was going to disappear and I don't know where he is. But I did promise him discretion. Until now, that is,' he said. 'Now I know you are involved, too, I have to go to the police — so that's what I'm doing next.'

'I'm not involved,' the handsome woman assured him. 'Really, it was just a guess, coming to you. I was desperate — I thought he might be dead — and I was certain he'd confided in you.'

184

Macy shook his head sadly. 'Wrong on both counts, I'm afraid. If you really thought he was dead, you wouldn't be looking for him. And actually, he didn't normally confide in me about personal things — we just talked business. He only told me this because he thought I could help, but . . .' He sighed and shook his head. 'If he has told even one other person, the risk for me is too great, so I just wanted you to be prepared. I don't need to mention anything about you, but that doesn't mean the police won't find out at some point. Then they will want to talk to you, no doubt.'

'I promise you, I really didn't know.' Kay Denby's face was strained with desperate calm. 'I just guessed, because Adrian and I often had fantasy chats about how we could be together. And when he disappeared, I just felt he wasn't dead. That's why I pursued you. I knew he trusted you and I thought you would have the answer. And, I was right, you do.' A long moment passed while she stared into his implacable brown eyes, and then she moved away from him slightly, grey-faced against the orange sofa. 'I really didn't think he would do it,' she said sorrowfully, eyes now downcast. 'And then not to tell me — or his wife. She will be bereft, too. Why did he suddenly decide, do you know?'

Macy lifted heavy shoulders. 'Maybe you're right, it was a sort of fantasy with him, which he'd probably been planning for years. But a man like Carmichael is not just a dreamer. He can make things happen. You would know that about him.' Across the table, she nodded silently, her eyes fixed on his. 'At first, I had some sympathy with him,' Macy admitted. 'Although I was very clear that I couldn't help him, I understand that everyone wants to break out some time, don't they?'

Kay Denby shook her well-groomed head, eyes clouded. 'Maybe. But to go through with it is unbelievably cruel and selfish, isn't it?'

Macy didn't answer, but after a minute or two, he said, 'If it helps, I am sure he wanted you to join him, but he didn't want to implicate you. He was waiting to see if he could get away with it. Then, maybe, after a few months, he was going to contact you. Possibly through me, I don't know.'

'And assume I would give up everything here.' She raised her ringed fingers lightly from the table to indicate the building around them, the wider world outside the windows. 'My friends, my family, my profession. No, that would never work. And yes, he used you unfairly, too.'

'Well, it will certainly never work if I do what I intend to do next,' Macy said, and gave her time to take this in.

She nodded slowly. 'I do see,' she said, as a tide of feelings washed behind the mask of make-up. 'It is like a death now, isn't it?'

They continued to sit in silence, and then she asked, surprising him, 'What will happen to you?'

'Me? I hope I will get off with a severe rap over the knuckles as I have come clean — admittedly with a small delay. And it is not as if I could have stopped him or prevented the rescue attempts. I found out that he'd gone missing in the news bulletins, like everyone else.' He met her grey eyes. 'So, that's me, hopefully. What about you?'

She pushed herself back from the table. 'I am going to give myself the rest of the day off and allow myself to start to grieve.' She stood up and held out her hand. 'After that, no doubt I will recover as we all do — given time. Thank you for preparing me. You're a gentleman.'

'Not many people say that,' he said wryly, shaking hands. He wished her well and took a little heart from that meeting with Kay Denby, which he needed to sustain him during a gruelling four hours at Coventry Police HQ.

* * *

Meanwhile, Jo was on her way to the manor house at Stokesly. She was driving very carefully and well within the speed limit. Although she told herself she had no regrets, she felt so bruised and tender after the conversation with Teddy last night that she felt the need to take things slowly. 'That

186

was a break-up,' she said out loud as she drove along the A38. 'Teddy and I have broken up.'

Being without her phone also made her feel strangely vulnerable. She had not called Duncan Ellerman before she left home, so she knew she was taking a chance he might not be at the manor house. Although her initial plan had been to visit him at his workshop in Great Yelding, she concluded that the likelihood of Lucia Hewitt still being there was remote, so she trusted her instincts. In addition, the manor house was closer, and driving wasn't easy with two bruised legs.

She made her approach slowly, driving past once to assess who was around. There was a police car stationed at one end of the driveway, tucked in against the gate. Jo rehearsed her story as she drove up. However, the police officer on the gate immediately recognized her. 'You're Jo Hughes,' she said, leaning cheerfully in through the car window. 'You were with Diane Watts yesterday. I was the one moving vehicles about,' she added. 'What do you want?'

'I remember.' Jo smiled back. 'DS Watts said she would be in touch but she hasn't called. Is she at the scene?' She pointed hopefully up the driveway.

'She's pretty busy, you know. I'm sure she'll call you when she's ready. There's no need to go following her about. Anyway, she's not here,' the PC said. 'It's just me on duty here, plus a colleague at the house.'

'No, I'm actually here to see Howard Ellerman-James. My friend left a crystal when we visited Irene Ellerman and her brother here the other day. It's not valuable — only sentimental value anyway — but I said I would pick it up for her.'

'Does DS Watts know about your visit?' The officer looked doubtful.

'Well, no, but she knows all about my involvement. She was the one who asked me to come here yesterday,' Jo said reasonably. 'We have an agreement.'

The PC nodded. 'OK, ten minutes only. I'm entering you on the visitors' log list and letting Diane Watts know.'

'No problem,' Jo said cheerily, and hoped she was right. At the end of the drive, as the PC had said, there was another uniformed officer stationed by the tower. He was clearly expecting to see her and nodded towards the substantial front door. She tried to chat to him while she waited on the doorstep in the patchy sunshine, but he was less trusting than his friendly colleague. 'Ten minutes only,' he said darkly.

Eventually, Duncan Ellerman's thin, drawn figure appeared at the door. He seemed unsurprised to see her, but then, she realized, given the shocks he had experienced, it was likely that nothing seemed odd to him anymore. 'Irene is not here, I'm afraid,' he said, his eyes focusing somewhere beyond her face. 'There has been a horrible accident, and I'm afraid to tell you—'

Jo stopped him. 'It's OK, I know, and I'm very sorry about what's happened to Irene. You probably didn't see me, but I was here with the police when they arrived yesterday.'

'You were? Why?' He stared at her, a grain of hostility running through his vague, distressed features.

'Because they asked me to. My name is Jo Hughes, and I'm a private investigator. We met the other day, when your sister asked my friend Hanni and I to come and talk to you about Leah.' She didn't want to say more with the police officer in earshot. She persisted quietly, 'Do you mind if I come in briefly?'

He opened the door with minimal energy and drifted ahead of her into a large and shabby sitting room to the right of the front door. From her quick glance around the hallway and rooms off it, he seemed to be in the house alone. 'Howard's upstairs,' he said, as if reading her mind. 'Unfortunately, he's refusing to get out of bed. It's one of the reasons I'm still here.' He flopped down on one of the sofas, which looked like it had been squashed and moulted on by many dogs and humans over the years. 'And it makes it easier for the police to reach me. Sergeant Watts said she would be back later. I will be sure to tell her about your visit,' he added.

'Yes, of course. I won't take long,' she said. 'The thing is, I'm still trying to find out what happened to Leah, and there's a question I've been wanting to ask you. Is that OK?'

'I suppose so.' Duncan Ellerman leaned over his knees with his hands clasped and his face pointed at Jo. 'But don't expect me to know anything. No one ever tells me anything in this family. I didn't even know that Irene had asked the builder to carry on with renovating the cottages until he turned up here yesterday. He was talking to me as if he expected me to oversee the plans.' He gave a hollow laugh. 'Of course, I soon disabused him of that idea. I've no interest in the renovations, I'm afraid.'

'This is not about the building work or the family — at least, I don't think it is,' Jo said, taking a seat on the other sofa and sinking uncomfortably low. 'It's about Lucia Hewitt. You know her, don't you? She was the holiday tenant in the canal cottages. Leah's first, in fact. Lucia told me she was on a self-imposed retreat from her job in London and knew nothing about Leah. Well, that might have been true, but the day she left, I am pretty sure she caught a cab to your workshop, not to the station.'

Duncan pushed his long fingers into his eyes and sat back against the sofa. 'Sergeant Watts asked me about Lucia.'

'What did you tell her?'

'It really isn't any of your business, you know.'

Jo waited as patiently as she could, knowing that the police officers outside would be keeping time. Eventually, he shook his head, his eyes hooded. 'I told her I didn't know Lucia. And that's because I didn't want them to go chasing off to London to interview her, dragging her into all the sordid family issues. She is a completely innocent person, a friend of mine. Not even a friend,' he corrected himself with a groan. 'Merely a colleague. And now I've embroiled poor Lucia in a murder inquiry, and, well, Christ knows what else.'

'Look, I don't tell Diane Watts everything,' Jo said. 'I've promised I'll tell her only if I discover something that will help them find Leah's murderer. And if Lucia Hewitt is innocent, I don't need to say anything. How do you know her?'

Duncan Ellerman lay back on the sofa, staring at the grubby chandelier suspended from the ceiling. 'Through my business. Lucia is a buyer for a department store and she bought some of my furniture. She placed a regular order, so we used to meet up in town now and again.' He glanced up at Jo briefly. 'It is just a work-based friendship, you understand, nothing more than that. I'm gay,' he added, 'and I'm telling you that because I don't want you leaping to conclusions about Lucia and I.'

'OK, I won't, but are you saying that your friend Lucia just happened to be staying here when your sister was murdered?'

He groaned. 'This is why I didn't want to tell the police. I knew they would pursue Lucia, and she is just an innocent victim in all this mess.'

'And you want to protect her?' Jo said, feeling her way through the labyrinth of Duncan's story.

'Of course,' he said. 'And to protect myself, too. The police would have no respect for this, but Lucia is an excellent customer. I can't afford to lose her and if I'd had any idea she'd be a witness—' He broke off, covering his face again. 'I can't believe I've been so stupid as to get her caught up in the family madness.'

Jo waited for a second while the obvious question hung in the air, and then she said, 'Why? What have you done?'

Duncan Ellerman hauled himself to a seated position, his expression defeated. 'All my life, my sisters were always trying to get me to take sides. I generally managed to stay out of their feuds, but lately, Irene was getting increasingly paranoid. She was convinced Leah was trying to get one over on her, trying to do us out of our inheritance.'

But you've already had your inheritance, Jo wanted to say, but decided on silence. It paid dividends, because Duncan went on, 'When Leah started to let the cottages as holiday homes, Irene asked me to find a tenant who could be a sort of spy in the camp. She suspected that Leah was going out with this builder chap, Sullivan, and she was sure he was bad news.'

'She might not have been wrong there,' Jo said, as the clandestine scene in the lane came back to her. 'What was she afraid of?'

He pulled a cynical face. 'Oh, it wasn't about Leah's well-being, if that's what you mean. She was afraid Leah would get married and therefore swindle her out of her inheritance — the rest of the estate, which Irene saw as rightly ours.' He turned a tired, defeated face to Jo. 'You can see why I kept out of it.'

'But you obviously suggested Lucia as a tenant,' Jo pointed out.

'Against my better judgement. I knew it was a mistake, but Irene could be very persistent, plus Lucia was genuinely looking for somewhere to have a little break. Once I'd suggested it, Irene wanted to know all the details, what the cottage was like and what Leah was up to.'

'Why didn't she just ask her sister these things?' Jo asked. She didn't have the closest relationship with her own sister, but if she really wanted to know something, Marie would tell her.

'They didn't really speak. You see, we Ellermans really are a sad bunch of misfits,' he sighed, meeting her eyes with a jaded, self-pitying look. 'And, of course, I didn't want to admit any of this to Lucia, so I was telling lies to her, playing stupid games to get information out of her. Then, when Leah died, of course I understood perfectly that Lucia would want to leave the cottage as soon as possible. So, out of common courtesy, I asked if she wanted to stay with me for a few days. Understandably, Lucia didn't need much persuading to stay quiet about her connection to us. Who would want to be connected to the Ellermans?' His last remark was flung out rhetorically to the faded room.

While Jo was wondering how much of this she believed, the door to the hallway creaked open a crack and Howard peered in, asking what was going on. The older man was in his dressing gown and slippers and looked confused and ill.

However, Jo suspected from the timing that he had been listening outside.

'Oh, go back to bed, Howard,' Duncan groaned, waving him away.

'I thought I heard shouting,' Howard said, staring from one to the other.

'I'm just leaving, don't worry,' Jo reassured him. She felt sorry for the poor man, and she guessed the PC would be banging on the door if she took much longer. In the doorway, she stopped and spoke a few words to Howard, giving her condolences and trying to sound reassuring, but she wasn't sure how much he took in. Duncan remained in an elegant slump on the old sofa. On her way back down the hall, towards the front door, she spotted a narrower panelled door with wrought-iron hinges across a corner just to the left. She'd never noticed it before, but surely it must lead to the tower?

Howard was standing watching her, half in and half out of the sitting room doorway. She gestured to him. 'Is this the tower door?' She pointed upwards. 'To your observatory?' He nodded sadly and she thanked him. She turned to the heavy front door and let herself out, feeling something of the same relief Hanni had described when they had driven off in the truck together. The house and the family made her shudder. But at least she had established how Irene had probably accessed the tower, on her way to an accident which proved fatal. Or maybe followed by her murderer?

Jo paused and thanked the PC on the gate. She opened her palm and showed her the selenite crystal which Hanni had given her the night of the séance. The officer looked unimpressed. 'Very nice. I've got a message for you from Detective Sergeant Watts,' she said. 'Can you get down to the station in Stroud now? She says not to hang about. Oh, and you can collect your phone, too.'

Jo had missed her phone even more than she'd expected. She had no idea how Macy's ordeal was going, nor if her clients were re-installed at the pub. She was also sure that Hanni would be trying to reach her. This was reason itself to obey DS Watts and head straight for the police station, but her independent spirit, which resisted being ordered about, meant that she drove first to the Rivermill.

As Jo arrived near lunch time, Chloe was busy in the café, and the bookshop had a few browsing customers, but Hanni waved her over urgently. 'Thank goodness you're here,' she said. 'I called, but it went straight to voicemail.' She paused and looked hard at her friend. 'Are you all right?'

Jo sighed. There was never any point in pretending to Hanni. 'I've been better. I told Teddy last night that I'm not ready for babies just yet.'

Hanni nodded, wide-eyed. 'And?'

'Well, he is,' Jo said. 'So, that's sort of that, really.'

They were both aware of a customer approaching the counter, but Hanni reached over and gave her a quick hug. 'We must talk later, but for now, thankfully, the angels directed you here—'

'I don't know about that. The police definitely want me at the police station. What's wrong? Did you give your statement to DC Williams?'

'Oh yes, that was no problem. It's Alys—'

Hanni had to break off to serve the customer while Jo waited impatiently. As soon as Hanni was free, she turned back to Jo, her face serious. 'She's desperate to get hold of you. I met her in the car park as I was leaving, and she said to tell you she's got some information, which she can't share with the police yet. She has to check it herself first, and she wants you to go with her.'

Jo frowned. 'Why me? Why can't she go on her own? I've got Diane Watts expecting me, and I don't think she will like being kept waiting much longer. And why can't she tell the police?'

'I've no idea, Josephine.' She held out her hands helplessly as another customer came up. 'Alys just said she needed you and she would meet you at Stokes Avon Museum this afternoon as soon as you could make it. Every time I asked anything, she kept on about the confidentiality of her sources.'

'Stokes Avon is the outdoor museum where Irene Ellerman was on the board,' Jo said, although she was talking to herself, as Hanni was serving the customer. She hesitated for a minute or so longer, torn between going straight to the station or following Alys's tip-off, and then realized that delay didn't help either option. She gave Hanni a quick wave, said she'd call, and hurried back to her car.

'Take care, Josephine,' her friend called after her.

CHAPTER TWENTY

How did people ever meet up before mobile phones? Jo pondered the question as she left her car on the flattened grass of the museum car park. All she had to go on was that Alys Parry would be at the museum some time this afternoon. She had never visited the place, although she knew it was a local tourist attraction. Now that she stood just inside the entrance, she realized it was a large park dotted with buildings of differing ages and with meandering paths suggesting various directions. In front of her was a wooden toll booth, beyond that, a church spire, and, in the distance to her left, she could make out the sails of a windmill.

Very aware of Diane Watts waiting for her to turn up at the police station, Jo went straight to the ticket office and spoke to the white-haired woman behind the counter. 'I'm here to meet a journalist, Alys Parry. She writes for the *Standard*,' Jo said. 'I don't suppose you've seen her, have you? Or know where she is?'

The woman blinked at her and then said, 'As a matter of fact, I have.' She retrieved some reading glasses and consulted a notepad on the counter. 'Are you Jo Hughes?' When Jo nodded, she was met with a triumphant smile. 'She left a message to say she will meet you at the windmill.' Jo thanked her and raced out before the woman could offer her directions and a map.

It was easy enough to follow the path towards the windmill sails, jogging as quickly as she could past a brightly clad couple striding out on a walk and two women in deep conversation, one pushing a pram. However, it swiftly became clear that the windmill was at the furthest end of the site, and she slowed, panting slightly. So far, the museum seemed like an idyllic spot, safe and peaceful. Each of the buildings were within easy reach of one little group of tourists or another. But this part of the site was by far the most isolated. The windmill stood alone in a field and, at the head of the path, a sign informed visitors that the mill was closed today.

Alys was not conveniently sitting waiting for her on the long flight of steps which led up the side of the windmill. Scouring the edges of the field, Jo saw no sign of her — or anyone else, either.

Jo continued in a vigilant walk, taking the solitary path across the field towards the old grain mill. She was not sure whether to feel stupid or vulnerable for following this breadcrumb trail, and for the hundredth time that day, she wished she had her phone. As she reached the bottom of the steep flight of open steps, which led to the closed mill door, she turned and surveyed the scene.

She was reluctant to give up, but neither did she have time to wait for Alys to show up. It would be useful if the woman had left a fuller message, explaining why she wanted to see her, or provided some timings, Jo thought irritably, and was equally annoyed with herself for not asking at the ticket office for more information. Then her attention was caught by something flapping near her right foot. Stuck under a stone below the lowest step, a copy of the *Standard* lay folded. She turned the paper over in her hands and on the back page, in the white space around an advertisement, Alys had written: *Jo, go through the gate and up the hill to the lane at the top. Will meet you there. AP.*

There was only one gate at the field border, which proved to be locked. Jo clambered over it and landed gracelessly on the hilly pasture outside the boundaries of the open-air museum. Glancing anxiously at her watch, Jo plodded up the hill and soon caught sight of the top of a car skimming the hedgerow, which indicated that the lane lay on the opposite side. There was, however, no sign of Alys once she reached the lane. Frustrated, Jo bawled her name a few times at the top of her voice. She was nearing the top of the lane when a pair of hands grabbed her from the thick hedgerow on the left. Instinctively, she fought back, bringing her fist across her body in a fierce right hook, and made contact with something hard beneath a halo of hair.

'Jo! Jo! It's me, don't hit me!'

'Alys! What the fuck are you playing at?' Jo stood back, panting. 'Why are you hiding in a hedge?'

'I've found it!' Alys announced, looking gleeful but unusually dishevelled, her long hair escaping from a ponytail and sticking to her face, any make-up long gone. 'I wasn't hiding,' she said. 'This leads to a track.' She jabbed at the hedge behind her and then rubbed the side of her head meaningfully. 'I heard you shouting, so I ran back down to meet you and then got clobbered for it. Thanks for that. It's so annoying you've got no phone,' she added.

'I know. This is what it must have been like in the eighties. I got your messages, though. What have you found?' She followed Alys through the thick hawthorn hedge, which opened out onto a narrow farm track. Alys didn't reply immediately, and Jo realized she was finding the climb hard. 'I'm carrying extra weight, remember,' she panted, pointing at her stomach.

'Sorry about hitting out,' Jo said guiltily. 'To be honest, I didn't know if I might be walking into some sort of trap. You know, given the threats we both got. So, I was a bit wary. And I'm meant to be at the police station, so I don't have much time.'

Alys nodded, saving her breath for the climb, and, as the track crested a hill, she pointed ahead. Stuck at an odd angle by a field gate on the downward slope was the blackened shell of a burnt-out car. There were no tyres, no discernible paint colour or number plates, and the driver's door hung on its hinge. But, as they drew closer, Jo recognized the shape — it was a Hyundai Tucson.

'Leah's car,' Jo breathed. 'How the hell did you find this?'

'One of the guys who lives on the Charwell Estate calls me sometimes with gossip — some made up, some genuine bits of news. He heard about this stolen car, which some idiot kids took on a joy ride and abandoned in a field. Because he's got nothing better to do, he strolled up and took a look at it yesterday, then he phoned me. Because he follows my reports and listens to police radio, he realized it was the missing car.'

Jo circled the car, although she was not sure what she was looking for. 'Why didn't he just tell the police?'

This gained her an eye roll from Alys. 'Just because he follows police activities doesn't mean he wants anything to do with them,' she said, and grinned at Jo. 'He likes me, though. Unfortunately, his directions were pants, so it has taken me ages to actually locate it. That's why I wanted some help. But you only turned up when the hard work was done.'

Jo accepted this with a sheepish nod. 'And I suppose you didn't want to tell the police until you were certain,' she said.

'That's the other reason I wanted you to see it,' she admitted. 'So we can both be sure. I didn't want to send Diane Watts out on a wild goose chase or they'd never listen to me again. It is Leah's, isn't it?' Alys brought out her phone and they compared photographs of the make and model of Leah Ellerman's car with the charred wreck in front of them.

'I'm no car expert, but it has got to be,' Jo said eventually. 'But what's it doing here? It looks like it's been here a while. Was it really just kids taking it for a joy ride? Don't you think it's a coincidence that it's close to the museum that Irene was involved with? She was on the board there, so she must have visited the site pretty regularly.'

'Are you suggesting that Irene drove it out here and set fire to it?' Alys stared at her. 'That would mean she killed her sister.'

'Well, no, but that family are weird,' Jo said succinctly. 'Look, I've got to get back to the police station. If only to pick up my phone. Why don't we both go, and we can tell them about your find?'

Alys agreed. 'I can't give them any details about my source, though,' she said. She took a few more photographs with her phone and they returned down the farm track at a slower pace. Alys's car was parked a little further along the lane and she offered to drive Jo back to hers. As she typed the address of Stokes Avon outdoor museum into the sat nav, Jo realized it was not far from the Charwell Estate, where Alys's source lived. She picked up the road map in the footwell and studied it on the short hop to the museum car park. The farm track where they had found the abandoned car was certainly an isolated spot, but Charwell was less than a mile away, albeit on twisty lanes. The canal cottages and the New Navigation lay only a couple of miles in the opposite direction and, as Alys sped down the lanes to the museum, she swept past the Stokes Avon Home for Elderly Residents, where Jo had visited Maureen at work.

'This place is closer to the canal cottages than I thought,' Jo said. 'God, no wonder everybody knows everybody else around here.'

'You didn't mean that about Irene Ellerman killing her own sister, did you?' Alys's tone was sceptical as they drew up in the museum car park. 'And then, what? She took her own life by throwing herself down the tower steps of the manor house?'

'I know, it sounds bizarre. But I keep coming back to the fact that she was the main beneficiary of Leah's will. Her and Duncan,' Jo said. 'Now it's just Duncan, of course.'

'Well, I'm glad I don't have to solve the thing. I only have to write about it,' Alys said blithely. 'See you at the police station for our bollocking.'

CHAPTER TWENTY-ONE

Jo was indeed anticipating a frosty reception from DS Watts, seeing as she was about three hours later than the sergeant was probably expecting to see her. However, as soon as she arrived, she could tell there was a change of atmosphere at the station. There was a subdued hum of activity behind the public counter, and she caught sight of DC Dom Williams hurrying purposefully through the office, carrying an open laptop, with a couple of plain clothes officers in tow. Alys glanced across at her. 'Something's up,' she muttered. 'My guess is they've made an arrest.'

DS Watts kept them waiting for half an hour or so, about which they could hardly complain, but Alys grew increasingly impatient and spent most of the time on her phone. Clearly, she was the sort of organized person who had two phones, Jo observed. Eventually, the detective leaned her head out of the security door and beckoned them in. 'I understand you want to see me,' she snapped. 'I haven't got long, so make it quick.'

'I thought you wanted to see me?' Jo said, genuinely puzzled, as they followed her to her office at the end of the long corridor.

'Things move on,' Diane Watts said enigmatically. 'Now, tell me what you've got to report.'

Alys launched into the discovery of the car, but before she got very far, DS Watts called in DC Williams to take down the location and other details. It was clear she intended to hurry away, so Jo halted her with a question. 'What's going on? We said we'd share information and I can see there is something happening.'

'I've noticed that sharing only cuts one way with you,' Diane Watts said, with a hard look at Jo. 'But, seeing as we will be issuing a press release in the next twenty-four hours, you may as well know. We have arrested Matty Sullivan in connection with the murders of Leah and Irene Ellerman.'

Alys sat down suddenly on one of the office chairs. 'On what evidence?'

'Traces of his DNA on Leah Ellerman's body—' DS Watts began.

'That could have come from his coat,' Alys interrupted. 'You know she was wearing his coat when she was struck.'

'And bodily fluids—'

'They were having an affair,' Alys said, her voice raw.

The detective set her jaw. 'I don't have to tell you any of this, let me remind you. And it's not for wider consumption, either.' She glared at Alys. 'You will get our press notice tomorrow.'

'But we've brought you the evidence on the car,' Alys protested, still seated. 'You can at least tell us what else you've got on Matty.'

'His van was captured on CCTV on the way to Stokes Manor on Friday morning,' the detective said grudgingly. 'It was an hour ahead of his agreed appointment with Irene, therefore, it seems likely that he arrived there early. He has no witnesses who can prove he was elsewhere.'

Alys opened her mouth to challenge this but clearly thought better of it, and the detective continued. 'While you're both here, there's something else you should know.' She turned to DC Williams. 'Dom, will you arrange for a patrol to check out the burnt-out car, please?' When he'd left the room, she reached across and closed the door firmly.

'This is about the threats you received on your phones yesterday. We traced the sender without too much difficulty.' Diane Watts remained by the doorway, arms folded, watching them both. 'It is Nora Hutchinson. We have her here now, together with her father and a social worker.'

'Oh no,' Jo groaned. 'How could she be so daft? She was probably doing it to protect Sarah — but of course, it hasn't helped at all.'

Alys turned to her, compassion making her eyes wide. 'Jo, she's only fifteen. Did you think everything through at that age?'

'No, of course not,' Jo admitted. She turned back to DS Watts. 'If it was so easy to trace her, maybe she actually wanted to be caught? So it might be more that she needs help, not policing.'

'Thank you, we have thought of that,' Diane Watts said, her tone heavy with sarcasm. 'But we still need to make sure she understands the seriousness of what she has done. I can assure you it will be done with a light touch — but it will be done properly.'

'Well, I won't be pressing any charges,' Jo said, and Alys murmured her agreement.

'Noted.' DS Watts pointedly opened her office door.

Jo hesitated. 'Can I ask what happens to my clients, Mr and Mrs Robart? Are they—?'

'They remain under suspicion,' the detective said, before Jo had finished her question. 'Look, I'm sure you realize that a great deal of precious police resources are being committed to this inquiry, and we are nearing the final stages. Not to put too fine a point on it, but I don't want either of you acting the maverick crusader and buggering it up now.' She looked pointedly at them both. 'So can I insist that you stay out of the Ellerman inquiries and keep to your own areas of expertise from now on, please?'

As she finished, she glanced down at her phone, which had buzzed while she was speaking. She waited until they had both acknowledged her request and then excused herself to take a call. 'Wait here. I will see if your phones are ready to collect,' she said, on her way out of the office.

Jo looked at Alys, who was still seated, biting the side of a fingernail.

'Do you think they know about Matty's other activities?' Jo asked. She was thinking of the scene in the layby the previous night. She had re-run the video of it in her head many times, looking for other explanations or details she might have missed, but still had to conclude one thing — it had looked very much like a drugs transaction. And Matty was the one supplying. The only question in her mind was, which drugs?

'What activities?' Alys was saying, as a reddish colour creeped up her neck. She shook her head and, as she tried to speak, tears sprang out onto her lashes. She wiped them briskly with the back of her hand. 'He told me he'd stopped. He used to deal a bit of coke, but he swore he'd stopped,' she whispered eventually. 'Don't say anything, please.'

Jo nodded. She guessed that if the police had pulled Matty in, nothing she said would make any difference anyway. They must be certain of their case. 'What will happen to Nora?' she wondered aloud. 'I hope they're not too hard on her.'

'She'll have good protection. Social workers, family, teachers, etc.,' Alys said, blowing her nose. 'And we won't report any details, obviously, because of her age.'

'So, if we stay quiet about the silly threats, who else is going to know?' Jo said. 'Apart from the officials, and we've got to assume they are there to help her.'

Alys nodded and they exchanged a look that was as resolute as a handshake.

Jo was mightily relieved to collect her phone from the front desk, but she didn't switch it on immediately. Instead, she turned to Alys, who was already scrolling through screens to find out what she'd missed. 'Thanks for contacting me about the car,' Jo said. 'And . . .' she sought the right words while Alys hovered between the glass doors, 'if you want to chat, any time, you know how to get me,' and held up her phone.

Alys smiled wanly, dark shadows around her eyes. 'I do now. And you,' she added. 'I don't really know what happened with you and Teddy, but . . . you know, same goes.'

Jo sighed. 'I suppose you could say, it ended well. As well as it could, anyway.'

She drove slowly and pensively home along the lanes. She could only assume the police had more evidence of Matty's guilt than Diane Watts had shared. Therefore, she told herself, the inquiry into the two Ellerman sisters was closed — and a quick resolution, too. No wonder DS Watts had been so keen to move on. It was over.

Jo knew she should feel a welcome sense of relief, but she didn't feel anything very much at all, except tired. She wished she could be a fly on the wall in the police interviews with Matty. There were so many directions they could take. How much did they know about his drug activities on the side? She wondered how seriously they were connecting him with Irene's death. Seeing his van on a CCTV did not seem like sufficient evidence to her. She could imagine that someone like Matty could explain that away easily.

At a red stop light, she stretched out her sore left leg and massaged it. On a purely personal note, she would like to get Matty in an interview room and drill him on what exactly happened to cause her to nearly fall into the canal. She still wasn't sure if he really had rescued her or if he had been the one to push the tile truck down the path.

This was just one of many issues still unresolved. She wished she could feel, as DS Watts assuredly did, that it was all cut and dried, but there were too many worries passing through her mind. It hadn't escaped her that the detective had also insisted that her clients were not out of the woods yet.

Therefore, instead of going home to an early dinner and bed, she found herself parking once again in the New Navigation car park. She limped over to stare across the low fence at the rough gravelled area behind it, and tried to imagine Leah's car being driven away by joy riders. Given that the car park wasn't visible from the lane and was reached by a short, steep track, Jo found it a stretch for her imagination. She noticed that the police tape had been removed and a cluster of cars were now parked against the fence of the pub and path leading to the beer garden. She recognized Matty's white transit van, and guessed that the three-year-old people mover belonged to Gil Hutchinson, and the red VW Polo to the Lilleys. Now she knew where to look, she could make out the two CCTV cameras on the beer garden lights, directed towards the pub, therefore leaving the private parking dark and unmonitored. The police would have trawled through this data for the relevant dates, she knew, so she gave a sigh and turned towards the lighted windows of the pub.

'What are you drinking?' Gary Robart demanded cheerfully, as soon as he caught sight of her. 'Sarah and I are celebrating our narrow escape.' His ruddy face beamed at her across the bar.

'I'll settle for a coffee, thanks,' Jo was saying, when Sarah shot across the busy pub to give her a hug. She smelt of cigarette smoke and red wine.

'Rubbish, not tonight,' she insisted. 'Go on, tell us your favourite tipple. Tonight, we must have our moment of celebration. After all, who knows what's round the corner? Honestly, Jo, Gary and I never thought we'd get back behind the bar when the detective sergeant carted us off this morning. When I called you, I was pretty desperate. I had us spending the night behind bars, to be honest. But you were so calm and gave us good advice — as you have all along.'

'Really, a coffee is all I want,' Jo insisted, as Sarah pulled her along the corridor and outside to their private picnic table behind the pub, where her own glass and a sneaky piled ashtray waited.

'Then that's what you shall have. Do you know, Jo, I am beginning to think we might just get through this,' Sarah said, her mercurial face suddenly serious. 'And if we do, it's partly due to you. I said at the start that we reward our friends, and I have a juicy little titbit for you. But you must tell us what's happening with Matty and Nora. Wait there while I get your coffee.'

It was another still, warm night. Jo sank down on the hard bench. She wanted to warn Sarah that they may be celebrating too early, but she recognized that the woman knew it.

From where she was sitting, she had an angled view of the beer garden, with a good sprinkling of customers. Clearly in her line of sight was the table by the canal where she and Teddy had sat the previous night, now unoccupied. She didn't want to think about their last evening together, so she shifted around and found she could make out the three canal-side residents' cars parked against the fence. Bright round bulbs strung from posts threw yellowish light on the path beside the pub and across the garden, but the covered lean-to woodshed and the door to the back room were in deep shadow. She shuddered suddenly at the thought of Leah's body being unceremoniously hidden in the cellar that lay directly beneath her feet.

'Are you cold, sweetie?' Sarah's voice cut through the dark behind her. 'I can get you one of the furry blankets if you need it. Here you are, Gary's best coffee brew!' She placed the cup in front of Jo, then plumped down on the bench opposite, lit a cigarette and launched into an account of their travails at the police station. They had been questioned in depth about the so-called paranormal evenings and about Gary's altercation with Leah. Sarah said it had been provoked by Leah, who had launched into a loud complaint in the crowded bar.

'Gary made an empty threat,' Sarah said. 'He wouldn't harm anybody, but he was an idiot to have said it. Thankfully, I think DS Watts began to see it our way — or they wouldn't have let us go. And hopefully, they have seen sense about Nora, too, as I saw her and her dad return home tonight. She can be thoughtless and impulsive, but she has a good heart.'

Jo listened, sipped her coffee, and answered questions about Matty as best she could. Sarah paid avid attention, cigarette and wine abandoned, as Jo explained he was arrested on suspicion of the murder of both sisters. She said nothing about his supplying drugs.

'Irene too,' Sarah breathed, shaking her head. 'Do you think that's it then? That it was a lover's quarrel that got out of hand?' Sarah's expressive eyes rested on Leah's house across the canal. She spoke softly, now seemingly fully sober. 'Leah was wearing Matty's coat, wasn't she? It was raining, so, perhaps she was staying in his caravan, as we know she did regularly, and pulled it on as she left. Maybe they'd had a row, but she still had to go to work.' Sarah paused, took a considered sip of wine and went on with a little nod, 'Then Leah took the path behind her house and over the bridge to her car, as she always did when she was travelling to London.' With her eyes, she traced the woman's journey to the car park just across the fence. 'But on this rainy morning, Matty must have followed her. Maybe they were still arguing,' she mused aloud. 'Or maybe he was quietly raging. He could have picked up any one of his tools and carried it with him. Whatever they rowed about, it made him so livid that he beat her to death.'

Sarah came to a sudden halt and a strange silence fell between the two women, then Sarah shivered. 'That's what he must be telling the police right now,' she said, then, shooting Jo an almost pleading look, added, 'Don't you think? It must be almost over now?'

'Almost over, yes,' Jo said quietly.

'Sorry.' Sarah gave a half-embarrassed laugh. 'That was me allowing my dramatic self to take over. It's my gift, I suppose. Sometimes I can be so scarily accurate, I frighten myself as well as everyone else. I hope I didn't alarm you?'

'No, just gave me something to think about,' Jo said.

'I expect your coffee's gone cold. Can I get you another?'

Jo thanked her but said she was going home. As she stood up, she gestured around her. 'Say it did happen in the morning, like you said, it would have been nearly dawn, if she was going to drive to the station to catch an early London train. Would these lights have been on?'

'Not the garden lights,' Sarah said. 'Just those two security lights.' She indicated the stanchions with the CCTV cameras. The square white lights, like the cameras, were directed at the pub garden, intensifying the shadows where Leah's car would have been parked. Jo walked to the edge of the path, which was in the deep shade provided by the hulk of the old building. The narrow door to the pub's back room, where they had sat for Sarah's séance, the trapdoor to the cellar and the lean-to woodshed lay behind her, also in darkness.

'Thanks, that's what I thought,' she said. 'And everyone around here would know your security arrangements, wouldn't they?'

'Such as they are,' Sarah said drily. 'That is something we are going to have to improve, for sure.' She linked arms with Jo in the dark as they walked alongside the pub, and gave her elbow a squeeze. 'But now it is looking as if Gary and I will be given another chance. When this is really over, you must come down one night for a proper celebration,' she insisted.

Jo made a non-committal response and was about to wave goodbye when she remembered something. 'You said you had some information for me?'

'So I did.' Sarah looked pleased with herself. 'It's actually more of a message. Maureen was here this morning before the police arrived. She cleans for us on Saturdays but not Sundays — that's her day off. Anyway, when you called to see her at the old people's home, she said you were interested in her other job with the Ellermans. It was something to do with that, she said, and could you give her a call. I can give you her number, if you like?'

Keen to finally make her escape, Jo assured her she would contact Maureen tomorrow. The prospect of a supper on the sofa, followed by an early night, was finally looking possible, and she hurried towards her car. Turning to give her client a quick, final wave, she saw the woman's face had turned anxious. Sarah cupped her hands around her mouth. 'She did say it was urgent,' she called.

CHAPTER TWENTY-TWO

By the time Jo was turning the key in the door of her flat, her mind had turned from murders towards the unavoidable fact that it was Saturday night, and normally she would be with Teddy. Of course, she didn't want to be with him right now, she reminded herself. She felt exhausted and grimy, and wanted to rest her sore leg, eat something comforting and go to bed early. Seeing Teddy was the very last thing she wanted, in fact. All the same, it was Saturday and usually they went to the movies or their favourite bistro. Or, more recently, the Tulip Lounge, where there were live bands and sometimes dancing.

'Dancing is out of the question anyway, Halifax,' she said to the cat, who bestirred himself to give her a cursory greeting. The other elements of her chosen Saturday night — dinner, sofa, TV and bed — were, however, all within easy reach. While she was heating some soup, she checked her phone and discovered missed calls from Macy and one from Maureen, with no message. There was nothing from Teddy. But then, she hadn't expected anything. It was past 8 p.m., so she decided not to phone Maureen back, despite Sarah's shouted plea. She reminded herself that she was leaving the Ellerman murders in the hands of the police, but, out of courtesy, she would call Maureen in the morning. She wanted no more phone calls tonight.

Apart from Macy, of course. He was the exception. She had been wondering all day how he had fared in confessing all he knew about Adrian Carmichael to the Coventry police. His messages gave nothing away, but that was to be expected of Macy. She turned the hob down low, poured herself a glass of wine and dialled his number. As the phone rang out, she realized she'd assumed he would emerge unscathed but, remembering his worried call at 2 a.m., she began to feel more doubtful. When he eventually picked up, his voice was muted. 'I can't really talk just now.'

'That's OK. I just wondered how it went with the police today?' There was a hushed background noise, which Jo struggled to identify. It didn't sound like a police station, she decided. 'Is everything all right?'

'Yes. I won't say it was easy, but at least I still have my licence.' Among the soft sounds behind him, Jo detected the unmistakable chime of cutlery and the clink of a glass. 'Look, I'll call you tomorrow,' he said.

She decided it was beneath her to wonder who he was celebrating his liberty with — although it was almost certainly Rowanna. The pan of soup on the hob no longer looked appealing, but a woman has to eat — and rest. So she poured it into a bowl, ate in front of the TV and tried not to recall previous Saturday nights with Teddy.

The following morning, in tune with Jo's mood, the fine weather finally broke. It wasn't the same downpour that had caused the recent floods, rather an overcast, steady drizzle, and she had overlooked the fact that building sites get muddy when it rains. Her sandals were not the best footwear for picking her way through the builder's rubble behind Leah's house that afternoon. Skirting a large puddle in the space where the new bi-fold doors would eventually open onto, she questioned herself for agreeing to return to the canal cottages to meet Maureen.

Her phone call that morning seemed to have caught Maureen by surprise. 'I'm afraid I'm on my way to church,' she'd explained, when Jo had reminded her about the message she'd left with Sarah. 'And my daughter, Charlotte, is home from university, so of course I'm cooking her a Sunday roast later. She'd never let me get away with less.'

'That's all right,' Jo said, somewhat relieved. She certainly didn't object to a lazy Sunday after the events of the last week. 'I just wanted to make sure it was nothing important. If it's regarding the case, then you'll probably know it's all in the hands of the police now anyway.'

But, once Maureen had been reminded, she was not to be easily deterred and soon came up with a plan. She explained that she had promised to check on Leah's house to ensure that Matty's workers had left the place in good order. 'I know you probably think it a bit odd in the circumstances, but Irene asked me to keep an eye on it and so I will,' she'd said.

Jo had agreed to meet her at Leah's house at 4 p.m., but ended the call no wiser as to what the rendezvous was about.

Jo had already circled the house and rung the front doorbell to no avail. Trying to shelter under the new guttering in the fine, soaking rain, she folded her arms and kept one eye on her watch, having decided to give Maureen five minutes to turn up. That morning, she had been more than happy to leave the Ellerman case to the police and, instead of brooding about Teddy or Macy, had found solace in her astrology work. Her mind had already drifted back to her planned newsletter on the planetary positions at the summer solstice when Maureen appeared around the corner, holding a bunch of keys.

The older woman was suitably equipped with wellies and a raincoat. She apologized earnestly to Jo, saying that she'd had to drop her daughter at the station, and she quickly unlocked the doors.

'I'm not sure what this is about,' Jo said, as she tramped across the heavy-duty plastic covering the floor of the new extension, following the other woman's efficient progress.

As they crossed the threshold from the new build into the kitchen of the existing house, Maureen automatically took off her shoes, switched on some lights and darted out to pick up the mail which was lying on the hall floor. Jo took the chance to cast her eyes around Leah's house. Having spent so many days trying to understand the dead woman, she had to admit she was curious to see where she had lived. In fact, it was one of the reasons she'd agreed to meet Maureen. The layout was different from the other canal cottages, with higher ceilings and a greater sense of space, and the kitchen was both homely and well-fitted. Jo spotted a top-of-the-range coffee machine, about which she experienced a pang of envy, and the chic, angled lighting glinted on a smart set of knives on the counter. Leah had clearly been a woman who had looked after her own home comforts, Jo concluded, and this made her feel a little sad.

'I'm so sorry you got wet waiting,' Maureen said, returning with some envelopes and flyers in her hand. 'Do you want a hot drink? There's no milk, but the electric is on, so I can make you a herbal tea?'

Jo refused politely. 'I really want to get back home soon,' she said. 'I know Sarah said you had some information for me, but really you'd be better off giving anything to the police now.'

Maureen's eyebrows shot up behind the metal frames of her glasses. 'Oh. Really? I hadn't realized that. Are you not interested any more, then?' She pulled out a heavy kitchen chair and sat down, her plain, square face dismayed. 'I'm afraid I'm a bit out of touch,' she said. 'I've been with Charlotte as much as I can all weekend. She doesn't come home very often, so I have to make the most of her.' She lowered her voice and spoke tentatively. 'Is it really Matty Sullivan, then?'

When Jo nodded, the woman rested her chin on her fists. 'It was terrible finding out about Irene. I don't think that has quite sunk in yet. It's hard to believe he could kill her too — in cold blood.'

'It seems so,' Jo said. 'Although I struggle to see a motive, personally,' she admitted, and sat down on the other chair.

Maureen's shoulders had dropped and her brown eyes clouded over. 'You can't understand people like that,' she said simply. She fished a handkerchief out of her coat pocket and blew her nose, recovering her normal no-nonsense manner. 'But how did they know it was him? Have they actually arrested him or what?'

'Yes, they took him in yesterday, arrested for both murders. As far as I know, he has been in overnight.'

'Well, he's not here.' Maureen gestured towards the window and the direction of Matty's caravan. 'That's one of the reasons I'm checking up. Without him in charge, God knows what his subbies will get up to. They're bad enough when he's here. Irene was right not to trust him. I never have,' she stated, glancing up defiantly. 'And I told you he was Leah's weakness. So, what happens next, do you know? What did the police say to you?'

'Not much. We probably just need to leave it to them now,' she said. 'So, it's not that I'm not interested, but there's no more I can do.'

Maureen nodded and got to her feet, glancing around the kitchen. 'All right, then. All seems in order here, so I'll walk out with you.'

'As a matter of interest,' Jo said, curiosity getting the better of her. 'What did you have to tell me?'

'It's more something to show you really,' Maureen said. She dug once again into the pocket of her raincoat and produced her phone. 'You were asking about the Ellermans when you came to see me at Stokes Avon, and I told you about Irene and Leah. I didn't say much about Duncan,' as she spoke, she was flicking through photographs, 'but when I got home, I remembered I had this.' She held up her phone.

Jo had to step forward to see the small screen and it took her half a minute to work out what she was looking at. The photograph was blurred and taken at night, but the fiery ginger hair of Lucia Hewitt, caught in a car headlight, was unmistakable. She was leaning back against a dark-coloured car door, her arm and the glint of her bangles clearly visible resting across a man's shoulder. The man kissing her, pinning her against the car, was distinguishable by his long, thin shape. It was Duncan Ellerman.

'He told me there was nothing between them,' Jo said. 'That they were just work colleagues. When did you take it? Is this in the lane outside?'

'Actually, Nora took it,' Maureen said. 'She was chatting about it in the pub the next morning. She acted like it was a bit of a drama. I wasn't that interested, to be honest, but she sent it to me anyway. I forgot about it until the other day, after your visit. Look at how he's gripping her. Maybe she's enjoying it, but you can't be sure.'

She held the phone near her face. Jo leaned in to get a closer look and, as she did, her own phone rang, vibrating noisily against the wooden table. It startled them both, and Maureen stepped back against the kitchen counter as Jo turned swiftly to pick it up. Macy's uninflected, level voice sounded in her ear. 'I said I'd call. Is this a good time?'

'Er, no. I'm with a . . . a friend of my client,' she said. As she watched, Maureen pocketed her phone and bustled out of the room. Jo could hear her opening and closing doors in the other downstairs rooms. 'Look, I'm leaving now. Can I call you back in ten minutes?' As she ended the call, she found her hands were shaking.

CHAPTER TWENTY-THREE

The 9.28 a.m. to Paddington on Monday morning was sparsely filled with passengers who mostly had a more leisurely day ahead of them than the commuters who had packed into the earlier trains. The man opposite Jo seemed to be struggling with the *Metro* crossword, and a woman across the aisle was trying to keep two small children amused with colouring books and various snacks. Jo herself was content to look out of the window and not think too much about the plans she had put in place for her day. Today was a day to trust her instinct, she felt.

At Paddington Station, she stepped out into the clamour of London, where there appeared to be a Tube strike, with confused crowds of people milling around the underground station. Jo didn't hesitate. It was important she wasn't late for her appointments, as she was reliant on the good will of others, so she headed straight for the taxi rank and took her place in the queue. There was a pack of tourists in front, squabbling over enormous suitcases, and three business people behind her, impatient with the queue. Jo allowed their frustrated chatter to flow over her. She felt tense with apprehension, but tried to take a leaf out of Hanni's book and closed her hand on the selenite crystal she was still carrying in her jacket pocket.

A woman hurried past with her phone to her ear, pulling a laptop bag on wheels, and with a baby in a sling clutching one of her lapels and staring around. It made her think of Alys and she wondered how she was feeling. There had been no more news about Matty. So far as they knew, he was still being held at the station. Jo decided she must give Alys a call later. Meanwhile, the baby looked at Jo, wide-eyed, and she waved back, watching the woman's determined progress through the station crowds. She could do that herself one day, she knew she could. But in her own time.

She gave an address in Victoria and sat back to enjoy the rare luxury of a black-cab ride through London. Staring out at the white-fronted town houses, the glimpses of Hyde Park, where the trees were a defiant green under the grey skies, and the comings and goings in front of the hotels on Park Lane, she felt a sudden rush of energy at being in the midst of all this urban activity. Despite what lay ahead, there was a broad smile on her face as she paid the cabbie.

She stepped out at a department store where she'd shopped a few times, usually for Christmas presents. Red stickers advertising the summer sales now filled the windows. Taking a deep breath, she pushed through the glass doors and made her way up to the offices on the top floor. The store itself seemed quiet once she was past the entrance where customers were mooching around the cosmetics counters and a kiosk selling coffee.

At the office suite, she gave her name at a reception desk and was shown to a sofa. Her stomach tensed as if she was in the dentist's waiting room as she peered down through the glass panes of the balcony to watch desultory shoppers drifting around the furniture department. She was wondering if any of the stock had originated from Duncan Ellerman's workshop when a small movement by her side caused her to glance up and she met the distracted hazel eyes of Lucia Hewitt.

'You said on the phone you wanted to meet,' Lucia said. 'To be honest, I hardly even remembered you when you rang yesterday. I know you came to the cottage on my last day, but there were so many other things going on, I don't recall much of what we talked about.'

'Astrology mostly,' Jo said with a smile. 'You were asking about sun signs, because you'd just read in the local paper that I'm an astrologer. Thank you for agreeing to talk. I know all this urgency must seem a bit weird.'

'Ye-es, it does. I hope you haven't come all this way just to see me, because I'm sure it won't be worth it.'

'I just need about ten or twenty minutes of your time,' Jo said. She lowered her voice, trying to get Lucia's attention, which seemed to be consistently elsewhere. 'A man has been arrested for Leah's murder, and I don't believe he did it. You may be able to help me set the record straight.'

'Are you bonkers?' Lucia's fair eyebrows shot up to her ginger hairline. Her voluminous hair was tied back today, but that was the only concession to a corporate look. Her blouse had a fussy little bow tied under the collar with a bright hand-knitted cardigan over the top. She glanced at the receptionist, who was conspicuously keeping her head down.

'Let's have this conversation away from here,' Lucia sighed. 'Come on, I have to buy my lunch. You can walk with me, but you'll have to talk fast because I have a meeting at twelve forty-five and I want time to eat my salad.'

'I'm trying to make sense of what happened at the canal cottages,' Jo explained, as they entered the lift together. 'My clients, who run the pub, are still under suspicion. I need to be clear in my own mind about something before I carry on working for them.'

'Those cottages,' Lucia groaned. 'People say that London is toxic, but they want to try spending a week in the middle of nowhere. Anything less like a retreat would be hard to imagine. I suppose the first week was all right, but after that, the place was swarming with police and journalists. I was sort of glad to get back,' she admitted, 'which is not what I expected.'

'Actually, it's the first week I'm interested in,' Jo said, and Lucia's expression closed up. 'I was one of those people

217

asking questions. Unfortunately, I didn't ask the right ones,' Jo went on. 'You said you didn't know Leah Ellerman.'

'That was true. I didn't know her from Adam. Or should I say Eve?' Lucia cast her eyes to the cloudy sky as they left the shop and threaded their way through the lunchtime throng.

'But you know her brother, Duncan Ellerman, don't you? And you didn't go to the station in the taxi when you left. Instead, you went to see him. I think that was because of something that happened in your first week.'

Lucia's expression became mutinous and her silence gained a purposeful edge. She swerved towards a crowded Pret and Jo followed, although any proper conversation was hopeless until Lucia had bought her salad and juice. Jo was convinced she was deliberately taking a long time choosing. When they were finally back outside, Jo pursued her question. 'Why did you go to Duncan's workshop when you left the holiday cottage? He says you're just work colleagues, but . . .'

Lucia's eyes narrowed. 'You've spoken to him?'

'Of course,' Jo said. 'He admitted you'd been to see him.' Frustratingly, she could feel her time with Lucia slipping away with each return step towards the large store.

'You know it all then, don't you?' Suddenly, the other woman spoke rapidly. 'He's a trusted supplier we use regularly, and has been for some years. Why shouldn't I go and see him? I didn't see the need to mention that on your flying visit. I don't know what else I can tell you.' She was still hurrying along the pavement, but Jo kept pace with her.

'You can tell me why he kissed you on the lane by the canal at night,' Jo said.

Lucia finally came to a halt, her forehead knitted into a frown. 'What do you mean?' Then, after a beat, she asked, 'Who saw us?'

'I can't tell you that,' Jo said. 'But they didn't just see you. They took a photo on their phone.' Lucia stopped, one hand on the door of the department store. 'Don't worry,' Jo added quickly. 'I don't think it will be widely shared. It's with the police.'

'The police?' Lucia blanched, staring at Jo, while other lunchtime commuters and shoppers parted around them. More slowly, she said, 'I suppose it doesn't really matter who sees it. We're both free and single grown-ups.'

'Yes, it's your business, and you don't have to tell me anything. And maybe it's OK if the police continue to believe that Leah's builder, Matty Sullivan, killed her.'

'Well, maybe he did, for all I know,' Lucia shot back, but Jo could hear a note of panic in her voice. 'It's really nothing to do with me.'

'Just by being there, at those cottages, at that time, you are involved,' Jo said, staying rooted to the spot as customers brushed past them through the glass doors.

Lucia paid attention to the paper carrier bag with her lunch in it and spoke off-handedly. 'It was nothing. Duncan drove over, took me out for dinner . . . it was really nothing special. In fact, we mainly talked about his family and the building work. But anyway, we got a bit tipsy, and, well, it was just a kiss.'

'So he . . . what? He tried it on?' Jo said, puzzled. 'But he told me he was gay. In fact, he made a point of it, to stress that there was nothing between you two.'

'No, he didn't. I did.' Lucia fixed her gaze over Jo's head. 'Sometimes things get out of hand, don't they? Especially out of context. There I was, in the depths of the Cotswolds, staying in his sister's cottage, and I'd always liked him. Maybe that was one of the reasons I'd gone along with the whole idea of the so-called retreat. We'd been out for dinner and work seemed a long way away. Deep down, I suppose I knew he was gay, but we'd never talked about it, so I . . . well, I kissed him. In the lane. Like a teenager.' She brought wide eyes back to Jo's, chewing her lip.

Jo brought back to her mind the picture she'd seen on Maureen's phone: Lucia leaning back against the wing of Duncan's ancient Audi with her hand on his shoulder. It had looked like he was pressing himself on her, but that bright hand could just as easily have been pulling him to her. 'So, when you went to see him—'

Lucia nodded swiftly. 'Yes, it was to apologize. After all, we have to work together, and I wanted to stay friends. And I still do,' she added, 'which is why I haven't told a soul.' She looked at Jo pleadingly.

'There's no need for me to tell anybody,' Jo assured her quickly. 'But you must see, it *is* important, because Duncan Ellerman is implicated in a murder. At least one. What happened when you went to his workshop? How did he seem?'

'Oh, he was very charming about it, of course. Though things are still a bit awkward.' Lucia brought her hazel eyes to a level with Jo's. 'But I don't believe this has anything to do with the death of his sisters. He has no interest in the Ellerman estate or making any money out of those little cottages, and he certainly doesn't resent Irene's manor house.' Her voice took on a pleading note. 'And there's no need for this to go any further.'

Jo didn't feel she could make any promises. In fact, watching Lucia weave her way back through the store towards the lifts, she felt uncertain about most things. It was not that she didn't believe Lucia, but she was not the sort of woman on whose judgement she wanted to rely. She lost a little faith in her instinct, and doubt seeped into the gap it left.

CHAPTER TWENTY-FOUR

'You took your time to get in touch,' Meena Sanyal said, as she strolled elegantly down the steps of her office building. But her smile and double kiss took the sting out of the words. 'I knew you would, though, so I just waited patiently. Now, where do you want to go?' Meena and Leah Ellerman's consultancy company appeared to have sole occupancy of a 1920s building behind Fleet Street. The inlaid marble steps led into a narrow lane, very different from Lucia's store in bustling, crowded Victoria.

'Somewhere quiet,' Jo said, looking round at the backs of office buildings and shops. 'And where I could maybe get a sandwich.'

Meena thought for a second and turned towards the river. 'So, what have you found out about Leah? I still miss her dreadfully, you know.' She shot a look across to Jo. 'Oh, I can see you're going to make me wait a bit longer. So, tell me about you instead. You look tired. No,' she corrected herself, 'not tired, but tense.'

'It is sort of tiring. I feel like I'm close to the end of something, but I'm still not sure,' Jo said. Then she smiled. 'Sorry to be so cryptic. I will explain in a minute.'

The café Meena chose was Colombian, situated under a railway arch on the embankment with the Thames a few metres away. She requested one of the wicker booths at the far end. 'You gave me a very welcome pot of tea when I came to visit you,' she said, as they took their seats, 'but something tells me you prefer coffee, and this place knows how to do coffee. Is it quiet enough?'

'You notice all sorts of things, don't you? You'd make a good PI.'

'I actually already make an excellent executive assistant, thank you. But yes, I can see there are many crossover skills.' The two women shared a look across the table and laughed. Jo relaxed for the first time in a while, but recalling what was ahead, her tight nerves soon returned.

'Go on,' Meena said, eyeing her. 'Let's get it over with. I suspect you've got something horrible to tell me. By the way, if you've come to tell me about Irene, it's OK. I already know that she died on Friday in some sort of accident at home. I picked it up through one of your local papers online.'

'I don't think it was an accident,' Jo said. Meena frowned, her expression becoming grave.

'Go on,' she said again. 'You'd better come out with it. Tell me everything.'

Jo took a breath. 'Actually, I'm not going to tell you anything bad about Leah. The more I come to understand her, the more I feel for her. I think she was a high achiever, very driven, and there was little — possibly nothing — she would let get in the way of executing her grand plan.'

Meena was nodding in agreement, and Jo went on. 'Maybe she lacked a bit of empathy, but she understood loyalty and maybe love, too. Though she didn't have the best role models, given her family.'

'I don't mean to say anything disrespectful about Irene Ellerman, but . . .' Meena sighed and raised her hands expressively. 'I've already told you, I thought she was a bully and a control freak. And they are all emotionally dysfunctional.'

'They're not a likeable bunch, the Ellermans,' Jo agreed. 'But it was a shock to find out about Irene's death. Where she fell, she could have slipped down the outside steps of the tower at the manor house, but someone could also have followed her up there and pushed her. The police are even considering whether it could have been suicide. Anyway, they are treating it as suspicious.'

'But you think that the same person who killed Leah, also killed her elder sister?' Meena said shrewdly.

Jo nodded briefly, and Meena's eyes widened. 'The police have switched their attention from my clients, Sarah and Gary Robart, to Matty Sullivan.'

'Leah's builder,' Meena said, her expression grave. 'Tell me they are wrong, because that would have been a terrible shock for Leah. She was fond of him. And what would he have to gain? Or are they suspecting a crime of passion?'

'They obviously have enough evidence to hold him. I know he's no angel, so I wouldn't be surprised if he has previous convictions.' Jo hesitated a moment. 'But yes, I think they are wrong. Because he, in his way, loved Leah. I don't believe he killed her.'

'So, who did?' Meena wisely didn't press Jo on this question, however, and they ordered coffee and omelettes, which she particularly recommended. She waited until the server had moved off, then said quietly, 'Duncan would be the one with the most to gain, of course.'

'It's true,' Jo agreed, 'but I've just come from a friend of his who insists he is innocent and not interested in the estate. And, I suppose, Irene's grown-up kids will inherit a chunk of it now, anyway.'

Meena pulled a sceptical face. 'Anyone would be interested in a legacy that size.'

'Maybe not, if Irene was debt-ridden,' Jo pointed out.

'Well, Leah certainly wasn't. She will have left a decent amount to her brother and sister, I predict. I can see why you wanted somewhere quiet to eat,' she added. 'My regular lunchtime conversations usually consist of plans for the weekend and moans about other people in the office, whereas this one has been steeped in suspicious deaths and murder.' She paused as their coffees and omelettes were set in front of them, then went on. 'When I picture that pretty little pub and the row of cute cottages by the canal, with their hanging baskets and flowers, it's hard to believe the family anguish and the tensions that have built up in such a tiny place. But, around Leah, passions always did run high.'

'I haven't finished yet,' Jo said. She reached into her bag, pulled out her phone and laid it on the table. 'This is why I needed to see you in person. Do you remember you told me you had taken one of the calls from Irene when she phoned in sick for Leah?' Jo took a welcome sip of the hot coffee and indicated her phone. 'After you came to my flat, I met Irene and Duncan at the manor house. While I was there, I recorded Irene's voice,' she said. 'You seemed pretty sure that you would recognize her again, so I thought we might try . . . ?'

Meena stared at the phone doubtfully, her plate of food untouched. 'And we know that Leah was already dead when her sister made that call,' she said. 'A lot rests on this, then.'

'Obviously, you might want some time to think it over,' Jo said, and made a valiant attempt to eat some of the ome-lette, realizing she probably looked as desperate as she felt.

'You think that this person . . .' Meena's brown, aquiline features paled. 'You mean, they killed her. Or they knew who did.'

'And you are the person who can identify this voice. I know you can do it, because you care about finding out the truth,' Jo said. 'When you came to see me, you couldn't understand why the police hadn't asked you to identify the voice, and I expect it's because this could never count as evi-dence. But you gave me the idea to try it out. Obviously, we've just got my phone and a couple of sentences to go on, but it would still tell us something, if you're prepared to give it a go?'

Meena pushed aside her plate and took a breath. 'All right,' she said, 'press play.' She clasped her hands into her chest and leaned forward over the mobile phone. Jo did as she was told, and into the little booth with its rafia walls, Duncan's cultured, light voice sounded first: *I'd be careful of taking that tack, if I were you. You are the only one with kids to inherit all this, you know.* Irene's irritable reply followed: *And you know that they are not in the least interested. Both are overseas. I mean, could they get much further away? Tom is working in Japan, for heaven's sake, and my daughter is busy saving the planet in Ethiopia.* There was a crackly pause and then Irene went on. *You must understand that although we are not a showy family and we don't do emotions well, it doesn't mean we don't care about each other.*

Meena's dark eyes met Jo's across the table, her brow creased in concentration. 'Can I hear it again?'

After the third hearing, she sat back and said with certainty, 'That's not the woman I spoke to. The woman had a younger voice, and more of a regional accent. Not strong, but—' She broke off and stared at Jo across the table. 'She said she was Leah's sister, but clearly she wasn't.'

'No,' Jo agreed. 'Irene told the truth about that. And it certainly couldn't have been Matty.'

Their food and coffee cups abandoned, both women were sitting back, staring at each other and at the phone. Meena looked drained, but she wriggled her shoulders and said she must get back to work. 'Can you spare another few minutes?' Jo said. 'I've got another couple of voices for you to listen to.'

'Have you been going around illicitly recording lots of people? That will get you into trouble.'

Jo smiled wanly. 'Not lots. Just my list of . . . well, suspects, I suppose. It's all I could think of to do, Meena.'

Meena glanced briefly at her watch. 'Go ahead, then,' she said, and resumed her listening position, hunched over the phone.

* * *

225

There were heavy issues weighing on Jo's mind and conscience when she walked into the brightly lit lobby of the Astoria Hotel in St James that evening, but she couldn't help a small, secret fizz of anticipation at seeing Macy. She sought him out among the little huddles of people around the grand white staircase. Some were overspilling from the Lichfield Bar, while for others, the gracious split staircase formed an obvious meeting point. She was still scouring the little clusters for his long-legged, lean form when she felt his light hand on her shoulder and whirled round.

Imprinted on his familiar face, she saw a reflection of her own taxing day. He returned her look for a long moment and, keeping his hand on her shoulder, pivoted them both towards the bar. Traversing the lobby at a pace, she tilted her head back to take in the sparkling chandeliers and the curves of the mezzanine balcony, with shaded lights on the tables. 'This place is a bit fancy, isn't it?' she said.

'Your Angry Cherub is paying,' Macy said. Jo came to a halt, staring at him.

'You said you didn't take any money from Carmichael. You said you refused to have anything to do with his escape.'

'I didn't,' he said, 'but Kay Denby deposited some money in the business account yesterday.'

'Why?' Jo demanded, leading the way into the bar.

'Because I'm a gentleman, apparently,' he said enigmatically, and produced two room keys from his jacket pocket. He handed her one. 'And I decided we both deserved some luxury. After a gruelling day with the Financial Crime Agency, in my case, and, well, you can tell me about yours later, but you look like you've earned it too.'

'Thanks. I'll find a way to see that as a compliment.' She took one of the keys. 'Two rooms. That *is* very thoughtful of you.'

'Don't worry, I've kept the best,' he said. 'Now, go and nab that little corner seat, and I will bring two large gins.'

Jo didn't argue. She felt all out of arguing, all out of convincing and persuading, all out of considering and concluding. Collapsing onto the cosy velvet banquette, she allowed the hum of voices and clink of glasses to mute her busy brain — until Macy returned with the drinks. Then she demanded to know what exactly Kay Denby was paying him for.

He raised an eyebrow. 'Services rendered,' he said, taking a long gulp of gin. Jo punched him lightly in the ribs. 'Be gentle with me,' he protested. 'I've spent all day with the finance police and I'm psychologically beaten.'

'So, she said you were a gentleman,' Jo persevered. 'Presumably for telling her the truth about the cherub.'

'Yes, so now I have standards to live up to,' he said flippantly.

'Hence the two rooms,' Jo giggled.

'I've got a table booked for dinner, too, and I suggest we go there soon or we'll be too silly to appreciate it. I also propose a rule.'

She sipped her gin and waited. 'You know I don't like rules.'

He held up a long, elegant finger. 'This is an incontrovertible rule: there is to be no discussion of cases at dinner. So, talking about anything that happened today is confined to the bar only.'

'I have no problem with that rule,' Jo said. 'You go first. You told me that the Financial Crime people wanted to talk to you about Carmichael. So, they suspect him of fraud, do they?'

'Yes. I thought I was home and dry when the local bobbies let me go home with my licence intact.' He sat back and let his shoulders drop. 'Then they called me on Sunday and told me, no, it's not all over, and I had to talk to this specialized division because Carmichael is a high-net-worth individual.'

'He's minted,' Jo said. 'Yes, you said that. But I thought he didn't take any money with him. He had no debts, you said, and there has been no life insurance claim.'

'I didn't say he didn't take any with him. I said he had left his family sorted and comfortably off. But I imagine he had salted a bit away in overseas accounts over the years, because he'd been planning this for some time. Now, I don't know if there is anything dodgy about that. So, thankfully,' he added fervently, 'for once, I could tell the plain truth. You don't know how hard that was. A whole day of telling the truth. It was like being back in court.'

Jo let her eyes roam around the dimly lit bar. The after-work drinkers were thinning out and the new arrivals looked more like tourists. 'I wonder what Kay Denby will do? Do you think she will try to find him? Or maybe he will contact her?'

Macy shrugged eloquently. 'As long as they leave me out of it, I really don't care.' He turned to her. 'Now you,' he said. 'Dinner is in about fifteen minutes, so you have a strict timescale.'

'Like I said on the phone, there were two people in London I really wanted to see, and I managed to meet up with both of them: Lucia Hewitt, because of her connection to Duncan Ellerman, and Meena, Leah's assistant.'

'And?'

'I felt almost as confused as Lucia herself by the time I'd left her,' Jo sighed. 'But I think that's just her natural state. I don't think she had anything to do with Leah's or Irene's death. She secretly fancied Duncan Ellerman, who is gay, so that was never going anywhere, but I think she is harmless.' She paused to finish her gin. 'How long have I got?'

He smiled at her. 'Take as long as you want. They can wait for us.'

'I met Meena at the office where they both worked and I played her the recording I'd made of Irene's voice.' She shook her head at him. 'It's not Irene. She's certain.'

'So, who was it?' Macy asked.

'I've got a sort of theory, and tomorrow I've got to go back to the New Navigation to test it out,' she said. 'But you're right, I can't think about it anymore tonight. Let's go and eat.'

Macy needed no further persuading, and they made their way up the curving staircase. 'There are only two things worrying me,' Jo said, while they waited to be shown their table.

'I thought we agreed—' Macy began.

She stopped him. 'This is not about either of our cases.'

He eyed her warily. 'Go on then.'

Jo bided her time until they were seated at one of the tables beside the balcony and wine had been ordered.

'Go on,' Macy prompted her again. 'Don't keep me in suspense. I've already told you I've had a traumatic day.'

'All right,' she laid down the menu and looked at him. 'Why am I here and not Rowanna?'

'Oh.' His dark eyes were familiar and yet unreadable. 'Well, she and I decided that it's over. Don't give me the third degree about it. Not just now, anyway.'

'All right,' Jo swallowed. 'And is this a recent thing?'

'Saturday night,' he said, matter-of-factly.

'That's why you couldn't talk when I rang.'

He nodded. 'This business over Carmichael clarified a few things for me. I suppose I don't want to get to my fifties and find I want to escape. I want to try and get it right now.'

'So, no Rowanna and no Teddy.' She looked at him steadily.

He smiled. 'Wait a minute, though. You said there were two things bothering you. You'd better hit me with the second. Let's get it out of the way so I can enjoy my dinner.'

Jo bit her lip. 'Well, you know that, as a Virgo, I hate to waste money, but—' she pushed the room key towards him across the table — 'I can't stay tonight. I have to be back tomorrow morning early to see Sarah and Gary. And it really can't wait.'

'Such devotion to duty,' Macy sighed, but he took back the keycard. 'And after that?'

'After that?' she hesitated. 'I don't know what happens next.'

'That makes two of us,' he said.

CHAPTER TWENTY-FIVE

The next morning found Jo at the New Navigation long before they were open. It was early enough for there still to be a quietness in the air, with no sound from the building works and all the canal cottages shuttered and sleepy. But it had required resolve on her part. The confusion of her emotions — delight about her encounter with Macy vying with sadness over Teddy and uncertainty about the future — would have occupied her for the whole of her late-night train journey if she hadn't been facing a confrontation she knew she couldn't avoid. After that, knowing what lay ahead, she'd had a disturbed night.

'You are doing the right thing for Leah,' Meena had said, when they'd hugged goodbye outside her office building the previous day. 'Just keep persevering.'

'I wish I could be so sure,' Jo had said, but she'd repeated Meena's advice to herself as she'd driven speedily down the now-familiar lanes to the New Navigation. She arrived just after 8.30 and diverted to the towpath first, tempted by the fresh scent of the water and the air, busy with birdsong. She breathed deeply to steel herself, then walked purposefully past Sarah's scarlet geraniums and pushed open the front door of the pub. She found Gary refilling stock behind the bar. He swung round to face her. 'Jo! Is there any news?' Anxiety was pressed into the creases around his eyes. 'Have you heard anything about what's happening to Matty?'

'He's still in police custody as far as I know,' Jo said cautiously. 'Is Sarah around?'

He jerked his head towards the back room. 'She's in there. All this is getting to her. To both of us.' He blew out his cheeks. 'The police seemed so certain we had something to do with the Ellerman deaths that I almost began to believe it myself.'

Jo paused on her way through the pub. 'What do you mean?'

'The paranormal evenings, for one thing. That's where things began to go wrong. Leah always objected to them, but of course, I should never have had a go at her like I did. It was out of order and the police made a lot of that.' He returned to stacking the fridges with bottled juices, but kept talking. 'And they asked about the cloth wrapped around the body, the one Sarah uses for her Thursday sessions. As soon as I laid eyes on it, I knew I had to get rid of it, but that's something else I should never have done.' He glanced up briefly as if checking she was still there. 'And Sarah said Irene felt wracked with guilt for not being closer to her sister, so what if . . . I mean, what if she took her own life as a result? Then we'd have played a part in both their deaths.'

Jo couldn't bring herself to give him the reassurance he was looking for. Instead, she said, 'It's not over yet, and Sarah is going to need you to support her,' then carried on through to the back room, where her client was sitting at the round table slowly shuffling the tarot cards. Sarah's jawline sagged, there were shadowed folds under her eyes and she barely acknowledged Jo's presence.

'I don't know much about the cards,' Jo said, taking a seat beside her. 'Only what I've learned from Hanni, but I know it's not a good idea to consult them when you're troubled.'

Sarah extended a rounded blue fingernail and tapped the single card turned up on the table. 'The tower,' she said.

'That's where we are, Jo. All we've built up is falling around our shoulders and taking our neighbours with it.' She fixed Jo with morose eyes. 'We've heard nothing from Matty. He hasn't even entrusted us with the dog. That's gone to the Hutchinsons. And Gil has stopped Nora from coming here. I can't even message her because she's not allowed her phone. They forget all the Sundays she spent with us making herself useful and then filling up with Sunday roast. They are only thinking of the Thursday nights.'

Sarah halted her monologue and turned over another card from the pack, which showed a woman holding a lion. 'This is your card — it stands for fortitude and courage,' she said. 'I remember, it came up the night we were preparing for our last spiritual soirée. I didn't mention it, but I knew it represented you.'

'That night didn't go as you'd hoped, did it?' Jo looked directly back at Sarah.

'Nothing is going as I'd hoped,' Sarah said flatly. She stacked the cards and started to wrap them in a thin Indian silk scarf at her elbow. 'I'm giving it up, Jo. No more spiritual soirées. I've seen the harm that my gift can cause. I've nearly lost us the pub and I've hurt poor Nora. I haven't used it wisely.'

Jo waited while Sarah placed the cards in a carved wooden box and closed it with a firm click. 'I know what you were trying to do on Thursday night,' she said, and Sarah glanced up warily. 'The knocking on the cellar door. That was Gary, wasn't it? You arranged it.'

'Of course it was,' the other woman responded impatiently. 'I've been doing this a long time, and sometimes I just know the feeling isn't right. There's too much tension or scepticism in the room and the spirits won't play with me. Then you need a little earthly help to bring proceedings to a quick close.'

'You and Gary have some sort of signal,' Jo said.

Sarah smiled, although her face remained melancholy. 'Don't be silly. Think how long Gary and I have been together. We don't need it.'

'I knew he was down there from the moment I switched on the cellar light,' Jo said. 'I saw a shadow and knew it must be him.'

'That's why you didn't let Alys go down. You knew you'd be exposed.' Sarah's face cleared as she stared back at Jo. She reached across the polished table and patted Jo's arm. 'Bless you.'

'But on Thursday, you didn't send Gary down there because the spirits weren't playing, did you? I believe you were trying to flush out Leah's murderer, but it didn't work,' Jo persevered, her eyes steady.

Sarah held her gaze. 'We were just doing what we could,' she said simply.

A silence fell between them while Jo wrestled with her decision. Then she took a breath and said, 'I want you to have another try. But we need to invite more people, so it can't be a séance.'

Sarah was quick to understand her meaning. 'No more séances, I promise. Let's make it a thank you from Gary and me to our friends instead. A little get-together for helping us through difficult times.'

'OK, but it must be soon.'

'Then let's plan,' Sarah said, a gleam back in her eyes.

By the time she left the pub, Jo felt confident she could leave the arrangements in Sarah's capable hands. But she had left herself the hardest job — somehow, she had to persuade Duncan Ellerman to attend. On her way to Stokes Manor, she rehearsed the arguments. She was trusting that, despite his jaded attitude, he wasn't immune to public duty or family loyalty, and she could persuade him that Irene would have been fully behind her plan.

* * *

She was still wondering whether he would actually go through with it when she picked him up at the manor house on Thursday morning. Although she'd managed to secure his agreement, she knew there was a chance he would change his mind after a couple of nights to reflect on it. However, Duncan and Howard were waiting for her outside. They were dressed as if for the funeral, which, owing to the inquest, could not be held for a couple of weeks.

Howard had proved to be a surprising ally. He had sat in abstract silence in the manor's decrepit lounge while she expounded her plan, seemingly obsessed with tracking the leaf patterns outside the lead-light windows. But then he had chimed in unexpectedly when Jo had run out of things to say, with a plea of his own. 'We've got to do it, Duncan. Irene would want us to.'

Reluctant to exert himself as ever, it had been part of Duncan's terms that she provided transport, but Jo was more than happy with this. At least it meant she knew he was going to be there. On the journey, their faces were as sober and conversation as stilted as if she was indeed taking them to a wake. So, when she finally arrived with her guests in the back room of the New Navigation, she felt she had cleared the first hurdle.

Sarah had been adept at transforming the room so that it looked cheery, and there was a hospitable buzz from the small party already gathered. The large round table had been pushed to the back wall with chairs turned outwards. The sideboard was set with plates of simple buffet food, and drinks were on a side table, where Alys Parry was helping herself to a cup of tea. The journalist caught Jo's eye meaningfully as soon as she arrived, but sat back while Jo made the introductions between the Ellermans and the Robarts. The residents from the canal cottages, including Gil Hutchinson and Nora, were seated around another table below the window. Maureen was circulating with glasses of Prosecco.

'Thought we'd best not be *too* festive,' Sarah muttered to Jo, while Gary was helping the two newcomers to drinks. 'Given recent events and with Matty in custody.' They both glanced towards Alys, who seemed as self-possessed as ever, but a closer look revealed the strain behind her eyes.

'It's fine,' Jo murmured, watching as people gathered in clusters. 'Duncan is going to be managing the estate until the will is sorted out, so he has a message for his tenants. Do you think you can make some time for him to tell them.'

'Leave that to Gary and me,' Sarah said firmly. 'Now, go and mingle.'

Valerie Lilley had helped herself to a Prosecco and, when Jo arrived at her side, was holding forth about the noise from the latest contractors who had been working on Leah's house.

'Matty Sullivan employs some shockingly careless workmen,' Maureen commented as she swung past with her tray. 'That's how he keeps his prices down.'

That, and dealing drugs on the side, Jo thought to herself, carefully avoiding Alys's gaze.

'You should see how the plasterer left cottage number two,' Maureen went on. 'I've lost count of the times I've cleaned it from top to bottom. No doubt I'll have to do it again after the tiler's finished.' She beamed at Jo. 'Prosecco?'

But Jo had seen her friend Hanni arrive, a little late and flustered, and politely refused. 'Thanks, I'll get myself a coffee.' She had only just managed to greet Hanni when Gary clapped his hands and the gathering drew to a murmuring quiet.

'We're not going to interrupt your lunch for long,' Gary said, surprisingly at ease addressing the room, 'but we wanted to say a heartfelt thank you for all your support. We realize this may seem an odd thing to be doing when we are all going through such difficult times,' his eyes rested on Alys, who looked away, 'but perhaps that makes it even more important. Sarah and I are grateful to each one of you, as you have helped us keep going and stay in business.'

Valerie Lilley led the little round of applause that greeted this, but Gary quickly held up his hand. 'No, no, we are just here to celebrate the neighbourliness and friendship in our little community, so please help yourselves . . .' He indicated the buffet table. 'First, though, Mr Ellerman has some news about the cottages which he wants to tell you.'

Duncan Ellerman had height and could summon up something of a presence when called upon. He was also clearly used to being in charge and he created a little space for himself in front of Gary, with Howard standing stiff-shouldered at his side. Duncan scanned the room with his blue-eyed patriarchal gaze. 'Thank you, Gary. It's very good of you and Mrs Robart to provide us with this opportunity to meet the folks who live in my sister's cottages. Leah would have known you all personally and she would be very grateful as well. She was very proud to own the cottages, and had great plans for them, as you know.'

A moment of awkwardness rustled through the group and Duncan paused. 'Or maybe you didn't know Leah very well,' he went on, and Jo guessed he was diverting away from his planned speech, 'but I can tell you, she was a kind and intelligent woman, who took her responsibilities very seriously. I was honoured to be her brother.' His voice faltered momentarily, and the attention in the room was rapt. 'I am also proud to be Irene's brother.' He turned to his brother-in-law, standing grey and taut at his side. 'Irene was my elder sister and Howard's wife. We are both getting over the terrible shock of losing them both. So, forgive me,' he added, 'if I'm a little . . .' He sought for a word for a few moments and, when he finally found it, Jo sensed it cost him a lot to use it. '. . . upset,' he finished.

Valerie Lilley murmured her understanding, which others echoed. Maureen had stopped circulating and had planted herself in front of the Ellermans. Duncan hastened on. 'Not that I come here looking for your sympathy. I have some news for you and it's good to be able to communicate it face to face.' He drew a breath. 'You will appreciate that it can be a long, drawn-out business to get an estate like ours sorted out, and two family deaths in close proximity will not make it any easier. Consequently, I have agreed to manage the estate in the short-to-medium term. My nephew and niece, who will ultimately inherit, are overseas and have assured me they will be happy with any decisions I take. With that in mind, I have decided to cease the renovations on the cottages, which means that current tenants need not be displaced.'

Nora Hutchinson looked round at her father, wide-eyed, and they squeezed hands. Valerie Lilley gave vent to a small cheer and her husband lifted his beer glass.

'The exception is Leah's own house,' Duncan went on. 'We will find another builder, in due course, to finish that work, and I suppose ultimately we will sell it.' He gave the group a sweeping glance. 'Well, I'm glad that seems to be good news. I've nothing left to say except that I will aim to be as diligent a landlord as my sister, and to thank Sarah and Gary for their hospitality. If you have any questions, I'll be happy to answer them.'

His small speech was greeted with a much warmer response than he probably expected — or wanted. He stepped back, flapping his hands dismissively. Sarah smartly took his place in front of the table, using her rich voice to cut across the excited murmur. 'Can I just add my own thanks to all of you?' she said, her mercurial green eyes today radiating warmth. 'And particularly to Jo, who had faith in us through thick and thin.'

Jo saw Hanni and Alys beaming and clapping at this, but she spoke up quickly. 'Actually, I have a question,' she said. The room fell quiet. 'It's not necessarily for you, Duncan, but I need to find out what caused that trolley of tiles to hit me and almost knock me into the canal. It happened virtually outside your front doors, so someone here must know what happened.'

It was Maureen who spoke up. 'Matty pushed the trolley down the slope himself, of course,' she said, matter-of-factly. Alys shot her a pointed look, but said nothing. 'Because he was worried about what you'd dug up on him.'

'That seems odd,' Jo said. 'After all, Matty pulled me clear and even took me to the hospital.'

'Yes, it's so easy to blame Matty for everything.' Alys's clear voice rang out, and heads turned towards her. 'I know he's no saint, but—'

'Did you see it happen?' Jo directed her question to Maureen, whose stocky form faced her in the centre of the room. 'Because I must have some evidence if I'm going to take this any further.'

Maureen gave a short laugh. 'I can't help you there,' she said. 'I'm not here in the afternoons, am I? I'm at Stokes Avon with the old dears.'

'Not that day.' Jo held her gaze. 'I checked, and that's your day off. So, you could have been here. Maybe you were waiting at number two for the tiler. After all, although you don't like him much, you are always doing jobs for Matty. Or maybe you were cleaning it up? And you have all the keys.'

'Only to the renovated cottages, and to Leah's, of course. I need it because she was often in London when I cleaned her house,' she explained for Duncan's benefit. Her brown eyes, shielded by the metal frames, turned back to Jo. 'But I can assure you, I don't spend my days off here if I can help it. I'm not that sad. Anyway, you'd have knocked at number two, wouldn't you? So, if I had been there, I'd have answered.'

'I did knock,' Jo said. 'And you were there, weren't you?'

'Can't we just be allowed to celebrate the good news?' Valerie Lilley interjected. 'It's unfair to pick on Maureen. Everyone knows how well she looks after Leah's holiday cottages. Especially number two — it's like a little palace.'

'Of course,' Duncan murmured, and threw a desperate glance at Jo, who appeared to ignore it. He began to button his jacket and glanced at Howard. 'We ought to leave you to your celebration,' he said easily. He reached out a hand to Gary, offering a farewell handshake, and Howard followed.

'Wait.' The word came out powerfully and the men turned. Maureen stood squarely in their way. 'You haven't said what happens to the cottage at number two,' she said.

Duncan frowned momentarily. 'That's the one that's as good as complete, isn't it? The tenants have already moved on, so we'll continue to let the first two as holiday cottages, of course.'

His words sucked all the air out of the room. Even those who didn't understand why knew this statement changed everything. It was Jo who spoke into the charged silence. 'But that cottage is like a second home to Maureen. She looks after it as if it was her own, her little palace. Everyone here knows that. It's like her second home.'

'It isn't *like* anything.' Maureen's face suddenly flared up, colour reaching the high points on her cheeks and her voice gaining strength. She directed it at Duncan. 'It *is* mine. That cottage is mine. It's the perfect house for me and Charlotte, and it has been mine for years. So, that will come to me now, won't it?'

'No, of course not. We'll continue with Leah's plan for the two finished cottages,' Duncan repeated with uncharacteristic force. 'They will be holiday lets.'

'Oh no. No, no.' Maureen shook her head, rejecting this outright, and the threat in her voice was patently clear. 'Leah and I had an understanding. And I had a long-standing agreement with Irene.' She turned to Howard, who visibly paled and took a step back. 'It's my reward for all the dirty work I've done for you Ellermans over the years.'

'I don't know anything about this,' Duncan began, 'and unless you've got something in writing, I'm sorry—'

But Maureen was shouting now and the little crowd were mesmerized. 'Irene promised it to me when Charlotte was five. She said it was instead of a pension or sick pay or holiday pay or any of the other things people get for their work and their . . . their loyalty.' The air seemed to reverberate on this word. 'My cottage is the reason I have stayed with your family.'

'But they are Leah's cottages,' Jo said, watching Maureen face off to the two men. On either side of her, she could feel Sarah and Gary tense, ready to act. 'So, how could Irene give one away?'

'Oh, Leah was well aware,' Maureen said scornfully. The deep fury within her strong body was palpable as she jabbed a finger at Duncan. 'When she started to get them renovated, I used to remind her regularly — "Number two is mine. You can do it up like a perfect palace for me and Charlotte, so when she comes home from university, she is proud of it." Leah knew it was our passage off that estate and out of that dingy, cold flat.' Maureen paused for breath. It came on an angry sob. 'It's right that it comes to me now.'

'Yes, you reminded Leah again before you killed her, I expect. And when Irene also let you down, you had to kill her too, didn't you?' Jo said, keeping her voice even. She thought of Meena's admiration for her boss and her own insights about Leah, the confidence and self-respect which she'd sensed when she'd visited the woman's house. She thought about Irene's awkward, clumsy determination for justice for her sister, and looked at Duncan. She took a steadying breath and went on, 'You killed both sisters because they broke their promise.'

'Not just because of that. And I gave Leah a chance,' Maureen said soberly, looking back at Jo. 'She said it was Irene's promise, and that she had nothing to do with it. She said it was a fairy tale and I'd been a fool to take it seriously.'

There was a rustle of reaction from the room. Jo felt, rather than saw, that Sarah stilled it with a look. Maureen turned her attention back to Duncan and Howard. 'And she was right. I was a fool, because in the end you've betrayed me,' the woman went on bitterly. 'And not just me. Leah had already evicted Kayleigh Thomas, and she had two kids under five. So, it's not just about me and Charlotte.' She turned to the other canal residents. 'She'd have turfed you out next. You know she would.' Gil had his arm tightly around his daughter. George and Valerie Lilley had moved closer together. Maureen drew herself up and regarded them all. 'Then she and Matty would have giggled about it in his dirty little van. I see things, you know. I'm not stupid. And I suppose I'll suffer for this now. But it's important you know that I was restoring order in our small world. Matty will go back to prison—' She broke off and swivelled towards Alys, her voice suddenly spiteful. 'Oh yes, Matty's done time for

240

dealing. I'm one of the few people around here who know — apart from the police. That's because Charlotte got mixed up in it when she was younger — until I found out. And Matty Sullivan knows I can read him like a book, and I can promise you, he will be no loss to society.'

Alys went white but held her gaze. 'Believe me, you can't shock me now,' she said levelly.

'Did you use that to make Matty help you?' Jo said. 'After you'd killed Leah?'

'Him? Help me?' Maureen's attention was pulled back to Jo. 'I didn't need any help. It all went according to plan. After I'd hit her, she fell forward over the steering wheel. I'd already chosen a piece of wood from the pile and it did the job. Later on, I burned it in the pub fire. I pulled her out, tied her in the plastic and dragged her to the cellar door. Then I just pushed.' She gave a little nod. 'I had to work quickly in the cellar to shove her under the shelf, but then I had all morning to clean up at the pub. In fact, I gave myself a few more days by calling in sick for her. I even had time to wrap the hideous tablecloth you use for your séances around the body.' She tilted her head towards Sarah with an air of satisfaction.

'You wanted to take us down,' Sarah breathed, shaking her head.

Maureen looked at her with disgust. 'What you do at those séances is evil, and preys on the young and vulnerable.'

'You had to get rid of the car, though. How did you do that?' Alys's clear voice interrupted with the question, her journalist's curiosity clearly undimmed.

Maureen answered without turning her head. 'I caught a taxi to work that day so, after I'd come out of the cellar, I could drive Leah's car back to my house and pick up mine. I stuck hers in my lock-up, had time for a shower and still arrived on time for work at seven.' A vestige of personal pride made its way into Maureen's eyes as she held the room with her story. 'Over the next week, I cleaned it up as much as I could. Then one night, I drove it to the reccy on the estate, where I knew some kids would find it and wreck it for me.

Which they did,' she said, matter-of-factly. 'That is one of the things I do well. I look after the details.'

'It needed that, didn't it? A fantastic grasp of detail and a desire for order.' Jo stepped closer to Maureen and sent Hanni the smallest nod. Her friend slipped out of the door which led to the bar. If the others in the room noticed, no one moved. 'I understand because I'm a Virgo, too,' she went on. 'Order and service to others are important to us. And detail. You even knew Leah's schedule, didn't you?'

'Irene expected it,' Maureen answered, almost conversationally. 'She liked reports on what exactly Leah was up to, and it was easy to do. Leah kept everything on her laptop and she was pretty lax about passwords. I could have sent emails from her if I wanted to.' Maureen gave a little chuckle. 'But it would have been too easy to spot, so I only did that once.'

'You sent the email to the brewery, didn't you?' Sarah said, blinking at Maureen as realization dawned. 'Because you so desperately wanted us thrown out of this place. And that's why you hid the body in our cellar.'

'I told you, I was restoring order,' Maureen said calmly, rocking slightly on the balls of her feet.

'How was killing Irene restoring order?' Duncan took a step forward, white with anger. Maureen flinched. 'Go on, I want to hear it all.' He pushed himself in front of Jo. 'Don't spare us now.'

Maureen dropped her eyes for the first time, and Jo saw that Valerie and George Lilley had moved subtly to cover one exit. Alys was near the other and Gary moved closer to her. 'I'm afraid I just lost it with Irene,' the woman went on, head lowered. 'When she told me she was carrying on with the renovations, I couldn't believe it. But we were in the house alone so it was easy enough to get her up that stupid tower. I just told her Howard was in trouble, and I followed her up the steps. Then I pushed her and I watched her fall. It was always dangerous up there.'

Maureen raised her head again to confront Duncan and Howard, her plain face open and reasonable. 'I'm not sorry.

Your sisters betrayed me, and now you have. Which just proves me right.'

As she spoke, Hanni slipped back into the room. This time Maureen noticed. She looked around her with sudden desperation, almost panting.

'That's enough,' said Gary. He stepped forward and pinned back her arms with surprising efficiency.

This seemed to be a signal for everyone to move at once. Sarah rushed to her husband's aid on Maureen's other side, and, with Duncan assisting, they manhandled her into one of the chairs.

'We've called the police,' Jo said, after exchanging a grateful look with Hanni. Maureen's jaw clamped shut.

Jo took a step backwards, shaking. Alys drew her away from the little crowd around Maureen into the corridor. She pushed a cup of coffee into her hand. 'Here, have this, although you could really do with something stronger. I don't know how you managed to work it all out. Bravo.' She gave her a quick hug. 'You knew very well that Matty didn't help her, didn't you?'

'I was pretty sure he didn't. But I knew she'd hate the idea. Though he still has some tricky questions to answer, you know.'

'I said he's no angel,' Alys said. 'But then which man is? Or,' she sent Jo a quick, teasing look, 'maybe Teddy Scarborough is? He's more the type.'

Despite herself, Jo laughed. 'Well, I wouldn't go that far. But maybe he's too angelic for me, anyway.'

'You dodged a bullet there,' Alys reassured her. 'I can't see you becoming one of the Scarboroughs with a horde of Scarborough babies.'

Jo became serious suddenly. 'Talking of babies, will you be OK? I mean, Matty will almost certainly go to prison.'

Alys looked back at her stoically. 'I told you before. What happens will be between my baby and me, and we will be absolutely fine on our own. I can look after her,' she added.

Jo shook her head in admiration. 'I know you can.' She leaned across to return the hug and found herself holding back tears.

243

Later, Jo examined her reflection in the speckled mirror above the sink in the ladies'. She began to repair her make-up. People had remained in the room, reliving and talking over Maureen's confession far longer than she had expected, even after DC Williams and another police officer had arrived to take Maureen to the station. Before Duncan and Howard left, she thanked them for playing their part.

That was when she'd made her escape to have a good cry. Now, as she re-applied her eyeliner, she acknowledged that it wasn't so much the morning's revelations that had upset her, as her own private sadness. Maybe Alys was right and she had dodged a bullet, but she knew she would miss Teddy, and the future he offered. But no regrets, no, never.

The door clicked open and Hanni's slight form appeared. 'Are you OK? I was getting worried,' she said. 'Nora was asking for you.'

Jo sniffed and smiled. 'This is such a cliché, isn't it? Crying in the ladies'. It's not even as if I've had six mojitos.'

Hanni hugged her unexpectedly. 'Thank you, Josephine. You only got into all this to help me and you've ended up injured, and I don't mean just cuts and bruises, either.'

'I'll get over Teddy,' Jo said. 'And in the meantime, life isn't all bad.'

Hanni stood back, scrutinizing her friend's reflection, arms folded. 'Is this something to do with David Macy? I notice he was absent from today's little party.'

'You know him, he doesn't like parties,' Jo said. 'But we might meet up later. We have got a few things to celebrate, too. He was at a court case last week, and he told me this morning that they've given a guilty verdict. Plus, I've successfully completed my first case.'

'Seems to me you might have more than that to celebrate,' Hanni said. Jo smiled at her in the mirror. 'Let's go back and join them,' she said.

THE END

ACKNOWLEDGEMENTS

Thank you to my agent, Vanessa Holt, and editors, Emma Grundy Haigh and Jasmine Callaghan, for your support, encouragement, for inspiring ideas and for having faith in me. A huge thank you to the whole team at Joffe who, as ever, have been supremely professional and supremely positive, which is the perfect balance. Thanks also to Meg Sanders, my writing mentor, for giving me wise advice amid lots of laughs.

Thank you to Angie, Annie and Glynis for your help, your diligence and great feedback, which made a significant contribution to the story. And for your friendship — best gift of all. Thanks also to author pals Daniel Sellers, Judith Cutler, Edward Marston and Biba Pearce for your generous guidance and practical help.

Thank you to the loving RTT for being there every step of the way and to my family; in particular, my big brother, Roy, my niece, Kirsty, and also to my best friend, Julie. Thank you for always believing in me and for all the listening and love.

Finally, thank you, reader, for reading this because you are at the heart of it all.

THE JOFFE BOOKS STORY

We began in 2014 when Jasper agreed to publish his mum's much-rejected romance novel and it became a bestseller.

Since then we've grown into the largest independent publisher in the UK. We're extremely proud to publish some of the very best writers in the world, including Joy Ellis, Faith Martin, Caro Ramsay, Helen Forrester, Simon Brett and Robert Goddard. Everyone at Joffe Books loves reading and we never forget that it all begins with the magic of an author telling a story.

We are proud to publish talented first-time authors, as well as established writers whose books we love introducing to a new generation of readers.

We have been shortlisted for Independent Publisher of the Year at the British Book Awards three times, in 2020, 2021 and 2022, and for the Diversity and Inclusivity Award at the Independent Publishing Awards in 2022.

We built this company with your help, and we love to hear from you, so please email us about absolutely anything bookish at: feedback@joffebooks.com.

If you want to receive free books every Friday and hear about all our new releases, join our mailing list: www.joffebooks.com/contact

And when you tell your friends about us, just remember: it's pronounced Joffe as in coffee or toffee!

ALSO BY LINDA MATHER

JO AND MACY MYSTERIES